DEVIL'S ROCK

GERRI HILL

Bella
BOOKS
2010

Bella Books, Inc.
P.O. Box 10543
Tallahassee, FL 32302

Printed in the United States of America on acid-free paper
First Edition

Editor: Anna Chinappi
Cover Designer: Linda Callaghan

ISBN 13: 978-1-59493-218-2

Also by Gerri Hill

Artist's Dream
Behind The Pine Curtain
The Cottage
Coyote Sky
Dawn Of Change
Gulf Breeze
Hunter's Way
In The Name Of The Father
The Killing Room
Love Waits
No Strings
One Summer Night
Partners
Sierra City
The Target
The Scorpion

About the Author

Gerri Hill has eighteen published works, including 2009 GCLS winner *Partners* and 2007 GCLS winners *Behind the Pine Curtain* and *The Killing Room*, as well as GCLS finalist *Hunter's Way* and Lambda finalist *In the Name of the Father*. She began writing lesbian romance as a way to amuse herself while snowed in one winter in the mountains of Colorado and hasn't looked back. Her first published work came in 2000 with *One Summer Night*. Hill's love of nature and of being outdoors usually makes its way into her stories as her characters often find themselves in beautiful natural settings. When she isn't writing, Hill and her longtime partner, Diane, can be found at their home in East Texas, where their vegetable garden, orchard and five acres of piney woods keep them busy. They share their lives with two Australian Shepherds and an assortment of furry felines. For more, see her website: www.gerrihill.com.

CHAPTER ONE

"You know, they say Sycamore Canyon is haunted."

Andrea Sullivan wiped the sweat from her brow, her eyes squinting against the glare of the hot sun. "You don't really believe that crap, do you?"

"There's just a lot of weird shit that's happened in this canyon."

Andrea pulled her horse to a stop. "Are you going to tell me the UFO story again?"

Randy shook his head, his long blond hair tied back in its usual ponytail as he took a drink of water from the old-fashioned canteen fastened to his saddle. He wiped his mouth with the back of his hand before speaking. "Not just that. The Native Americans thought it was haunted too."

"So because we find a body with her throat slashed, you assume it's because of the canyon?"

"Two bodies. A week apart."

"Don't jump to conclusions. We don't know if this second body is for real. Hikers have been known to mistake bear carcasses for humans before. You can't assume it's related. Besides, we haven't found it yet."

"Haven't had a murder in the ten years I've worked here."

Andrea urged her horse on. "And you probably still won't get to work one. She was killed and dumped. That wasn't the crime scene. Chances are the case will be handed off to someone else."

"I bet you saw plenty of murders when you were in LA, didn't you?"

"More than I can remember." And plenty she couldn't forget.

"Why won't you ever talk about it?"

"It what?"

"Being a cop in LA. Must have been exciting."

"A blast," she said dryly. "Come on. We're close. GPS says about two hundred more yards."

"Hey, Andi. Wait up," he said, trying to get the mule he led behind his horse to pick up the pace.

She ignored his request and rode on ahead, her horse following the trail without much direction from her. She'd only been on the Rim Trail a handful of times in the two years she'd been working for the sheriff's department. Never in the middle of summer. She normally hiked the lower Dogie Trail, deep in the canyon. While most people found Sycamore Canyon to have a wildness to it—albeit in a weird sort of way, as Randy had said—she found peace here. With the shadows of the canyon drifting about, the outcroppings and spires seemed almost ghost-like from below. The sandstone walls changed colors with the shadows—orange, then red. Junipers, scrub oaks, mesquites and pinyons lined the rocks, taking hold where no tree should ever grow. Deep in the gut of the canyon, where spring water flowed, cypress and sycamore trees flourished. When she hiked alone in the canyon, the quiet was nearly overpowering. The canyon was wild and remote, yet it was where she found some peace.

It all looked different from up here along the rim though. The sun beat down, making the red rocks glow like hot embers in a campfire. There was a quietness in the air, the only sound that of their horses' hooves as they crunched along the rock, and the occasional call of the ravens as they soared past, inspecting their progress. Rim Trail was an eleven-mile loop, but six miles into it, a side trail veered off that would take hikers farther into the wilderness, the red rock cliffs and canyons a challenge for even the most seasoned individual. That was one reason she suspected the body they were searching for wasn't a victim of homicide. More likely a hiker who succumbed to the elements.

She was still twenty yards away when she smelled it. She glanced over her shoulder as Randy and the mule caught up to her.

"Jesus Christ," Randy mumbled as he covered his mouth and nose with his shirt.

"Decomp," she said. "That's a smell I'd hoped to never encounter again." She reined in her mount, then slid from the saddle. She didn't want to spook the animal by walking upon a rotting corpse. Her handheld GPS guided her on and she too covered her mouth and nose. The stench was unbearable.

She stopped when she saw it. It was definitely not a bear.

"What is it?"

She walked closer, seeing the remnants of blond hair, although the face was nearly gone, the skin turned nearly black. The ribcage was exposed, the organs missing as was most of the flesh. What remained was being consumed by maggots and beetles. The arms and legs had been badly gnawed, most likely by coyotes. She took the small, digital camera from her pocket, taking pictures from different angles.

"I'm guessing blond female," she said. "We're missing part of a leg here," she said, pointing where the right lower leg should have been. She took a closer picture of that. "Wild animals probably carried it off." She looked up. "See if you can find it."

"Are you serious? You want me to look for her leg?"

"We came up here to retrieve this body. Let's try to bring all of it back."

Randy shook his head. "No way. I'm not touching that. We can't bring it down."

She turned to him and put her hands on her hips. "So you want to just leave her here? Let the animals finish with her?"

"How the hell are we going to get her down?"

"The aluminum rack we brought."

"Yeah. For a body. That's...that'll fall apart if we try to move her."

"We don't have a choice. Now put your gloves on."

She shook her head, seeing the squeamish look on his face. He'd been a sheriff's deputy for ten years. The other guys on staff had all been here at least six years. Yet they always turned to her for instruction. That wasn't always the case. She was a woman and she was new to the area, new to the department. But it didn't take long for them to realize her knowledge of law enforcement far surpassed their own. Sheriff Baker was the only one who didn't defer to her. Not in public, anyway.

She tried not to think about what they were doing or how the bones were barely intact when they moved her. Not that she suspected this was a crime scene, but she tried to get as much physical evidence as possible. The lab in Phoenix would give them cause of death. If it was a homicide, perhaps there was some usable trace evidence under and around the body.

"This is the grossest thing I've ever done in my entire life," Randy said when they'd finished taping up the plastic tarp. The smell was only slightly better.

"Yeah, it ranks pretty high on my list too." She stripped off the latex gloves she wore, stuffing them into a crease of the tarp. "Put yours there too. I'll tape them down." She motioned to the horses. "Go get the mule."

Andrea led the way back down the trail, pulling the mule behind her. The last thing she wanted was for the mule to get spooked and take off. Not that she didn't trust Randy, but his history with horses was legendary. They usually did what they wanted and he held on for dear life. She didn't want the mule—and their body—to take off down the canyon.

"Hey, Andi, why'd you leave LA anyway?"

She looked over her shoulder. It was a question she'd heard numerous times in the last two years. You'd think her evasiveness would have given them a clue she didn't want to discuss it. "I wanted to," she said, using the answer she normally gave. Wanted to, needed to, *had* to.

"Yeah, but who leaves LA to come to Sedona, Arizona? It doesn't make sense."

"Why are you here?"

"Crystal's an artist. This is where she wanted to come."

"Right. You came from Las Vegas. Who'd leave Las Vegas to come to Sedona?"

He laughed. "Yeah, but I came for a woman. What's your excuse?"

CHAPTER TWO

"Heard back from Phoenix on that first body," Sheriff Baker said, handing her a note. "Student."

She skimmed over it. Sandy Reynolds, age twenty-one. University of Northern Arizona, Flagstaff. Reported missing by her roommate. "Last seen at a bar?"

"Yep. I've already called Flagstaff and handed it over. Sorry."

She shrugged. "Oh well. I think Randy was more interested in working a homicide than I was. I've done my share."

"Yeah. But it's a shame your skills are wasted up here."

She looked at him affectionately. She'd only known Jim the two years, but he'd become the father figure in her life that had been missing. Her own father would have been a few years younger than Jim. And while they didn't resemble each other physically—her father had been a large, robust man—Jim was just as straightforward and honest with her as her own father had been. He was willing to hear her story without judgment. In fact, he was the only one here who knew the details of why she left LA.

"I don't look at it as wasted," she said. "I've loved my time here."

He nodded and stuck the ever-present toothpick back in his mouth. "So what about this other one? Crawford thinks it might be linked."

"How the hell would he know? I'm pretty sure he had his eyes closed the whole time we were bagging her. But if it is linked, then our timeline is all wrong. This one's been out there at least three weeks, I'd guess. Sandy Reynolds was found after two days."

"Sandy Reynolds was on a well-traveled trail in Oak Creek Canyon," he reminded her.

"She was dumped. If this new one was dumped as well, the killer would have had a hell of a trek carrying a dead body."

"So you're thinking accident?"

"If it's an accident, why hasn't somebody missed her? Three weeks?"

"Not everyone leaves an agenda. We've learned that." He shrugged. "Maybe she's got no one to miss her."

"Did Phoenix give you a time?"

"They'll have a preliminary COD in a day or so, they said. Don't know about ID." He narrowed his eyes. "What does your gut tell you?"

She met his stare without flinching. "Before we found her, I was convinced it was a hiker who had a bit of bad luck." She shrugged. "Now, after seeing her, I think they're linked somehow. She was laid out too perfectly. Even after the animals had their way with her, you could tell she'd been placed there. Just like Sandy Reynolds."

"But you just said it was too far for a dump."

"If he was on horseback, just a couple of hours. I suppose he could have disguised the body as gear on the back of a horse."

"That'd mean he'd have access to a horse."

"Well, anybody can rent a horse," she said.

He sat down across from her desk. "Did I ever tell you about Bigfoot being spotted in Sycamore Canyon?"

"Several times." She smiled at the playful glint in his eyes.

"What about the UFO?"

"A hundred times."

"You don't believe me?"

"What? That two hikers shined their flashlights on a spacecraft that was flying over the canyon? Or the part about them being abducted for a day?"

"Yeah. Nobody believed them back then either. But under hypnosis, it all came out. Spacemen with big bald heads and almond-shaped eyes."

"Right."

"I kid you not," he said. "True story." He scooted his chair closer and she waited for the next part of his story, the one about *him* seeing the UFO. "Lived here my whole life, Andi. I've seen all sorts of things coming and going in the canyon. In the mornings, when the sun is just right, you can see it reflecting off of...stuff."

"Like alien spaceships?"

"Exactly. Bright, shiny objects. Seen it myself," he said. "Several times."

At first, she'd thought that maybe they were just playing with the newbie when they told their stories. But no, the story of the two hikers being abducted by a UFO was legendary. So was the story of Bigfoot roaming the canyon. That story held more credence to her than the UFO. The Bigfoot legend was enough to scare sheepherders away and even some cattle ranchers back in the day. But she drew the line at UFOs.

"So, on our two dead girls, you want to go with the spacemen story or Bigfoot?"

"Oh, hell, I'm not that dense," he said as he stood up. "I don't really believe in Bigfoot."

She laughed when she saw the twinkle in his eyes as he walked away. Another thing about Jim that reminded her of her own father—his playfulness. Her father used to tease her with his own stories, making up elaborate tales at bedtime. Maybe it had been an outlet for his stress or maybe he just genuinely enjoyed entertaining her, but those were memories she would always hold dear. She glanced at Jim as he filled his coffee cup, his smile still playing on his face. Yes, if he packed on about a hundred pounds and shaved that gray, wiry mustache, he could nearly pass for her father.

Randy Crawford came busting in the door just then, Joey Turner on his heels. He flashed a grin at Andrea, then hurried over to Jim.

"Sheriff? I heard on the radio when Sheila said Phoenix had called. What's the word? Need me to go out again and—"

"Slow down, Randy. Damn, I never seen someone so excited about a murder before."

"Well, it's just that we've never had one here."

"I know. And we still don't. She was a student up in Flagstaff. She was last seen out at a bar. I've already turned it over to the PD up there."

"Oh, man. You're kidding? They don't need us for anything?"

"Nope. She wasn't killed here, just dumped."

"Well, maybe we need to go back to the scene and see if there's some evidence left behind."

Andrea snorted. "You wouldn't know trace evidence if it bit you in the ass."

"No. That's why I'd take you along. Then I could listen to all that forensic shit you talk about."

It was true. She did tend to know more about the forensic side of police work than most, mainly because her best friend had worked in the crime lab. It was something she thought she'd want to do and spent nearly a year there, but she soon found she missed the action of being on the streets. Still, even with her limited exposure, forensic science was way over her head.

"Well, I've been back to the scene myself, Randy, so you can rest easy," Jim said. "I didn't see any of that trace stuff Andi talks about. Just rocks, gravel and sand."

"Maybe you want to go up Rim Trail," Andrea suggested. "Take Joey. You can collect some more evidence up there."

"Hell, no. I'm not going near that spot again."

"It could be the murder scene you've been waiting on," Andrea teased.

"I'll pass on that one."

CHAPTER THREE

It was an hour from daybreak and Andrea filled her water bottle, her routine so practiced now, she didn't even think about it. Up before dawn, a quick fifteen minutes of yoga stretches, then out the door with a full water bottle, her trail runners already laced up and ready. Not that she actually ran the trails. But she liked the lightness of the shoes rather than the heaviness of the hiking boots she normally wore while working.

The Jeep that Jim had issued to her was old and dusty, with dents on both sides. But she loved it. The guys fought over the two new SUVs the county had purchased but she was happy with her Jeep, not even wanting to trade it in for the newer and now discarded trucks Randy and Joey used to drive. No, she was comfortable in this, the top down most days, loving the freedom of the wind, the sun.

She drove up Oak Creek Canyon, not venturing from her route. She parked in the same spot at the trailhead, pausing to stretch out her legs again before hurrying up the trail. The nightmares she'd lived with for so long were finally subsiding, but she didn't want to jinx it by stopping. Each morning, she'd hike up the trail to the flat outcropping of rocks facing east. She'd stand still, waiting on the sun, her mind blank. As soon as color showed in the sky, she glided into her Tai Chi routine. At first, she was very disciplined in her routine, staying within the Taijiquan form as she'd first learned. As she became more comfortable with her body and her ability, she strayed from the practiced session, incorporating her own positions and movements. She feared a true Tai Chi master would cringe if they saw her now, but it worked for her. It kept her mind free, focusing on her body, the sun, the earth. Her reasons now for practicing it had nothing to do with the purity of the martial art form of Tai Chi and everything to do with her own psyche.

This morning was no different. The summer nighttime sky of a million stars slowly gave way to the brightness of the day. She knew the trail like the back of her hand, knew where every rock would cause her to stumble, knew when to duck from a low-hanging branch. She slipped off the main trail, taking the side route to her slab of rock.

She stood still, taking deep, even breaths. Slowly, she spread out her arms as if welcoming the sun. In essence, she was. There were many a night when she was certain she'd never see another sunrise, see another day. But years of healing had gotten her past that. Now, she relished each new day, enjoying the simplicity of nature's wakeup call. As the sun showed itself, a deep red color filled the canyon. She held her palms up, nodding slowly, her mind drifting away as her body took over. She bent her knees, then started her routine, moving into each position effortlessly, gliding along the surface of the rock, paying homage to the new day and being thankful she was a part of it.

"You're joking," she said. "Same COD?"
Jim nodded. "Yep. Throat slashed, just like the other one."
"ID?"

"Yeah, that's the scary part." He took the toothpick out of his mouth. "Maggie O'Brien. College student too. Only this one is Arizona State at the Tempe campus."

"That means it's the same killer."

"Most likely."

"And he's targeting college students."

"Different colleges, different cities."

"Jesus. And we're the dumping ground."

He put the toothpick back into his mouth. "And I'm too goddamn old for this crap."

Andrea was already on her computer, pulling up the FBI database. Serial killers normally didn't invent themselves overnight. Most took years to earn that label. And most weren't caught after only two murders. She looked up. "This second body wasn't an easy drop off. He either had help or brought it up on horseback. We should check the stables."

"I can have Randy check the rentals in the area," Jim said.

"She'd been up there several weeks. You think anyone is going to remember back that far?"

"Maybe that was his plan. Dump her far enough so that she wouldn't be stumbled upon right away."

"Making it less likely people would remember him." She shook her head. "Still, he leaves Sandy Reynolds right off a trail in Oak Creek Canyon. As if begging for someone to find her."

"I don't pretend to understand killers, Andi." He motioned to her computer. "What're you looking for?"

"Same MO."

"Slashed throat? Or dumped body?"

"Both."

"Good luck with that."

"Too vague?"

"I would imagine there are a lot of throat-slashing artists out there," he said.

"You think so? It's a messy, nasty way to kill someone. I wouldn't think too many people have the stomach for it."

"A killer is a killer, Andi."

She shook her head. "No. A lot of serial killers use strangulation as the means. No blood. No mess."

He raised his eyebrows. "So, two bodies and you want to say serial killer?"

"Don't you?"

"Those words generally cause panic. Maybe we ought to let the experts determine that."

"Experts? Who? Police in Flagstaff? Tempe?" She shook her head. "They have one body each. No, they're not thinking serial killer. They're looking for boyfriends or whoever Sandy Reynolds saw at the bar last."

"Well, like you said, we're just the dumping ground. There's no crime scene here." He paused. "Thank God."

She wanted to argue with him, but she let him walk away. Technically, no, it wasn't the scene of the crime. But it was a *scene* just the same. She went back to her searching, finding many unsolved murders where the body was dumped. However, not many of those had cause of death as slashed throat. She stored that data, then did a different search. This one for young, college-aged women with no specific cause of death.

"Good Lord," she murmured. She limited her search to the last ten years and got one hundred and thirty-seven hits. She then went back to her first search, that with dumped bodies. She narrowed that down to rural areas. She played with the data, sorting and resorting, trying to find every possible scenario. After five hours—well after Jim had told her to go home for the night—she found a pattern. An alternating pattern.

Ten years ago, two young women were found in the woods near Pine Knot, Kentucky, not far from the Tennessee border. Both had been strangled and dumped approximately two weeks apart. One year later, three women were killed over a two-month period near the University of Tennessee in Knoxville. Two were strangled, one had her throat cut. All three were found at the murder scene. Their bodies had not been moved.

Eleven months later, in the small town of Hillsboro, Georgia, four women were found dumped in the Oconee National Forest. All four were students at the University of Georgia in Athens, some seventy miles north. Three were strangled, one had her throat cut.

Thirteen months later, three women were found murdered

in their apartments in Birmingham, Alabama over a stretch of six days. Only one was a college student. All three had their throats slashed.

Then, only five months later, in Pondville, southeast of Tuscaloosa, four bodies were found in the woods, all within a few hundred yards of each other. Again, two were strangled, two had their throats cut. They never found the murder scene.

The pattern continued, alternating between rural areas and cities, moving from state to state. The most recent of the pattern occurred in Dallas. However, it was the only one where DNA was left. Semen was found at each scene, yet no signs of sexual assault. Three victims, all tied, all with throats slashed. The pattern veered here and Andrea thought maybe the detectives got it wrong. A fourth victim, a male, was also attributed to the same killer. A homeless man was found with his throat cut. Fibers at the scene matched fibers at one of the victim's apartment.

Patrick Doe.

She read the file in more detail. They weren't certain Patrick was his real name, but that's what his brother referred to him as. The brother, John Doe, was dead. Shot and killed by Tori Hunter after he'd slashed the throat of her partner. She frowned. *He dressed like a woman.*

"Jesus, what the hell is this?" she murmured, making a note to call the Dallas PD in the morning. She wanted more information before she lumped these killings in with the others. Leaving semen deviated from the normal pattern. Killing a male also was new. But the overall pattern fit. Rural, city, rural again, then city. The Dallas murders happened eighteen months ago. If it was indeed the same killer, it apparently was the first time Patrick had nearly been caught. None of the other cases even had a suspect.

She read through the notes again, nearly convincing herself the Dallas murders weren't related to the others she'd been researching. Too much was different. But she wanted to be thorough. She'd still call them, get a better feel.

CHAPTER FOUR

Jim read through the notes she'd made. He wasn't much for computers so she'd printed them out. He leaned back in his chair, working his toothpick over as he read. She studied his expression, trying to see if he thought she'd been too liberal in her linking of the murders. If you looked for patterns, you could link almost anything if you allowed for subtle differences. The only real difference she'd found was the homeless man murdered in Dallas. When she read through the file more thoroughly, she determined he was killed for a completely different reason and wasn't a part of the serial killings, even though he was killed by the same man.

"How long did it take you to find all this?"

"Five or six hours."

He took his toothpick out and pointed it at her. "So you didn't go home when I told you to."

"You didn't really think I would, did you?"

"No." He tossed the toothpick in the trash, then tidied the papers she'd given him. "This is interesting, to say the least. How the hell were you able to find this?"

"Now I know you've been on the FBI's database before, Jim, if only to poke around. They've got a great search and sort program. I'm just worried I might be trying to link some that shouldn't be. What if these are two serial killers, one who dumps in rural areas and one who kills in the city?"

"No, I think your scenario is plausible. Go ahead and call Dallas. See if you can talk to this Detective Hunter. Maybe they've got a photo or a sketch of him."

"Great. Thanks, Jim."

She already had the number, hoping he would agree. She dialed it quickly, wanting to talk to them before Randy or the others came in. They would be hovering, she was certain.

"Homicide. Donaldson."

"Good morning. I'm calling from Coconino Sheriff's department in Sedona, Arizona," she said. "I'm wondering if Detective Hunter is available."

"Hunter? No, she's not here anymore. She's working for the FBI now."

Damn. "I see. Well, I'm calling about a particular case...about eighteen months ago. Patrick Doe. Is there another detective who could answer some questions?"

"Yeah. Hang on. Let me see if O'Connor is around."

She skimmed through the file again, finding Detective Casey O'Connor listed, along with John Sikes and Leslie Tucker. Surely one of them would be able to help her.

"O'Connor here. How can I help you?"

"Detective O'Connor, I'm Andrea Sullivan from Coconino Sheriff's department in Sedona, Arizona. I wanted to speak to you about Patrick Doe." There was only silence. "Are you still there?"

"Yeah. Sorry. That's a name I hoped I'd never hear again."

"I'm sorry. And this may sound strange, but we've had two women killed here, both with their throats slashed. College students. They weren't actually killed here in Sedona, but their bodies were dumped here. I've been looking through the FBI's database and came upon your case."

"Patrick didn't dump his bodies. He killed them in their own apartments, tied to their beds."

"Can you tell me something that's not in the file?"

"Hunter was usually very thorough in her notes. This one, though, I think she just wanted it over with."

"Her partner was injured, nearly killed. You can't blame her."

"Sikes never recovered fully. He doesn't get out in the field much, but he's still a part of the team."

"But he wasn't a victim of Patrick, rather his brother, John. Do I understand that correctly?"

"John was slow, mentally slow. He was also innocent. Patrick forced him to do some things, including pretending to be Patrick that day. John was a peeping Tom. We think that's how Patrick found his victims, by following John. We also suspect Patrick dressed as a woman, knocked on their doors and got them to open up for him."

"Why do you think that?"

"John and Patrick were twins. We found John wearing a dress one day. He said Patrick made him wear it but that Patrick was usually the one who wore the dress. I mean, a young woman is much more likely to open the door to a stranger if it's a woman, right?"

"I guess." She skimmed through her notes. "Do you have a sketch of Patrick? Or better, a photo?"

"No. He and John were twins, but not identical. At least, not according to DNA. The semen and John's DNA showed related male. But they looked eerily alike. It's hard to believe they weren't identical."

"You have a photo of John?" she asked.

"Yes. E-mail or fax?"

Andrea glanced at the ancient fax machine, knowing Sheriff Baker would prefer that. "Both?" she asked, then gave Detective O'Connor the number and her e-mail address.

"What makes you think our Patrick is in Arizona?" O'Connor asked.

Andrea didn't want to go into all of her six hours of research, but decided to share some of it. "It may be rushing things to

17

assume two bodies equal a serial killer, but I was curious. Our victims aren't from here and weren't killed here. One is from Flagstaff, one from Phoenix. In the last ten years, I was able to find similar cases. They alternated from killings in cities where the body is not moved, to killings in rural or smaller cities, and the bodies are dumped, sometimes up to a hundred miles away."

"Yeah. My partner did some research into that too. But she couldn't find anything where the killer left semen."

"Right. I didn't either. But there were just too many other similarities. I didn't want to dismiss your case just because of the semen."

"Well, if it is Patrick, he's very smart. We failed with him and he got away. Maybe that's how he avoids capture. He moves from state to state."

"Maybe he won't be so lucky this time," she said.

"Well, good luck. If you need any more information, just let me know."

"I will, Detective. Thanks for your time."

Only a few minutes later, the fax came to life. She then checked her e-mail, finding the file Detective O'Connor had sent. Not only was there a photo of John Doe, but she'd included the entire file on the case. There was much more information there than she'd been able to get from the FBI database.

"Any luck?"

She pointed to the fax machine. "They sent me a photo. That's John Doe, not Patrick."

He studied the photo. "How does this help?"

"They're twins. Not identical, but Detective O'Connor said they looked alike."

"This is all assuming that this Patrick Doe is our serial killer." He tossed the photo on her desk. "Which is questionable at best."

"I know. But it's something."

CHAPTER FIVE

"Son of a bitch."

Andrea took her cap off and tousled her damp hair, letting the breeze dry her skin. They had left the coolness of Oak Creek Canyon a half hour ago. Now, near the rim, they stared at the body of a young woman, her throat gashed open, a gaping hole staring back at them.

Sheriff Baker walked closer and Andrea could see his fists clenched tight, could feel the tension in his body. Two hikers had found the body this morning. By the looks of it, it was dumped during the night.

"Goddamn son of a bitch," he said again.

She pulled her eyes from the body, searching the ground around them, looking for shoeprints, looking for some evidence left behind by the killer. Other than a few rocks being disturbed, there was nothing. She moved closer to the body, noting the bloodstained T-shirt. University of Arizona Wildcats.

"Surely he didn't drive her all the way from Tucson," she said.

"I want to know how the hell he carries a goddamn body up this trail to the rim. That's what I want to know."

"This isn't a horse trail so we know he didn't pack her in." She raised her eyebrows. "You think he's got help? A partner?"

"Serial killers, as a rule, work alone. Isn't that what you said?"

"Yeah. But Patrick Doe had a partner. His brother."

"Who is dead." Jim turned away from the body and looked skyward, into the clear, blue sky. She followed his gaze, wondering if he was praying. "I need to call the FBI," he said after a few minutes. "This is too big for us."

"I know," she said.

He looked at her. "I figured you'd fight me tooth and nail before you'd let me call in the feds."

"Our hands are tied here. We can't do anything except report the bodies and have Phoenix do the lab work. If he's killing in different cities, then the only certainty is his dumping ground. Here."

"Yep. But we both know how vast this is. Even with the so-called professionals working the case, it'll still be blind luck to catch him out here." He glanced back at the body. "We need the equipment so you can process this. Call Crawford. Tell him to bring a mule up the trail so we can get her down. I'll sit with her. You go show Randy the way."

She nodded. This was the third body they'd found but the first one Jim had been along on for the search. It was affecting him probably more than he thought it would. He'd been in this county his whole career. He'd probably never seen anything this disturbing. What was unsettling to Andrea was how *unaffected* she was. Did twelve years in LA do that to her? Or was it the culmination of everything that had happened when she left LA? When Erin was killed, did her compassion die with her?

She stared again at the body, trying to envision the young woman alive, trying to envision the heartbreak her family would feel. She knew all about heartbreak. That, she understood.

CHAPTER SIX

"Get off my lap." Cameron picked the kitten up for the fourth time and placed it again in the passenger seat. "I should have left you at that rest area." The solid black kitten tilted its head. "Don't think I won't leave you at the next one if you keep this up."

Cameron drew her attention again to the road. Not only had she picked up the damn cat in the first place, but now, three days later, she was talking to it. She glanced at it again, glad to see it was finally settling down on the towel and not her lap. The first day, the kitten had hidden from her and she'd searched the large motor home from end to end, finally finding it hiding under her pillow on the bed. She had remedied that by closing the door. The second day of travel, the cat had curled into a corner of the sofa, its eyes wide with fear. Not only was it a starving stray, it surely had never been in a vehicle, especially one as large as the motor home.

She thought she'd give it a week and see how they both adjusted. Cameron had never had a pet before so she assumed she'd be the one doing most of the adjusting. If after a week they seemed to get along, she'd find a vet for the necessary shots...and to find out what sex it was.

"You're a sweet girl, aren't you?" She smiled at it. "Or boy."

She shook her head, glad no one was here to witness this. She doubted anyone would believe it. And this probably wasn't the best time to get a pet. She'd gotten the call the day she'd picked it up. She hadn't had an assignment in two weeks and she was aimlessly traveling, following the cooler weather north. She was in the Utah high country when she stopped to rest, having driven five hours without a break. As she'd walked around stretching her legs, she saw the black ball of fur. It darted under a thick spruce, warily watching her. She didn't know why she was intrigued by it. Maybe subconsciously she was tired of traveling alone. Or maybe it was the frightened, lost look in its eyes that drew her. Regardless, she squatted down, talking softly to it, hoping to entice it out from under the brush. The kitten was just curious enough, or hungry enough, to come out to inspect her. She snatched it up, fighting tiny claws that hurt like hell as she held it tight against her chest.

She looked at her hand now, the deepest scratch healing nicely. The others were practically gone. "And you're such a smart little girl, learning how to use the litter box," she said. Talk about lost. That was her as she walked into the pet store. Her mistake was telling the sales clerk she had her very first kitten. A hundred bucks later, she had every toy and necessity any kitten could want.

"And I don't even know if I'm going to keep you."

Oh, who was she kidding? In three short days the little kitten was already a fixture. Especially at night. Cameron couldn't believe how attached she'd gotten as the kitten curled up close to her head both nights, purring profusely until she fell asleep.

Her phone rang and she touched the large screen on the dash, answering.

"Ross," she said, her voice hard and professional, so different than how she spoke to the kitten.

"Please hold for Special Agent Murdock."

"Yes." She waited only a few seconds.

"Ross? Where are you?"

"En route. What's up?"

"I e-mailed you the file. I also was able to get profiles of the deputies there. Only one has extensive training and experience. The others are pretty much local boys with limited skills. If you want me to get a team in there, I can."

"Let me check them out first. I'm not the one hunting the killer. I'm the one trying to establish a drop pattern, right?"

"Right. I've got a team in Phoenix. Agent Collie is heading that up."

"Collie? Jesus, Murdock, he's an arrogant ass. A goddamn jerk."

"Then you should get along with him fine."

"I won't get along with him fine. I should have shot him the last time we worked together."

"It's not him I'm worried about. Please don't shoot one of the locals."

"That happened one time, Murdock. One time. How long are you going to keep bringing that up?"

"I'm just saying."

She sighed. "I'll try not to shoot the locals. As long as they don't piss me off," she added, getting a laugh out of Special Agent Murdock.

"Okay. Do you have a place lined up to park tonight? Do I need to make some calls?"

"I found what I needed online."

"You're surely not parking that rig in a public campground, are you?"

"Why? Worried about your investment?"

"Hell, yeah. That thing cost twice as much as my house."

"This rig has so much security, no one could break in. But I contacted the ranger at the Coconino National Forest. He put me in touch with one of the guys at a state park right outside of Sedona. Red Rocks. He says he's got a spot I can park her, away from the public."

"Okay. Well, as always, let me know if you need anything.

And please be in touch with Collie. He'll have the most current data on the case."

"I don't know if I can contain my excitement. I'll call him as soon as I get there."

"Read the file first, Cameron. It took me hours to compile all that."

"Right. You mean it took Joanne hours."

She touched the screen, disconnecting the call. Murdock was really the only one she'd call a friend. He was technically her boss. *Technically.* They both knew that was an ambiguous title. If she didn't like something, she didn't do it. She could walk away at any time. The FBI needed her much more than she needed them. However, the military had invested too much training her to just let her walk away into the sunset. She grudgingly accepted the FBI assignment in the first place but found she was good at it. Her problem was playing nice with others, or so she was told. This latest assignment—manning the rig—suited her. She liked the solitude. She liked working alone. And maybe if this experiment paid off, after a few years she could come off the road and train other agents. Or, she could do as she envisioned years ago—walk away into the sunset.

She glanced at the kitten who was fast asleep. Or at least pretending to sleep. "Wonder how you're going to like the desert." The kitten opened one eye, then promptly closed it again.

Cameron drove on as Clair, the onboard navigation system, told her she was a little over two hours away. She'd gotten an early start that morning so she should have plenty of time to set the rig up and read over the file before contacting the sheriff's department. She reached across the console and control panels to the large captain's chair that was the passenger seat, rubbing the kitten's ear affectionately. Maybe it was good she had a pet. She had become far too friendly with Clair, often making inquiries just to hear the computer's voice. At least she hadn't started conversing with Clair. Not much, anyway.

"No. That's what you're for," she told the cat.

"Are you sure you don't need some help with that, ma'am."

Cameron glared at him. "It's Agent Ross, and no, I don't need any help." She'd already unhitched the truck she pulled behind the rig. All she had to do was level it out—which required a push of a button—and put the four slides out, another push of a button.

"I suppose something that big has a generator onboard. There's no power out here. We don't have campsites, but I could rig up something for you, I suppose," he offered.

"I have solar panels," she said, pointing to the roof, "and a backup generator. I should be fine."

"What about water?"

"My tanks are full. Look, Mr. Winfield, the FBI appreciates you cooperating, but I need to get to work." She held out her hand. "So if you don't mind," she said, squeezing his tightly in a handshake, "you need to leave."

"Of course. I suppose you're here because of those young women they found. Sheriff Baker said—"

"I can't really discuss it," she said. "Now, if you'll excuse me."

"Well, I'll be sure to swing by here a couple times a day, make sure everything's fine. I'm going to put that PARK PERSONNEL ONLY sign down there at the road. That should keep any civilians from coming down here to take a look."

"I'd appreciate that. Goodbye now."

"You let me know if you need anything."

"I will. Goodbye."

She lost what little patience she had when she went inside and practically slammed the door in his face.

"Everybody's nosy," she told the cat, who was waiting by her food bowl on the floor—tiny, pitiful meows ensuing. "Didn't take you long to learn how to beg, did it?" She dished out a little of the kitten food she'd bought, then paused to rub the tiny ears on the cat before going to her office.

She unlocked the sliding doors, revealing a small, cramped

room with her computers and electronic equipment. She'd gone a little overboard when designing this, but she'd been given carte blanche on the cost. The FBI was footing the bill on this mobile crime fighting vehicle so she thought she'd at least fix it up how she wanted. It was a fully functioning office, with Internet and satellite, thanks to the gadgets on the roof. The rig itself was totally self-contained, the solar panels her idea. The main reason for the vehicle was to have a working office even in remote areas such as this. Their agreement was for her to use it for one year, then they'd reevaluate the cost and effectiveness of the rig. It had been five and a half months and she'd had eight assignments. This made number nine.

Instead of sitting down at the stationary computer, she picked up the small laptop and went to the sofa, stretching her legs out as she sorted through her e-mail. She opened the file from Murdock, skimming over the details of the murdered women—she'd already read a preliminary report on them—and reading more thoroughly the profiles of the sheriff's deputies who would assist her. Six men and one woman. The woman was the only one with experience, having worked in LA for twelve years. There was a side note from Murdock on her.

Questionable departure from LA. Didn't have time to dig that up but I can if you need it. Let me know.

"Shouldn't matter," she murmured. Actually, she wasn't certain how much she'd even need them. Her assignment was to develop a drop pattern. She had at her disposal various algorithms where she could plug in data and hopefully get accurate results. The hard part was finding what data to plug in.

"Okay, time to meet the troops," she said, going into her bedroom and kicking off her comfortable driving shoes to exchange them for the more sturdy boots. She didn't bother changing out of her jeans or T-shirt. Murdock had given up on her professional FBI attire years ago. The last time they'd tried to put her in a damn business suit she'd threatened to retire. She had a reputation with the others as being a recluse and *extremely* hard to get along with and a whole lot inflexible. Most were probably glad she'd gotten this assignment of solitary travel. She wasn't really a recluse. She just didn't like most people and found it annoying to pretend she did. And she certainly didn't think she was hard to get along with. She wanted things done a certain way—her way—and she wanted them done on her time schedule. That didn't make her hard to get along with. She'd give them the inflexible part. She didn't like to compromise. Maybe it came from being on her own so much as a child.

Or maybe it was because she was usually always right, she mused with a smile.

She grabbed her phone, deciding to call Agent Collie while she drove. No sense wasting time talking to him here. Driving would at least distract her from the aggravating tone that usually encompassed their phone conversations.

"Be back later. Don't get into any trouble."

She paused, smiling at the cat who had resumed its spot on the sofa. Then she took a deep breath, wiping the smile from her face. Time to turn into Cameron Ross, irritating FBI agent.

She locked the door, then using the remote, activated the security system and outside motion-sensitive cameras. There were no loud, obnoxious alarms should someone breach the perimeter. No, it was just her voice. Clear, distinct—warning that they would have ten seconds to back away.

And then the sound of a shotgun snapping a shell into the barrel.

She didn't worry that the warning wouldn't be heeded. If it wasn't, the low-voltage electric shock they would get upon touching the rig would do the trick. That was the real security. The shotgun warning was just for her amusement.

CHAPTER SEVEN

"I'm on my way to the sheriff's department now," she said. "I wanted to see if you had anything of note."

"I just got back from Tucson, Ross. The last victim, Angela Myers, was apparently killed in her apartment. Preliminary, of course, but I'm convinced it's the scene. A hell of a lot of blood."

"The first two victims, you haven't found the crime scene yet?"

"Nothing. I'm wondering if maybe he didn't kill them out in the desert."

"The sheriff here claims this was a dumping ground only, per Murdock's report."

"Yeah, Ross. Since when do you believe a small-town county sheriff?"

"Since I haven't talked to him yet or visited the dump sites, I'll give him the benefit of the doubt."

"Well, be careful with that group. I think they might be a bit gung-ho. One of their deputies worked up a scenario— Sullivan—linking this guy to unsolved murders going back ten years." He laughed. "Yeah, right, as if the FBI can't find patterns in their own database, they need some local deputy to find them. Unbelievable."

"Sullivan's the only one with experience. She spent most of her career in LA. Why don't you send me the file and I'll take a look."

"I already read through it, Ross. It's garbage. Ten years? Come on."

Cameron gritted her teeth, trying to play nice. "I'd still like to read it, Collie. If you don't mind," she added.

"Waste of time, Ross. Why don't you concentrate on the dump sites and let my team work on identifying the killer." He paused. "I think that's your assignment, isn't it?"

"Don't even think about dictating to me what my assignment is. Christ, Collie, I should have shot you when I had the chance." She disconnected without another word, hating that he could push her buttons so easily.

"Fucker. Asshole."

Goddamn jerk.

Talk about a waste of time. Minutes spent talking to him ranked right up there. She took several deep breaths, letting her anger subside. She really needed to do something about her relationship with Collie. He enjoyed pissing her off, and she let him, playing right into his hands. *Fucker.*

She checked the GPS, following its direction to the sheriff's department. Sedona, while a somewhat sprawling town, was larger than she'd first thought. A quick check told her the population was about twelve thousand people and had become quite a tourist destination. Hardly the remote wilderness Murdock had indicated. The town was in a valley, surrounded by the beautiful and wild red rocks that made it famous. She'd had little chance to familiarize herself with the area, other than a quick browse through a few websites. She planned on doing more thorough research tonight.

The cream-colored adobe building that housed the sheriff's

department sat on a corner on the outskirts of town. She counted a car, two trucks, a newer SUV and an old beat-to-hell yellow Jeep, all with sheriff's department insignia plastered to the sides. She pulled her truck into a visitor's spot, next to the lone handicapped parking slot. Shoving her sunglasses on top of her head, she got out and strode purposefully to the door, opening it without hesitation.

An older lady whom she assumed to be a receptionist smiled at her. Cameron ignored her, going instead to the attractive woman sitting behind a very cluttered desk. She looked uncomfortable in her pressed uniform, the beige sandy color zapping the life from her face. Her hair was dark—brown, not black—cut in a shaggy sort of way that nearly begged for someone to brush it away from her face.

Cameron couldn't help herself. She bent down, meeting the woman's eyes, a lighter shade of brown than her hair. She flashed what she hoped was a charming smile, shamelessly flirting.

"Andrea Sullivan, I'm hoping," she said.

"Excuse me?"

"I said I hope you're Andrea Sullivan." Cameron held out her hand. "It would be a pleasure to have someone as lovely as you show me around town, maybe take me to dinner tonight," she said with a wink.

Brown eyes narrowed as they ignored her outstretched hand. "Who the hell are you?"

She straightened. "Cameron Ross. Pleased to meet you." Her statement was met with a blank stare. "Oh, yeah. Here," she said, pulling the leather case from her back pocket. "This might help." She held up her FBI credentials. "I always forget that part of it."

The brown eyes looked her over, head to toe. "You're FBI?"

"Yep. Agent Ross. You can call me Cameron," she said, still smiling.

A fake smile flashed. "Agent Ross, how can I help you?"

"I thought we covered that already. Show me around. Dinner." She shrugged. "Are you free this evening? I would love to get together."

The woman stood. "I am most definitely *not* free this evening. I believe Sheriff Baker is who you want to see."

Cameron followed her down a very short hallway, but it was long enough for an uninterrupted stare at a very nice backside. Pity she had a case. This woman would definitely be worth a chase.

"Sheriff Baker? The FBI agent is here."

Cameron paused at the door, turning back to Andrea Sullivan. She couldn't resist. "I'll bet you a hundred bucks we have dinner tonight," she said quietly, hoping Baker couldn't hear.

This time she got a genuine smile. "I'll be happy to take your money, Agent Ross. You can pay me in the morning because I will *not* have dinner with you tonight."

Cameron had to use all of her professional decorum not to tell her exactly how she'd pay her in the morning. She gave a slight nod, then walked into Sheriff Baker's office, shutting the door behind her. He was older than she'd hoped he would be. Collie was right on that account. He was an old-timer. A tall, slight man with graying hair and a bushy mustache—he stood quickly, offering her a firm handshake.

"I'm Jim Baker," he said. "Thank you for coming."

"Cameron Ross," she said, following his lead of omitting the tiresome titles most law enforcement personnel insisted on using. Perhaps if she ranked as a *Special* Agent, she might be more inclined to use it.

"I've worked with the FBI a handful of times in my career. Most times I've felt like they just want me to get the hell out of the way."

"Well, actually, it's just me so I'll probably need all the help I can get."

"I talked to a Murdock, I believe his name was. He said he had an agent working out of Phoenix too," he said, sticking a toothpick in his mouth. "Andi has been in touch with him."

"Agent Collie. He's working on trying to pinpoint the murder scenes, talk to whoever saw the women last. That angle. I'm here to try to find some sort of pattern in the dump sites." She paused, not wanting to offend him right off the bat. "I read your report. You're certain none of the dump sites could have also been the murder scene?"

He laughed good-naturedly. "You probably think an old man

like me, stuck out here in the middle of nowhere, has never seen a crime scene before." He tilted his head. "You'd be mostly right. We're not a high crime area, that's for sure. But Andi, she's taken the lead on this. She went to all three sites, she found the bodies. If she says it's not the murder scene, then I believe her."

"That would be Andrea Sullivan, the deputy who showed me in?"

He nodded. "She's seen enough horrors in LA. She did say that just because the dump site wasn't the scene of the murder didn't mean they weren't murdered out here somewhere. But this is a pretty vast area. Without a clue as to where, it'd be hard to stumble upon that."

"That could very well be, seeing as how they've not been able to find the murder scenes yet. Well, they have a possible one in Tucson but they're waiting on lab results to be sure."

"I had Andi e-mail that Agent Collie. She shared that scenario with him. She also sent him a file of some stuff she'd dug up on other unsolved murders. He seemed to think she was out of line for even suggesting that. He didn't give her serial killer angle much credence, let alone murdered somewhere out here and then dumped someplace else."

"Well, Agent Collie is..." *A fucker.* "He's not one to take suggestions, really, unless it comes from his boss," she said as diplomatically as she could. "People have different definitions as to what constitutes a serial killer. But if you don't mind, I'd like to have a look at her findings."

"Yeah, sure," he said, rummaging on his desk. "I've got a copy of it somewhere here."

She smiled. "It would be helpful if it was an electronic file, Jim."

He laughed. "I guess I'm one of the few who still like to hold paper in my hands." He got up and opened his door. "Andi? Come on in here." He turned back to her. "If you need someone in my office to assist you, Andi's who you want. She's got the most experience."

"Thanks. I think I'll take you up on that offer."

"What a cutie," Joey said, his neck still stretched out as he tried to stare into Sheriff Baker's office.

"Cutie? That woman would probably break your arm if she heard you say that."

"Did you see her biceps? Did you see how her T-shirt *clung* to everything? Man, I bet she's got six-pack abs."

Andrea smiled. "Trust me, Joey, you're not her type."

"Oh, I know. I saw the way she was looking at you, Andi. But a guy can look, can't he? I mean, she's really cute."

She shoved her chair back, shaking her head. *Cutie?* The woman was far too arrogant to be called cute, although Andrea conceded she was attractive. She stood at Sheriff Baker's door, waiting for them to finish their conversation. He waved her in immediately.

"Andi, come in. Agent Ross here—"

"Cameron, please," the agent said, interrupting him.

"Cameron, yes. Andi, Cameron wants to read your file. The one you sent to that other agent."

Andrea nodded. "I e-mailed Agent Collie a file I'd worked up. He told me I was way out in left field, I believe those were his words."

"Yes, well, Collie is an ass," Agent Ross said bluntly. "I'd be interested to read it."

"Okay, sure." Andrea took the business card Agent Ross handed her, noting the e-mail address as well as cell number.

"I've got a few things to tend to this afternoon, but I'd like to take a look at the dump sites first thing in the morning. Jim said you'd be the one to take me."

"Okay. Two are close to town, up Oak Creek Canyon. The other is up on Rim Trail in Sycamore Canyon. We'll need horses for that one, unless you want to hike eleven miles." She arched an eyebrow, noting Cameron Ross looked more like a beach bum than an FBI agent. Her hair was thick, sandy blond, her eyes piercing blue, her skin tan. She epitomized the word *casual*. "You do know how to ride a horse, right?"

33

"I can ride pretty much anything, yes."

A teasing smile and twinkling blue eyes actually caused Andrea to blush. She hated women who flirted so easily. You could never trust them.

"No doubt," she said dryly.

"What I'd like to do—and Jim, I hope this is okay with you—but I'd like for the three of us to get together for an early dinner and discuss our plan, if you will. That'll give me a chance to read the file and do a little research myself."

Andrea stared at her, then flicked her eyes to Jim. *Dinner?*

"That's fine with me," Jim said. "Andi? About six? Is that too early?" he asked, glancing at Agent Ross for confirmation.

"Six is great." Agent Ross turned those confident blue eyes on her. "Dinner? Six?"

"You have got to be kidding me," Andrea mumbled, just loud enough for Agent Ross to hear.

Again, that arrogant smile. "I rarely lose a bet." She stood, holding her hand out to Jim. "Thanks for your time, Jim. Should we meet here at six or do you have a favorite spot?"

Jim looked at Andrea, waiting. She sighed. "Steaks? Mexican? Local?"

"I'm not much for steaks. How about Mexican? As long as I can get a cold beer to go with it and maybe a nice shot of tequila."

"Juanita's Café. It's off of Eighty-nine, Oak Creek Boulevard."

"I'll find it." She nodded slightly in her direction. "See you at six."

As soon as she left the room, Andrea whipped around, glaring at Jim. "Dinner? You just had to agree to dinner, didn't you?"

"What's wrong with that?"

"She bet me a hundred bucks I'd have dinner with her tonight."

Jim smiled. "Oh. I see. She was hitting on you?"

"She's arrogant. Very conceited."

"You think so? I didn't get that at all. She seemed really nice. Down to earth. Not like most of those FBI agents. What did you call Agent Collie again?"

"A prick."

"Yeah. A prick. I like this girl. Unless of course she's just blowing smoke up my ass."

Andrea wouldn't be surprised if that was the case. While Agent Cameron Ross was nothing if not smooth, she was just a little *too* smooth. Proof being the effortless way she'd won a hundred dollar bet. Andrea thought it wise to keep her distance from Agent Ross.

Cameron took a quick tour through town, just trying to familiarize herself with Sedona. Of course, as she relied on her GPS for practically everything, she didn't know why she bothered. She did find the café they were to meet at later. It looked like a local hangout and not one frequented by tourists. That would be a plus.

She soon turned back to the south and headed for the rig. She wanted to read through Sullivan's file on her suspected serial killer before dinner. She was also just a little anxious to get back and see how the kitten had fared. This was the first time it had been left alone.

After disabling the alarm, she quietly opened the door, not wanting to startle it. The kitten was curled up on the throw blanket on the sofa. It yawned widely, then sat up, stretching out tiny legs.

"Hey, you," Cameron said softly. "Miss me?" She scooped it up, cuddling it under her chin, again silently admonishing herself for turning into such a mush ball with the little thing. For never having had a pet, she was sure getting attached to it. She scratched it a few times under its chin then put it back on the sofa.

Her laptop was where she'd left it and she quickly opened her e-mail, finding the file Andrea Sullivan had sent. Before starting, she went to the fridge and got a water bottle, then sat down next to the kitten. It didn't take long for the black ball of fur to worm its way onto her stomach. Instead of tossing it back to the blanket—as she'd done yesterday—she scooted the laptop down to her thighs, giving the kitten room to curl up.

"God, I hope you're a girl. I'd hate to think I'm falling in love with a boy kitty," she said, forcing her eyes to the monitor and away from her new friend.

Cameron was soon enthralled with the data that Sullivan had assembled. She wouldn't have had the clearance to do more than superficial searching of the database, so some of it was rudimentary, but still, she was quite impressed with the file she'd put together. She imagined it had taken hours to compile it all.

Cameron logged in with her credentials, pulling up some of the early cases where Sullivan had only the bare minimum of details. Unfortunately, there wasn't a whole lot else that Cameron could find. Dallas was the only case where DNA was found. It was also going to be the one most helpful. If they could match wounds and knife patterns, then they'd know if Andrea Sullivan was on to something or not. If there was no match, then her angle was wrong and they were dealing with someone other than Patrick Doe.

She picked up her phone, putting in a call to Agent Collie. She half expected it to go to voice mail so she was surprised to hear his voice.

"I read over the file from Deputy Sullivan," she said. "I think it's quite impressive."

"Oh, come on Ross. Get serious. I told you, I've already looked it over. It's crap."

"I disagree. I think you should have the ME request the records from Dallas. See if they can match the knife, see if the wounds are similar."

"Waste of time, Ross. Even if they are similar, it's hardly conclusive without DNA. Or at the very least, a weapon to match it with."

"I'm not talking about conclusive evidence to use in court, Collie. I'm talking about being able to identify the killer."

He laughed, causing Cameron to bite her lip.

"Identify the killer? As Patrick Doe? Yeah, that helps a lot, Ross. Listen, why don't you just stick to your thing and I'll do mine." He disconnected before Cameron could reply.

"Asshole. Fucker." *God, I hate that man.* She quickly called Murdock, impatiently tapping her fingers.

"Yeah, Ross. What is it?"

"I need to get a file to the ME in Phoenix," she said.

"Collie is—"

"A goddamn asshole."

He laughed. "Oh. So you've already run this by him. Okay, Cameron. What do you need?"

"There was a case in Dallas about eighteen months ago. The deputy here, Sullivan, pieced together some unsolved cases, pretty much the same MO. I'd like for the ME to examine knife cuts, wounds, and see if it's the same as the Dallas case."

"Okay. Send me what you have. I'll bypass Collie."

"Thanks, Murdock. That'll prevent me from having to shoot him the next time I see him."

Truth was, Collie was right. It would do little good to link the cases. It wouldn't help them solve this one. But the possibility of identifying a serial killer—one who's been moving from state to state at will—was enough for her to go over Collie's head. And it would piss him off that she did.

CHAPTER EIGHT

"Do you think she got lost?"

"In this town?"

Andrea glanced again at her watch. It was only ten after six, but still, the least Agent Ross could do—since this was her idea to begin with—was to be on time. And yes, she was childishly pissed that she'd been *forced* to accept the dinner invitation.

"Here she is," Jim said, waving Ross over to their table.

"Sorry I'm late. I was doing a little research." She smiled at Andrea. "Your file was quite impressive, even with your limited access. I took the liberty of expanding the search and came up with a few more possible victims." She pulled out a chair and joined them. "I also got some more information on the cases you'd targeted. I e-mailed that to you, if you're interested."

"Thank you. Do you think it's possible that—"

"Far too early to tell," she said, interrupting her question. "To be honest, Agent Collie thinks it's crap, but you already knew that. I've requested the ME's findings in Dallas be sent here for comparison." She shrugged. "If it's a match, then we have a suspect. However, seeing as Patrick Doe is just that, an unidentified person, it's not going to help us all that much."

"No. But if we catch him, it'll bring closure to the unsolved cases in Dallas. And it may lead to tying up these others I found." Andrea gave a friendly smile to their waitress as she came over. "Hi, Rosa."

"Andi. Jim." She placed a glass of water in front of each of them. "I missed you Saturday night," she said, her voice low. "We had fun."

Andrea nodded. "I had a lot going on. Sorry."

"Maybe next time." She took a step back, assuming a more professional stance. "Drinks? Appetizer?"

"I'll have my usual beer," Andrea said.

"Me too," Jim said.

"Dos Equis, please. With a shot of tequila." Agent Ross gave Rosa a flirty smile, causing the waitress to blush.

"Of course. Can I interest you in anything else?"

Andrea glanced at Jim and rolled her eyes, getting a wink in return. Jim was well aware of Rosa's intent to date her. Even though Andrea had shown zero interest in her, Rosa continued to ask.

"That will get us started. Thank you," Ross said. As soon as Rosa was out of earshot, Cameron grinned at Andrea. "She's cute. Are you two an item?"

"No. Not that it's any of your business," she added.

"True." She took a sip from her water. "Jim said you'd been to all three sites," she said, changing the subject back to the case.

"Yes."

"And you're certain they were just the dump site? Is there any possibility that it was the murder scene?"

Andrea shook her head. "No. Victims with their throats severed like that—there would be a lot of blood. These sites were too clean. In fact, very little blood. There was no evidence of a struggle, no evidence that the victims were dragged. They were placed very carefully, all laid out in a similar pattern."

"Please don't think I'm questioning your ability, Andrea.

I just need to be certain." She paused as Rosa brought their drinks.

"Here you go," she said, placing a beer in front of Jim, then Andrea. She saved the Dos Equis and tequila for last, smiling brightly at Agent Ross. "I hope the tequila is to your liking. It's our best."

"I'm sure it'll be fine. Thank you."

"I'll come by a little later to check on you. You're staying for dinner, I assume?"

"Yes. But we have some business to discuss first, so we're in no hurry."

Rosa nodded. "Let me know if you need another drink." She smiled slightly at Andrea, and Andrea wondered if Rosa thought she was making her jealous by fawning all over Agent Ross.

As soon as she left, Ross was all business again.

"Do you have exact locations of all the bodies?"

"What do you mean? Can I find the spot again?"

"Longitude. Latitude," she explained. "I'll need exact locations. I don't know which algorithm I'll use. For that matter, I'm not sure what data to use."

"I don't understand," Andrea said. *Algorithm? What the hell?*

"My assignment isn't actually to try to find the killer," she said.

"Then what the hell are you doing here?"

Agent Ross looked at Jim. "I'm sorry. I thought I explained—"

"You did. I didn't fill Andi in. My fault."

Andrea glanced between them, waiting for one of them to explain. Agent Ross downed her shot of tequila first, following that with a large sip of her beer. She cleared her throat.

"Good stuff," she said. "Excellent tequila."

"I'm happy for you," Andrea murmured, quickly losing her patience.

But Ross laughed and pushed her beer aside. "My job is to find some sort of pattern in the dump sites using an algorithm. The FBI has spent a lot of money and research time developing several different equations."

"So you're like a math geek or something?"

The agent laughed again. "Hardly. My training has been to

enter the data then decipher the results. How it all works, I don't have a clue."

"And how exactly is this going to help with this case?"

"Well, ideally, you would get other potential sites and you would use the one with the highest probability."

"Are you serious? And what? Catch him in the act?"

"That would be the plan, yes. Providing the group in Phoenix doesn't catch him first."

"And that's Agent Collie?"

"Yes."

"So that's the plan?" Andrea put her elbows on the table and leaned forward. "I don't know much about math, and I know nothing about algorithms, but I'd guess you'd need more than three sites to hope to get a pattern."

"Yes. The more data you have, obviously the more accurate the results are."

Jim, who had been quietly sipping his beer as he watched the exchange, finally spoke. "No offense, Cameron, but this plan seems a little high-tech for Sedona. And like Andi, I don't know anything about your algorithm stuff—in fact, I don't even know what an algorithm is—but just because your computer can tell you the next potential dump site, doesn't mean it's true. A killer may be a poor excuse for a human being, but he's still that—human. Something could come up. He could change his mind at the last minute. Anything. And we're sitting somewhere with our heads up our asses waiting on him and he goes someplace different." He drank the last of his beer. "Just my opinion, of course."

"I understand. In fact, I used to think the same way. But when it works, it works." She too, finished off her beer. "Like I said, that's my assignment. And until Collie and his team can find a murder scene, can find some evidence, then there's nothing much else to do."

"So Collie has a team? Why don't you?"

"I work alone," she said. "Besides, I was offered your services."

Andrea frowned. "Excuse me?" She glanced at Jim, her eyebrows raised expectantly.

"You have the most experience, Andi. You've been to all

three sites." Jim gave her a somewhat sheepish smile. "What? Should I have offered up Randy?"

"Tell me about LA," Agent Ross said. "How long were you there?"

"A number of years," Andrea said evasively. She didn't talk about LA with her own department, she certainly wasn't about to with this arrogant FBI agent.

"Yeah? That's quite a change, going from LA to out here. Why did you leave?"

Andrea clenched her jaw. "That's none of your goddamn business," she said evenly. Agent Ross's blue eyes turned a bit sharper, but she appeared to shrug off Andrea's refusal to discuss it.

"Well, if we're going to work together, I'd like to know who I'm trusting to watch my back. That's all." She raised her hand, getting Rosa's attention. "Another round before we order dinner?"

Andrea nodded, wishing for nothing more than to be able to get up and leave. This was her town, her people. She shouldn't be the one feeling uncomfortable, but uncomfortable she was. Three years, yet she still didn't want to discuss LA and her departure. She didn't want to talk about that night. She didn't want to talk about Erin.

"So, tell me about the dump sites. You said horses would be needed for one," Agent Ross said, pausing to smile—flirt— with Rosa. "We'll have another round, please. That tequila was excellent."

"Thank you. I'll have your drinks right out."

When Rosa left, the agent leaned closer to Andrea. "Are you sure you're not involved with her?"

"I guess I would know, wouldn't I?"

"I'm just getting this vibe, you know."

"Rosa's been asking Andi out for two years," Jim said.

Andrea glared at him.

"Oh, and she keeps turning her down. I see."

"Can we get back to business, please?"

"Sorry. The dump sites. You were going to tell me about them."

"The first victim found was right off the trail, going up Oak Creek Canyon. It's a popular hiking trail so the killer wasn't trying to hide the body. It was left in plain sight."

"This would be Sandy Reynolds, a student from Flagstaff?"

"Yes. First body found, not the first killed." Andrea waited as Rosa placed fresh drinks in front of them. She didn't stay for conversation as customers at another table got her attention. "The victim at Sycamore Canyon was badly decomposed."

"The ME estimated the body had been there three, four weeks before it was found," Jim said. "But I guess you already know that."

Agent Ross nodded. "I read a briefing, yes. They'll have a more concrete time of death after test results are back. This was the student from Tempe?"

"Yes. She was found by hikers up on Rim Trail. They called it in."

"The one we'll need horses for?"

"Yes. Randy has agreed to drive the trailer with the horses over to Sycamore. It'll be noon before we make it back down, I'd guess. Then we can hike up Oak Creek Canyon for the other two sites. They're not far apart."

"Okay. I'd like to get started at first light. Is there an online version of the trails in this area? I'm going to need that data."

"I can send you a file with that information," Andrea said. "What do you need? Coordinates? Elevation?"

"Yes. As well as distance."

"Okay, no problem."

"No problem? We have all that other than in my file cabinet?" Jim asked.

Andrea smiled affectionately at him. "The Forest Service has that information electronically. And I'll get the Oak Creek trails from Bethany over at the park."

"Now you see why I keep saying we're lucky to have you." He tipped his beer bottle at her. "If it were left up to me and the guys, Cameron here would be hard-pressed for assistance."

While Andrea knew that was true, she hated when he belittled himself. Andrea knew when it came to real police work, Jim Baker was top-notch. He knew the law in the books, but he also knew the law of the land. He was fair and honest, the main reason he'd kept his job all these years.

"I'm sure you would manage just fine," Andrea said. "Now, if we're through talking about decomposing bodies, I'd like to eat." And get out of here, she added silently. She'd had enough for one night. And if Agent Ross wanted to get started at first light, that would mean she'd miss her solo hike to her rock ledge, something she suspected she'd need now more than ever.

Cameron watched Andrea Sullivan drive away in the old dented, yellow Jeep, her mind filled with questions. She picked up her phone, speed-dialing without looking. She leaned against her truck, waiting four rings before his sleepy voice sounded in her ear. She'd forgotten the time difference to the East Coast.

"Sorry. I didn't think you'd be in bed already. You could have let it go to voice mail," she said.

"No, it's just been a long week, that's all," Murdock said around a yawn. "What's up?"

"I need a favor."

"Another one?"

"Andrea Sullivan. I want the full workup. How deep can you dig?"

"You know my clearance level, Cameron. I can get anything you want."

"I want to know about LA, why she left, why she's here, who she was involved with—the works."

"You don't trust her?"

"I'm not sure. But she's hiding something. I want to know what it is."

"Okay. Give me a day."

"Thanks. Get some sleep."

She paused before getting in her truck, her gaze following the outline of the distant mountains and rock formations. It was nearly nine but enough light still colored the sky for her to see the red glow from the spires to the west. She'd never spent time in the desert before, certainly not in the wilderness like this.

But in the five and a half months she'd been on this assignment, she'd hit nearly every state in the west, except Washington and Oregon. She found she loved the vastness of the high mountain desert, the endless vistas, the varied terrain. She was actually looking forward to their trip on horseback tomorrow. It would give her a close-up view of the canyon, of the rock formations.

She shoved off her truck, reminding herself she had a kitten waiting for her. And that thought brought an unexpected smile to her face.

CHAPTER NINE

Cameron turned, the leather of the saddle squeaking with her movement. She pulled her horse to a stop, the beauty of the sunrise too awesome to miss.

"Wow," she whispered. They'd been heading west, the sky still heavy with darkness. But to the east, the sun shimmered behind the red rock formations, making the whole landscape glow and pulse with light. She glanced at Andrea, noting she too stared at the colors. "That's incredible."

"Yes. It used to make me sad to think so many people sleep this time away," Andrea said, pulling her eyes away from the sunrise to look at her. "Now I realize how lucky I am. You can't make someone love this."

"True. But still, everyone should experience this at least once. It's breathtaking up here."

Andrea pointed across the canyon. "That's Devil's Tower," she said. "The rock formations around it are quite impressive. Devil's Bridge still stands. Devil's Kitchen was once a natural bridge that collapsed in a sinkhole. At this time of morning, with the sun shining—"

"It looks like the gates of hell," Cameron finished.

"Exactly." Andrea nudged her horse on. "We should head up. It gets blistering hot once the sun is high."

Cameron followed, reminding herself of the reason they were up here in the first place. It wasn't intended to be a pleasure trip, but that didn't keep her from enjoying the scenery just the same. She was amazed at the changing colors as the sun rose higher. Ahead of them, she could see the red glow as it raced across the earth, waking the land to the new day, changing from dark to light, from dull brown to bright crimson.

Cameron finally brought her attention to the woman in front of her. She felt a bit guilty at having Murdock do a background workup on her. Some things are meant to be private and obviously Andrea Sullivan felt the same way. Unfortunately, Cameron wasn't in a position to blindly trust someone, especially if they were going to be working closely together. Perhaps she would give her another chance today, before Murdock filled in the gaps.

"So, you ready to talk about LA?" She saw the stiffening of Andrea's shoulders, but she didn't turn around.

"What do you want to talk about?"

"I want to know why someone would give up an exciting career in LA and come to a sleepy little town as this."

"Yeah? Well maybe it was too exciting."

"Why did you leave LA?" Cameron asked again.

"As I said last night, it's none of your goddamn business."

"And I didn't want to argue with you last night in front of Jim, but it is my goddamn business. I want to know who I'm working with."

Andrea jerked her horse to a stop and turned around. "Fine. Then get someone else to work with," she snapped. "I didn't volunteer for this, you know."

Wow. Who would have thought that anger could make someone more attractive than they already were? But Andrea's eyes flashed nearly black, her jaw clenched tightly, the look on her face daring Cameron to argue with her.

"True." Cameron smiled, knowing it was a bit condescending, but she smiled all the same. "But you're stuck with the job now. Sorry."

"The hell I am. I'll head right back down this trail and leave you on your own."

Cameron laughed. "Are you serious? That's your retort? That you're going to leave me?" Cameron nudged her horse up beside Andrea's. "Listen, I just thought I'd give you the chance to tell me about yourself before I read the file on you."

Brown eyes widened. "What file?"

"The file I requested on your background."

"You son of a bitch. You have no right."

"Actually, I have every right. I'm FBI. Remember? I can do whatever I want."

"Goddamn...arrogant," Andrea muttered, "...bitch."

Cameron laughed again. "Oh, come on. Surely you can do better than that."

"I hate you," she shot back as she kicked her horse, trotting up the trail away from Cameron.

"Like I haven't heard that before," Cameron called as she followed. "So what did you do? Have an affair with a superior?"

"Shut up."

"We all have skeletons, Andrea." No response. "I noticed that most everyone calls you Andi. Is that what you go by to your friends?"

"Don't you dare," she threatened. "Don't even try to pretend we're friends."

"Why can't we talk?"

"I don't want to talk to you."

"Look, I'll let you ask me some questions," she offered.

"Don't care."

"Come on. Don't you want to know something about me? Like if I'm seeing anyone?" Cameron called, still trying to catch up. "I'm single, by the way," she added.

"Oh, I don't doubt that for a minute," Andrea said. "I can't imagine that someone would actually date you, much less stay with you."

"Why not? I'm cute enough."

"Your looks will get you a first date. I seriously doubt anyone would suffer through a second one."

"What are you saying?"

"I'm saying you're arrogant. Conceited. A bully."

"A *bully*? Okay, I might give you the first two. But a bully?"

Andrea led her horse off the trail and Cameron followed. "Yes, a bully. You're trying to bully me into telling you about my past. You're threatening me. You're running a goddamn FBI background check, for God's sake."

"I told you, if I'm going to work with you, I need to be able to trust you."

"Well, that works both ways. How do I know I can trust you?"

"The FBI trusts me. That should be enough."

Andrea shook her head. "What exactly is it that you do for the FBI?"

"What do you mean?"

Andrea looked over her shoulder at her. "I've worked with my share of FBI agents in LA. Suits and ties for the men, business suits and jackets for the women. You don't fit the FBI profile."

"Oh. Well, that's where you're at a disadvantage. I can't really tell you anything."

"No? See, that's why I don't trust you."

"I'd like to tell you, but I can't. It's classified."

"Classified? I thought you were FBI, not military?"

"Currently, I'm FBI."

"Currently?"

Cameron knew she could reveal more than she was, but she was having too much fun pushing Andrea's buttons. "I was military. Special Ops."

"What did you do?"

"Sorry. It's classified." That, at least, was true. But again, she was surprised by the flash of anger on Andrea's face. "Most of my past is classified."

"I see. So your offer of sharing—you ask me questions and I ask you—is just a joke. You can hide behind the *classified* line. But I'm not afforded the same luxury."

"I don't believe the LAPD had classified missions, did they?"

"If your past can remain a mystery, why can't mine?"

"You know, if you had told me just a little, even just something insignificant, I'd probably be okay. But your adamant refusal has now piqued my curiosity to a point where you're forcing me to dig into your past. And the FBI can dig as deep as we like." She shrugged. "That was your choice. Not mine."

"My God. You're not just a bully. You're mean. I think you take pleasure in hurting others." Andrea pulled her horse to a stop and slid out of the saddle.

"Hurting?" Cameron did the same, sliding to the ground on legs that were sore from two hours on the horse.

"Yes, hurting. Did you ever think that maybe my departure from LA was painful for me? Maybe I don't want to talk about it. Maybe I don't want to relive it. I spent three goddamn years trying to forget it. Three long years where I wasn't sure I would see the next day, the next week. I'm finally past that. This last year has been almost normal. So I don't *want* to tell you about it." Her angry eyes filled with tears. "I lost my whole team. I don't want to go back and relive it. I have enough scars."

Cameron knew she should just let it go, but she didn't. She suddenly got very angry. "Scars? You're not the only one with scars. You're not the only who's lost a team." Cameron yanked her T-shirt over her head, standing still as Andrea's eyes raked across her body, landing on the numerous wounds of her past. "We all have scars we have to live with. We all have memories we'd just as soon forget. But we can't. They sneak in, they make you relive it every damn day." She pulled her shirt back on, now angry with herself for losing control but unable to stop. "Don't tell me about scars," she said loudly. "I can match every one of yours, both physical and emotional. I've got scars on my soul that are so deep, nothing can heal them."

She walked away, taking deep breaths, trying to regain some composure. She was out of line, and she knew it. But that wasn't enough to make her offer an apology. She wasn't here to make friends. And if Andrea Sullivan hated her, so be it.

"I'm sorry."

Cameron turned, the quiet voice filled with sadness. She lost every ounce of her anger just by the look on Andrea's face. She shook her head. "No. My fault." She cleared her throat. "Is this it?" she asked, getting back to business.

"Yes." Andrea walked about twenty feet away, then stopped. "She was here."

Cameron took her digital camera from her pack, along with her notebook computer and the handheld GPS. There was very little evidence that a body was once there.

"The ME said she'd been dead...what? Three, four weeks?" she asked, already knowing the answer.

"Yes. That coincides with when she was last seen."

"And it's been three weeks since you removed her?"

"Yes."

Cameron took pictures of the site, then recorded the coordinates in her notebook, along with the elevation. "Did anyone take photos of the body?"

"Yes."

"They weren't in the file I read."

"They were in the file we submitted to Agent Collie."

"Figures." *Fucker.* "He hates me and enjoys making my life miserable," she explained. "Can you e-mail me the file you sent him?"

"Sure."

"In fact, any correspondence you have with him from now on, please copy me."

"Okay, but it's not like we actually correspond. We were instructed to send him our files after the third body was found. He never responded back. I sent him my findings on the serial killer angle, and he did respond, but you already know how he feels about that."

"You want arrogant? Spend some time with Collie. He'll make you want to slit your wrists."

She got a slight smile out of Andrea with that, so Cameron went closer. "Look, I'm sorry about earlier. I was out of line." She held out her hand. "Truce?"

Andrea stared at her hand for a few seconds, finally reaching for it. "Truce."

"Good. And I'll refrain from reading your file. If you want to tell me, fine." She shrugged. "If not, well, I guess I'll just have to trust you on what I see."

"Thank you. I appreciate that."

Cameron turned a circle, looking around them. She was no longer seeing the rock formations, no longer looking at the scenery. She raised an eyebrow.

"How the hell did he get a body up here?"

"We have to assume on horseback. There are several stables that rent horses."

"Four-wheeler?"

Andrea shook her head. "They aren't allowed on this trail."

"Just because they aren't allowed doesn't mean it didn't happen. Could have come up here at night, dumped her then back down in less than an hour. Possible?"

"Possible, yes. Probable, no. The trail is narrow and steep in places. What are the chances our killer is an experienced rider? A night trip up in a four-wheeler would take skill."

"You're probably right, but it's still something to consider. Maybe on our way down we could look for signs," she suggested.

Andrea looked up at the sun which was now higher in the sky, the summer heat starting to show itself. She had droplets of sweat on her forehead and Cameron watched as she took her cap off and shook out her hair.

"Are you ready to head down?" Andrea asked. "We don't want to be up here on the rim much longer. The heat radiates off the rocks making it feel about twenty degrees hotter than it is."

"Yeah, I'm done here."

The ride back down was made in relative silence, and Cameron enjoyed the views nearly as much as on the way up. The multitude of rock formations had her imagination jumping, but her mind kept going back to the same question: How did he get the body up here? Horseback seemed the logical answer, but it also was very risky. For that matter, taking a four-wheeler out on an equestrian trail was risky as well but not nearly as risky at night. Even if someone reported you, you could be back down and gone before anyone of authority showed up.

"Can you get a signal up here?"

"Cell?"

"Yes."

"On a good day, yes."

She looked for signs along the trail to indicate a vehicle had traveled up the trail, but the red rocks and gravel all blended together, making it nearly impossible to tell if anything was disturbed. "Do you see anything that looks odd?"

"No. But then it's been nearly two months since she would have been dumped."

"Right. Making searching for anything futile."

"Pretty much."

"Who found her?"

"Don't know. A hiker. He called it in."

"You didn't interview him?"

"No. He called it in anonymously."

"Does Collie know that?"

"I would assume. It's in the file."

"Okay, so our killer dumps his first victim. Weeks go by, yet no one finds her. So, he dumps his second victim where she's sure to be found. Still, his first one lays unnoticed."

"Oh my God. You think he's the one who called it in?"

Cameron nodded, knowing she needed to go back and read the file more thoroughly. "It's possible. He wants credit for it, don't you think? So he calls it in, you find it. Then, a week later, a third victim is found. By now, you of course know all three are linked."

"And serial killers want the notoriety. Three murders are better than two."

"And four is better than three and so on," Cameron said. "Which leads us back to our question. How the hell did he get a body up here?"

"I've been thinking about your four-wheeler possibility. This is an equestrian trail, obviously used by hikers as well," Andrea said. "But farther north, there are four-wheeler trails. While the Rim Trail is essentially a loop around the canyon, there's a connecting trail between this one and one used by four-wheelers. I've never been on it, but Joey's hiked it before. He would know whether it's passable for four-wheelers or not."

"Good. Because it makes this dumping more logical then. He carries her up on a four-wheeler. We assume at night. Gets off the main trail, takes the connecting one to the rim, dumps the body fairly close to the trail where he assumes it'll be found rather easily."

"But it's not."

"So he's forced to call in the location himself."

Andrea grinned. "As scary as it seems, we're thinking alike on this."

"That's what partners do. They bounce ideas off each other." As soon as the words were out, she saw a cloud cover Andrea's face. Obviously, it was the wrong thing to say. Andrea gave a quick nod and continued down the trail, leaving Cameron to speculate on what caused the distressed look. It didn't take much thought. Andrea had said she'd lost her whole team, which most likely meant her partner as well.

And with that, too, Cameron could relate. She'd lost close friends, she'd lost lovers, and she'd lost partners. Yet, she survived, being forced to pick up new friends, new lovers. And yes, new partners. It was the most difficult—and painful—part of her job. Which was why she liked the current setup. She worked alone. There was no one to lose but herself.

CHAPTER TEN

Andrea stood near her Jeep and downed her second bottle of water, the heat of the summer day taking its toll on her. Agent Ross had left as soon as they'd made it back down Oak Creek Canyon, offering only a quiet "see you later." That, of course, was fine with her. She wasn't in the mood to chitchat.

After they'd made it down the mountain from the Rim Trail and left their horses with Randy, she'd lost all her enthusiasm for the day. She'd hoped that Agent Ross would put off the other two sites. But no, they barely took a break before they were hiking up Oak Creek Canyon.

And as before, Cameron marked the coordinates and entered them in her notebook computer along with the elevation. Andrea had watched her carefully as she studied each site, walking a wide circle, her eyes darting around, obviously looking for something—anything—that could be considered evidence. Andrea hadn't interrupted her, even though she'd been over both sites several times herself.

They'd hiked back down in near silence as Andrea had withdrawn again, not wanting to talk, afraid Cameron would say something to trigger old memories. She hadn't had a partner, not since Erin. They patrolled alone here, not needing to ride in pairs. And even when they did, it wasn't like she always went with Randy or always went with Joey, although they were her closest friends, if she'd even call them that. Other than Sheriff Baker, they had six deputies and Janet the receptionist who only worked part-time. Besides Jim, Randy and Joey, she had only a working relationship with the others, including Janet. And while Janet had always been cordial toward her, she suspected Janet was a bit of a homophobe. And Andrea could really care less. When she first arrived in Sedona, she hadn't been in the right frame of mind to make friends and was content to live a solitary life. But Jim, Randy and Joey had slowly drawn her out, and she joined them often out socially. Little by little, she'd returned to normal.

But today, when Cameron Ross had lightly tossed out the word "*partner*," Andrea was taken back, her mind flashing to Erin—her partner and lover—as she lay covered in blood, her eyes, so cold and lifeless, staring up at nothing, both legs missing below the knees.

"Christ," she murmured, feeling her chest tighten as memories crashed in. She turned, staring out at Thunder Mountain, taking deep breaths as she tried to focus. She closed her eyes, imagining herself in the early morning, her feet moving effortlessly across the rock slab, her body going through its movements without thought, her mind's eye watching as the sun rose above the canyon. Slowly, her tension eased, her anxiety lessened.

She opened her eyes again, seeing Thunder Mountain in the late afternoon, the sun beating down on Sedona. Middle to upper nineties were normal for this time of year, but it would cool off nicely after the sun went down, cool enough for a light jacket some nights.

She got in her Jeep, reminding herself that she'd missed her workout that morning. Perhaps that was why she let her emotions take over. After the incident—the ambush—she'd seen a therapist, hoping it would help her understand why her team was killed and she was left to live. They were a close-knit unit, and besides Erin, she'd also lost Mark, her best friend. They'd gone through the academy together, they rode patrol together in the early days, and they'd both made detective at the same time. At her urging, they both moved on to narcotics where she met Erin.

But nothing could take her grief away, not even Mark's wife, who—after the initial shock was over—sought out Andrea, perhaps knowing that Andrea was blaming herself, placing guilt where none belonged. She didn't want anything to do with Paige, however. She didn't want anything to do with anyone who reminded her of what she lost. When she realized her therapist wasn't helping, her grief turned to despair. She had never felt so helpless, so hopeless, so terribly alone. Each day was a struggle to go on, almost to the point of giving up.

In was quite by accident she found Tai Chi. The only solace she had at the time were solitary hikes in the mountains outside Los Angeles. She'd leave early, well before dawn, getting to the trailhead as the day was beginning. On one such hike, she saw him. He was standing high on the rocks, his arms spread out to the rising sun. When he went though his movements, he was graceful and elegant, and she thought it was the most beautiful thing she'd ever seen.

She began to study Tai Chi, learning the various forms of the art. She only took formal lessons for six months as she wasn't interested in becoming an expert. She simply needed something to focus her energy on and she combined the meditation techniques she'd been studying with the Tai Chi movements she'd learned, creating her own form.

When she felt strong enough—a year after the ambush—she left LA. She didn't think she'd return to law enforcement, she didn't think she'd be able to, but she soon learned she had no skills for anything else. Even then, she wasn't certain she'd work again as no one would hire her. Apparently, the little incident with her captain labeled her a high risk.

Fortunately, Jim Baker was willing to take a chance on her, even after she refused to discuss it with him, telling him her past was off limits. He hired her anyway. That was two years ago, the last of which—as she'd told Cameron—was almost normal. And every morning during those times, she'd hiked up Oak Creek Canyon to the rock slab, going through her routine, focusing on the present, not the past. Every morning, that is, until today.

She wasn't foolish enough to think that even if she had gone, Cameron's words wouldn't have had the same affect on her. But she realized it was something she still needed. Unfortunately, for the first time, she was on a case. She wouldn't always have the opportunity for her early morning hike. For now, at least, she was at the mercy of Cameron Ross.

And as much as she told herself she didn't like the woman, that she was arrogant and conceited, she still knew she owed Cameron an explanation. Or at the very least, an apology. It was very presumptuous of her to assume she was the only one carrying around scars. But Cameron Ross was literally covered with them. In the few moments Cameron had stood before her in nothing but her sleek bra, Andrea had counted six wounds marring what was otherwise a beautiful body. The most prominent one, a huge slash of a scar from her shoulder across her torso, the black bra hiding the part that crossed her breast. The wound was obviously from a knife or a sword, and Andrea was surprised Cameron had survived it.

She pulled into the driveway of the little house she rented, unmindful of the long neglected yard and flower beds. After living in apartments for so long, she thought she'd enjoy having the space of a small house, thought she might actually plant a flower or two. But it was one of those things she just never got around to. She went inside, the air cool, refreshing. She headed straight for her bedroom, shedding her clothes as she went. She was tired and hungry, but she lingered in the shower, closing her eyes and holding her face in the water, feeling a strange peacefulness settle over her. For once, her thoughts weren't jumping in all directions as she tried to steer them away from that fateful night. No, for once, she felt focused. She felt like she had direction.

She leaned back out of the water and opened her eyes. Yes, this was good. She had a case. She felt like she was actually doing police work, something she was trained to do. She had something to focus her mind and energy on, something other than the past.

And if she had to suffer through a few days—or even weeks—of Cameron Ross, so be it. At least she had a purpose now. Amazing how trying to solve a murder could make her feel so alive.

And inclined to talk. She left the house forty-five minutes later with a bottle of wine and an order placed for pizza. Jim said Cameron was staying out at Red Rocks Park. Why, Andrea had no idea. Surely she wasn't camping, but she couldn't imagine she was staying in the old, tiny cabins they rented. Well, didn't matter. She'd find Sonny Winfield. He'd know where she was. Not much happened at Red Rocks without Sonny knowing about it.

CHAPTER ELEVEN

"I haven't had a chance to look at it yet," she said. "I just got out of the shower."

"Well, you were right. She's got a few demons," Murdock said.

Cameron hesitated. She'd all but told Andrea she would not read the file, but now Murdock was tempting her with demons. "Give me the short version," she said as she sat down and opened her laptop, smiling as the black ball of fur immediately joined her.

"She and her team were supposed to be intercepting a drug deal. They had someone on the inside, had been working it for months. It was a setup. Her team was ambushed."

Cameron glanced through the file quickly, feeling a twinge of guilt as she read through it.

"There was a blast and two of her team members landed on her. She was protected from the automatic weapon fire that the rest of her team suffered. Five killed."

"Protected? Says here she suffered two wounds."

Murdock cleared his throat. "Protected in that she didn't die," he said.

Cameron smiled as she read more. "Wow. She pulled her weapon on her captain. How cool is that?"

Murdock laughed. "Thought you'd like that part."

"Why are there two files?"

"One is personal. I didn't know how much you wanted. One of her team members, Erin Rogers—they were lovers."

Cameron hesitated, then decided not to open it. Losing your team is one thing, losing your lover quite another. No wonder Andrea Sullivan didn't want to talk about it.

"From what I gather, Sullivan was invested more in the relationship than Rogers."

"What do you mean?"

"Oh, read the file, Ross. I don't want to get into all of that and it may not even be relevant. Let's just say Rogers played the field and Andrea Sullivan had no idea."

"Great. So she's suffering guilt because her lover was killed, yet her lover was—"

"Sleeping with four other women."

"Wonderful." She quickly closed the file she had opened. As Andrea had so bluntly told her earlier—it was none of her goddamn business.

"They never found where the breakdown was, so no one was prosecuted. However, after the scene with her captain where she threatened to shoot him, well, she was relieved of her duties. She had a hell of a time finding another job."

"No doubt. Okay, Murdock. Thanks. I'll read it more thoroughly later," she said.

"Anything new on the case?"

"No. Collie?"

"Yeah. But he's supposed to call you and fill you in. Apparently, the crime scene in Tucson was faked. None of the blood belonged to the victim. DNA matched it to Sandy Reynolds, the student from Flagstaff."

"The first body found. He's fucking with us."

"Amazing. You and Collie are more alike than you think. He said those very words."

"Don't insult me."

"Anyway, he's supposed to be in touch with you. And I let him know about the file I sent to the ME there. He wasn't happy with you, but the ME in Phoenix said he'd have results in a day or so."

"Okay. I've got the particulars on the dump sites. I'll start feeding the info and see what comes up."

"Keep me posted."

She sat there for a few minutes, listening to the gentle purring of the kitten as she rubbed its head. She decided having the cat was good for her. It brought a quiet peace to her life that had been sorely missing.

She was about to get up and see what she had on hand for dinner when the silent alarm flashed, signaling an approach. She waited, curious to see how close someone would get. It was obvious she was there. Her truck was right outside, lights were on. She went into her small office and flipped on the monitor, surprised to see Andrea Sullivan outside. She nearly laughed as Andrea took several steps back as her warning was heard, followed by the sound of the shotgun.

"Agent Ross? Are you there?" Andrea called.

"She's got pizza." She glanced at the cat. "You think we should let her in?"

"Cameron? I swear, if you have a shotgun pointing at me, I'll kick your ass when I get in there."

She laughed outright at this, turning on the speaker as she flipped off the security. "As if you could kick my ass," she said. "The security is off. Come on in." She closed the doors to her office and locked it. Not that she didn't trust Andrea Sullivan. She just wasn't in the mood to explain what all the equipment was.

"The only reason I let you in was for the pizza. I'm starving," she said when Andrea stepped aboard.

Andrea put the pizza and a bottle of wine on the counter and looked around. "What the hell is this?"

"Home," she said. "Home and office, actually."

"A motor home? The FBI has motor homes?"

"It's an experimental model," she said, the enticing aroma of the pizza making her stomach rumble. "How did you find me?"

"Sonny Winfield. He was very protective of your location. He only told me where you were because I told him we were partners on this case," she said, turning a circle. "You live in this alone? And just travel around?"

"Well, obviously, if there's something happening in New York, I'm not going to get that assignment. I'm pretty much relegated to the western states." A tiny meow brought her attention to the sofa. "And I don't live alone."

"Oh, my God," she said, scooping up the tiny kitten. "You have a cat? *You?*"

"Why not me?"

Andrea rubbed her face in the fur. "You don't seem the type."

"You've known me two days," Cameron countered.

"Right. And you don't seem the type." Andrea held it under her chin. "What's its name?"

Cameron paused. "Cat."

"Cat? You can't name it Cat."

She opened the cabinet and took out two plates. "Well, I wasn't sure if I was even going to keep it. I found it at a rest area in Utah," she said. "Besides, I don't know if it's a boy or girl, so I didn't come up with a name." She stared as Andrea turned the kitten around and lifted up its tail. "What are you doing?"

"It's a girl."

"How can you tell? It's like they're missing some parts or something."

Andrea laughed. "They're not like dogs. But trust me...it's a girl." She put the kitten down on the floor. "We had a momma cat when I was a kid. When she had a litter, part of the fun was finding the sex."

She handed Andrea a plate with two slices of pizza loaded with everything. "I'm not going to touch that statement." She held the wine bottle tightly as she turned the corkscrew. "But I'm really glad she's a girl. I've fallen in love with her. I think it would just be wrong if it were a boy." She pulled, loving the sound of the distinctive *pop* of the cork. Andrea slid the glasses closer and Cameron filled them both.

"Take the sofa," she said, choosing her recliner instead. The sofa was really nothing more than a loveseat. Cameron had chosen to have the recliner instead of a full-sized sofa as she knew she'd rarely have visitors, and she wanted the comfort of the recliner.

"This is nice. It's not as cramped as I'd imagined."

"Four slide-outs," she explained before taking a bite. "This is great," she said with a mouthful. "What are you doing here, anyway? I doubt just to bring me dinner."

"I thought I owed you an apology."

"Really? For what? The arrogant, conceited, bully, bitch names you called me?"

"No. You deserved those," Andrea said with a slight smile. "I meant for the way I treated you this afternoon."

"Oh. The ignoring me and not talking part?"

"Yes."

"Well, I obviously said something that—"

"You know what you said."

Cameron nodded. "Yes."

"Have you read my file yet?"

"No," Cameron said. And it wasn't really a lie. She'd only skimmed her professional file. The personal file, she didn't open. "Should I?"

"I guess I've accepted the fact that you will, regardless if you should or not." Again, a slight smile. "Even though you said you wouldn't. You know, curiosity and all."

"Okay. Then do you want to be the one to tell me instead of me going by only what your file says?"

"Yes." She held up her last slice of pizza. "The pizza was just an excuse," she admitted. "And I figured you were as hungry as I was."

"And the wine?"

"Well, I thought if you have a couple of glasses, you might not be quite as judgmental."

"So you plan a total confession? We might need two bottles then."

They were quiet for a minute as they both finished their pizza. Cameron was surprised that the kitten was ignoring her and was instead pressed against Andrea's leg. Of course, Andrea had picked it up and cuddled it, obviously knowing how to interact with the animal. Cameron, on the other hand, hadn't a clue.

"Can I ask you something?"

Cameron pulled her eyes away from the kitten, nodding at Andrea. "Sure."

"Why did you come into the office the way you did yesterday?"

"What do you mean?"

"You walked in without identifying yourself and asked me to dinner."

Cameron smiled. "You mean why didn't I say I was FBI or why did I ask you to dinner?"

"Why did you assume I'd have dinner with you?"

Cameron got up, taking both their empty plates to the sink and returning with the wine bottle. "I had every intention of identifying myself and meeting with Jim," she said. She debated telling Andrea the truth, but was afraid she'd see through a casual lie. "When I saw you, I somehow forgot why I was there. Your hair was all windblown," she said, pointing at it, "and you had a bit of a wild look in your eyes." She sat down again. "So, that arrogant, conceited side of me took over." She smiled. "I gave it my best shot."

"And you just assumed I'd fall for it?"

"Well, you still owe me a hundred bucks. I guess you did fall for it."

"You're crazy as hell if you think that little trick won a bet for you."

Cameron leaned back in her recliner, enjoying the conversation, but wondering if Andrea was stalling. Andrea must have sensed her question as she, too, leaned back with a heavy sigh.

"I worked...narcotics," she finally said. "We'd had someone on the inside, took us months for him to establish a relationship with the supplier. There were six of us going in. We were...we were very close. All of us. We were a good team." She looked up, meeting Cameron's eyes. "We were ambushed. I'm the only one who survived." She looked away quickly. "Mark, Mark was my

65

best friend, going all the way back to the academy. And Erin, she was my partner."

Cameron saw the misting of tears and leaned forward. "And lover?"

Andrea nodded. "Yes. Stupid, I know. Never, ever get involved with your partner. How many times have we heard that?"

"Yes. It's a good rule. It's there for a reason. But it's probably the one rule that gets broken most often." She waited a few seconds, seeing the faraway look in Andrea's eyes. She sympathized with her, she really did. She'd been there herself. "How long were you together?"

"About a year."

"Lived together too?"

"No. No we didn't. We didn't want to raise any questions."

Cameron nodded. That also made it easier for Erin Rogers to date other women at the same time. She wondered if those other women grieved as much as Andrea.

"That didn't make what we had any less," she continued, as if Cameron had questioned it. Or perhaps it was Andrea wanting to question it but her guilt wouldn't let her.

"No, it didn't," Cameron said. "Were you injured?" she asked.

"Yes. Not badly." Her eyes closed and Cameron assumed this was where the real guilt stemmed from. The fact that she was protected by her dying team. "There was an initial blast and two of them—Kevin and Mitch—were thrown on top of me. What the bomb didn't do, automatic weapons did. I didn't think they would ever stop. I couldn't believe I was still alive. Amazing that I only took two hits, really. One to the leg and one to the shoulder where the vest didn't cover me." She slowly slid her fingers into her hair, trying to tame it. "They pulled seven slugs from my vest."

"When did backup come?"

Andrea looked back at her, her eyes again far away. "They came right away, but it was too late. They were all dead, the shooters got away." She shrugged. "Never to be seen again."

Cameron waited for Andrea to collect her thoughts, not wanting to push.

"I was left to grieve alone," she finally said. "My team, they were my closest friends. I couldn't even be there for Mark's wife when she needed me. No one outside of my team knew about me and Erin, so..." she said, her voice trailing off.

Cameron wondered if it would ease some of Andrea's guilt if she knew the truth about Erin. Whether it would or wouldn't, she decided it wasn't her place to tell her. All she had were words in a file. Andrea had a life with this woman.

"Anyway, I did something really, really stupid."

"We all do stupid things when we let our emotions take over. I don't know if anyone can be rational after that."

"No one had answers for me. No one knew how the drug dealer was tipped off. No one was tearing apart the department, looking for the leak." She held her wineglass out. "Can I have some more?"

"Of course." Cameron filled it nearly to the top, noticing the trembling in Andrea's hand.

"When you read my file you'll see that I pulled my weapon on my captain. Not only that, I threatened to shoot him."

Cameron couldn't help but laugh, and she was immediately sorry as soon as she did. "It's not funny, I know. It's just... I've been there," she said. "Twice."

"You threatened to shoot a superior?"

Cameron smiled and arched an eyebrow.

"Oh, my God. You *shot* them?"

"I only shot *at* one of them, and he had it coming. The other, well, he eventually saw things my way."

"How much trouble did you get into?"

"My punishment was a mission no one wanted. I got sent to the desert for three months with enough supplies for a week. I think I bathed only four times during those months."

"Gross."

"Yes. But back to you," she said. "Those three months are something I don't want to think about." She refilled her own wineglass. "What happened with your captain?"

"Well, obviously, I didn't really shoot him. And because of what had happened, they didn't take any formal action against me. In fact, it wasn't publicized at all."

"But you got fired?"

"Oh yeah. It didn't matter. I couldn't have worked anyway. I wasn't in the right frame of mind."

"And you are now?"

"Yes."

"Therapy?"

"Yes. At first. But it wasn't really helping. Or at least I didn't think it was." She rubbed the kitten's fur, a smile on her face as they listened to the loud purring. "I started taking hikes, getting out of the city where I could be alone, where there were no distractions. I saw this guy doing Tai Chi. I was fascinated by him. So I started studying it, learned about meditation, about internal focusing." She paused, chancing a look at Cameron. "It was amazing how I was able to drift away, almost like leaving my body behind as I took a spiritual journey." Andrea smiled. "You probably think that sounds silly. I know I would, if it hadn't happened to me."

"No, not at all. I'm familiar with Tai Chi. In fact, I practiced it some, but went on to Tae Kwon Do and even karate."

"Do you still practice?"

Cameron shook her head. "No. In the military, I had to use my skills as a weapon. It ceased being an art."

"You've killed with your hands?" she guessed.

Cameron met her eyes without blinking. "That's classified," she said quietly, knowing that Andrea took that as an affirmation to her question.

"I'm sorry."

"No need. Like I said this morning, we all have skeletons, we all have scars to live with."

"Tell me about yours," Andrea urged.

Cameron gave a half-hearted laugh. "Which one?"

"Why so many?"

"Just been in a few scrapes in my time."

"It's classified?"

"Some, yes."

"What did you do in the military?"

Yeah, what did you do, Cameron? Sniper? Kidnapper? Liar and cheat? Killer? Spy? Not so flattering when you think of it that way, she supposed. "Special Ops," she said.

"That's vague."

"Yes."

"Tell me about the scars," she said again.

"Battle scars," she said. "Nothing more."

"You ever lost a partner? A lover?"

Cameron nodded. "Once, yes." She swallowed hard. "It was my fault."

"Tell me."

"Why? Will it help you?"

"No. But it might help you."

"You think I need help?"

"I've known you two days. You seem...intact," she said. "Or maybe your bravado and arrogance are a cover."

"It happened a long time ago, Andrea. I doubt I'm still harboring guilt for it. Not after...well, not after everything else I've done." She had always been proud to serve her country, but she'd never been proud of some of the things she'd had to do. Like kill.

"Were you military police or—"

"Look, really, most of my missions are classified."

"But you're retired?"

"I wanted out, yes. They weren't ready to let me go."

"So FBI?"

"It was a compromise," she said evasively. It was basically the truth. It was either that or walk away from her career at a relatively young age. She knew after the last assignment, in Darfur, that she had reached the end. She had become nothing more than an assassin. The life of a sniper and eliminating long-range targets was one thing to deal with. But planning and calculating the murders of three government officials from a hostile country—and going through with it—was quite another.

"You don't like to talk about yourself, do you?"

"Nor do you," she countered.

Andrea nodded, acknowledging the standoff. After a few moments, she asked, "So, what's the plan?"

Cameron didn't think she'd change the subject quite so easily or give up her inquisition without a fight. She was thankful Andrea did. For all the digging she'd done into Andrea's past, she had no desire to reciprocate and share the details of her own miserable past. "I'll input the data from the sites into some of the equations I have. I really don't think there's enough data to establish any sort of pattern though."

"Meaning we have to wait for more bodies?"

"Yes. And Collie is no closer to having a murder scene. The blood found in the apartment of the third victim—"

"The one from Tucson?"

"Yes. Angela Myers was her name. Anyway, the blood wasn't hers. It was from the first body you found, Sandy Reynolds."

Andrea stood, pacing as well as she could in the small space. "So that means he abducted her and killed her later."

"And he wants to make sure we know the murders are linked."

Andrea walked away, then turned, retracing her steps. "Sorry, I think better when I pace."

"No problem."

"I'm trying to remember," she said. "The file I put together, wasn't there a group of killings where they never found the murder scene? In Alabama, maybe?"

Cameron reached for her laptop. "I think you're right. They were all students. Dumped in the woods."

"Yes. Not all of the killings involved college students. But it seemed that in each group of killings, at least one was a student."

Cameron opened the file and searched, finding the section Andrea was talking about. "Here," she said, motioning Andrea over. "Pondville, Alabama."

Andrea leaned over her shoulder, reading. "Yes. Five months after the Birmingham murders. Those women were found murdered in their apartments, leaving the crime scene all nice and tidy."

"Then five months later, he moved on to Tuscaloosa, abducting four women, killing them—those murder scenes were never found—and dumping their bodies in the woods near Pondville."

Andrea straightened up. "Why the hell did Collie think this was so far out in left field? It's a perfect pattern."

Cameron nodded. "I think you're right. But I haven't had a chance to do anything with this data yet. I may pass this on to the geeks who wrote these programs and see what they can do with it. My training is geared toward concrete figures, numbers, locations, that sort of thing," she explained.

Andrea put her hands on her hips. "Seriously? You travel around in this thing, this moving computer, and only enter data into equations? That's your job?"

"I take it you're not saying that with envy. Like, wow, what a cushy job."

"I'm saying it like, wow, what a boring job."

Cameron wasn't in the least offended by the comment. "After everything I've done in the name of... *democracy*, something that borders on boring is a welcome relief."

"And guys like Collie get to have all the fun?"

"Well, like I said, I've had my share of fun."

CHAPTER TWELVE

Andrea wasn't all that excited to be back in the saddle, but she figured there was little else to do. Cameron wanted to take the connecting trail across the canyon rim to where the four-wheel drive trails were, hoping to get an idea of how he carried a body up here without anyone spotting him.

"This trail doesn't look well used," Cameron said.

"It's not. Years ago, before dirt bikes and four-wheelers became popular, all these trails were equestrian. Now, if you're on horseback, you avoid the motorized trails. I assume mountain bikers might use this trail or hikers looking for a shortcut down the mountain."

"But it's plenty passable for a four-wheeler, don't you think?"

"Yes, I think so. There's not—" She paused, seeing overturned rocks to the right of the trail. She pulled her horse to a stop, then hopped off.

"What do you see?" Cameron asked.

"These rocks are disturbed," she said. She heard the leather of Cameron's saddle cracking as she got off her horse too.

"Don't get too close."

Andrea tossed an annoyed look at Cameron. "It's not like I haven't done this before, Ross."

"Sorry."

Andrea squatted down, her eyes scanning the rocks, finally finding what she was looking for. "There," she said, pointing.

"Tire tracks," Cameron said as she squatted down beside her. "Wide. More than a dirt bike."

"Definitely." Andrea stood, walking a wide berth around the rocks, looking for more. Cameron still studied what they'd found before taking out her camera. Andrea watched as she entered data into the digital notebook she carried.

"Anything else?"

"No. Looks like he was heading south, got off of the trail here," she said, pointing. "Possibly to avoid those boulders."

"If he was carrying a body, he wouldn't have wanted to chance any mishaps," Cameron said.

"Right. Avoid the boulder trap, go around it, then back on the trail." She shrugged. "Of course, that's been a month. Small chance these tracks are from our guy." She walked back to the trail where they'd come from, looking for signs of where the four-wheeler would have gotten back on track. She didn't see anything that looked disturbed. She turned back around, feeling Cameron's eyes on her. Her eyebrows shot up when she saw just what Cameron had been looking at. "You were checking out my ass? Seriously?"

"What? You have a very nice...derriere. There's nothing wrong with looking."

"Really? Nothing at all?"

Cameron smiled. "I haven't made it a secret that I find you attractive."

Andrea put her hands on her hips and stared at her. "Your original dinner date notwithstanding—I'm not interested."

"No? Still holding out for Rosa, the waitress?"

"For your information, I'm not holding out for anyone, least of all you," she said as she stomped back to her horse.

"Oh, I see. Still grieving." Cameron shrugged. "It's been what? Three years now? How long are you going to carry that torch?"

Andrea pulled herself into the saddle, turning her horse around to face Cameron. "That's cruel, even for you. How long I grieve for someone I loved is my own damn business." She nudged her horse, then stopped. "Or is that something you can't relate to? Loving someone?"

"Now who's being cruel?" Cameron took the reins of her horse and walked closer. "I have loved before, you know."

"Oh really? And is it *classified* as well?"

"Look, my whole damn life is classified."

"Of course it is. It's easier that way. Then you don't have to talk about it. I just wish you would afford me the same luxury."

Cameron held out her hands. "Why are we fighting?"

"You started it."

"Me? All I did was look at your ass."

"Exactly."

Andrea jerked her horse around Cameron, continuing down the trail. She didn't know why she'd gotten so upset. So Cameron was ogling her ass? Frankly, other than Rosa, no one had even bothered to flirt with her since she'd been in Sedona. She should be flattered.

"Look, I'm sorry," Cameron called from behind her. "So you've got a nice ass? I'll refrain from looking at it."

Andrea hid her smile. She knew she'd severely overreacted, but she was enjoying hearing Cameron grovel in her apology. "Sure," she called back, as sarcastically as she could manage.

"I mean it. I'll also quit trying to imagine you naked."

Andrea whipped her head around, her retort dying on her lips when she saw the grin Cameron sported. "Oh, so now you're teasing me."

Cameron kneed her horse, breaking into a trot to catch up with Andrea. "Teasing? No." Her eyes raked across Andrea's body, pausing at her breasts. "I would just imagine you'd have—"

"Stop."

Cameron laughed. "Okay, I'll stop. But really, you went a little nuts—"

"I know. I'm sorry," Andrea said.

"I wasn't trying to belittle your relationship," Cameron said. "But if you carry your grief too long, you stop living yourself."

And as quick as that, Andrea got angry all over again. "You have no idea how difficult that was for me. Maybe you can relate. Maybe you've had something similar happen to you, but you don't know *me*. And you don't know what I went through. Alone. So don't tell me when to stop grieving."

"You weren't the one killed, Andrea."

"Yeah? Well maybe sometimes I wish I had been." She kicked her horse harder than she intended, sending it bolting down the trail, away from Cameron Ross.

Cameron knew she should heed Andrea's words that it was none of her concern. She also failed to take her own advice. *Mind your own business.* Truth was, she liked Andrea and she hated to see that haunted, soulless look in her eyes sometimes. Grief was a powerful emotion, especially if you had to endure it alone. And especially if the line blurred between grief and guilt.

She went inside the sheriff's department with only a curt nod at the receptionist. The only deputy she knew by name was Randy and that only because he tended to the horses for them. The young man who looked at her now was the one who had sat next to Andrea the other day when she'd first arrived.

"I'm Cameron Ross," she said, offering her hand.

"Joey Turner," he replied, squeezing her hand firmly. He looked behind her. "Where's Andi?"

"She wasn't feeling well. She decided to call it a day."

"Well, what's wrong? Andi is never sick. I don't think she's ever missed a day."

Cameron lost her patience and moved past him. "I'm sure she's fine. Is Jim in?"

"He's in his office."

Cameron saw the worried look on his face as he picked up the phone, no doubt to call Andrea to check on her. Good luck with that, she thought. After the way she and Andrea had spent the last three hours, she wouldn't imagine his phone call would be answered.

She knocked lightly on Jim's opened door, smiling when he looked up.

"Cameron, come on in." He, too, looked behind her. "Andi?"

"She went home." Cameron shut the door. "I guess she did, anyway," she added.

"What's wrong?"

"You tell me."

"What do you mean?"

Cameron leaned forward, resting her elbows on her thighs. "How much do you know about her past?"

Jim tossed the toothpick he'd been chewing on his desk and folded his hands together. "I know more than she thinks if that's what you mean."

"You pulled her file?"

"Of course."

"And you hired her anyway?"

He twisted the edge of his wiry mustache between his thumb and forefinger, a slight smile playing on his lips. "I liked her so much, I wanted to hire her first thing. But then when she wouldn't tell me anything other than superficial stuff, well, I got curious."

"And?"

"And I've wanted to pull my weapon on a superior or two before," he said with a laugh. But his smile faded quickly. "It's tragic what happened and she's told me a little about it over the last year. She's never mentioned a word of it to the others, and I've kept her confidence." He watched her. "I'm assuming you know."

She nodded. "Yes. FBI background check."

"On all of us? Did you find any skeletons in my closet?"

At the look he gave her, Cameron was nearly embarrassed they'd done any checking at all. "Actually, it was all pretty much preliminary," she said. "We wanted to check prior experience and see who might be best able to assist." She shrugged apologetically. "When I tried to find out more from Andrea, she refused to discuss it. I didn't want to take any chances."

"I see." He leaned back in his chair and linked his hands behind his head. "So now you want a new partner?"

"No. Quite the opposite. She's extremely competent. She knows her way around out there," she said. "I told her I'd done a background check on her and she was pissed as hell."

"No doubt."

"It prompted her to tell me some," she said.

"I'm surprised. As I said, she's not mentioned a word of it to anyone here. In fact, she pretty much keeps to herself, other than a few dinners out with us once in awhile."

"So she doesn't have a crowd she hangs with, people she dates?"

Jim snorted. "Rosa is the closest she's come to dating and that's not saying much, seeing as how they've *not* dated."

"You know about her partner then?"

"You mean that they were...*involved*?"

Cameron nodded. "I see you do."

He looked at her thoughtfully, then leaned forward again, resting his elbows on his desk. "Did she tell you about her parents?"

"No. What?"

But Jim shook his head. "I'll save that for her, if she chooses. It has no bearing on this," he said. He tapped his desk with his fingers. "You're worried about her though?"

"Yes. I feel like she's a good cop, but I want to be sure."

"She's the best I got. She'll have your back, Cameron. She lost her team, lost her partner, lost her best friend. I doubt she'll ever let that happen again."

"Sometimes those things are out of our control. Like it was for her then."

"And she won't be able to handle it, is that what you're saying?"

"I think she's walking a very thin line right now, Jim. She's trying to keep her past and her present separate. Almost like two different lifetimes. They're bound to collide sooner or later."

Again he studied her, making her nearly uncomfortable under his thoughtful gaze.

"May I ask you a personal question?"

"Ask away," she said easily. That, of course, didn't mean she'd answer him.

"You've been here a handful of days, you've spent time with Andi. I'm assuming your concern for her is professional, not personal."

It was a statement that surprised her and she flashed a quick grin. "I don't mix business with pleasure, Jim, if that's what you're asking."

"Good. Because Andi would cringe to hear me say this, but I've always thought of her as tough as nails when it came to the job. But emotionally, she's always carried a look of vulnerability about her." He met her gaze head on. "I would hate to see her get hurt."

"Understood. Like I said, my interest in her is totally professional."

"Wonderful." He picked up his earlier discarded toothpick and plopped it back in his mouth. "Now, are you making any progress with the case?"

CHAPTER THIRTEEN

"I swear, Collie, you're so goddamn stubborn, a clue could bite you in the ass and you'd ignore it."

"The fact that the ME has established a match in the knife wounds is irrelevant. It gets us nowhere closer to solving this case."

"No. It just links seven murders and establishes a serial killer's pattern," she said. "And I think you owe Deputy Sullivan an apology for trashing her research."

"What? Her linking of nearly every unsolved murder in the U.S. going back ten years? That's real genius."

"Apparently so. They're still analyzing the data, but they're prepared to link the cases."

"They? The computer geeks the FBI hires?" He laughed. "Unless I get a confession from the killer or have concrete DNA evidence, I don't link anything. You'd be wise to do the same."

Cameron had tired of this conversation. "Okay, Collie, so

we've given you the name of the killer. What do you have? Crime scene? DNA? You found a murder weapon yet?"

"The name? Patrick Doe? Yeah, that's real helpful, Ross. That'll get us going for sure."

She heard the dead space and looked at her cell, seeing that the call had ended. Oh, she missed the good old days where you could actually hang up on someone with the slam of the phone.

"Asshole." *Fucker.*

She had just tossed her phone on the sofa and picked up the kitten when it rang. She lightly nuzzled the kitten's fur, much like she'd seen Andrea do.

"Maybe he's calling to apologize for hanging up on me, huh?" She let it ring a couple more times before picking it up. "Ross."

"It's me. There's another body."

"Oak Creek Canyon again?"

"No. Sycamore. The Dogie Trail. It runs along the creek."

"Okay. Are you on your way?" She filled the kitten's food bowl as she passed by, then unlocked the file cabinet in her office, carefully taking out her service weapon.

"I'll wait on you. I sent Joey out to close the trail."

"Good. I'll be there in five."

"Look, about yesterday—"

"Can we just not talk about it, please."

"I just wanted to apologize," Cameron said.

"Fine. Accepted. Let's move on."

"You don't want to discuss—"

"No." Andrea gave a forced smile. "I don't."

She turned her attention back to the road, thankful the drive to Sycamore Canyon wasn't a long one. She should have known Cameron would want to *discuss* their little argument. When she first met her, she would never have guessed Cameron was the type to talk so much.

"Who found the body?" Cameron asked after the silence apparently became too much for her.

"Hikers," she said. "Locals, actually. Ben Speers and his wife. They own the tire place on the north side, on the road to Flagstaff." She smiled, knowing Cameron could care less who they are. "In case you wanted to question them," she added.

"I assume you already have."

"Just briefly. Sheriff Baker took their statement, not me."

"I'm sure Jim got all the details we need. Namely, did they disturb the scene?"

"They assured me they didn't get close enough for that."

"I guess it is a little unnerving to the people who live here."

"You mean because we've become a dumping ground? Yes," Andrea said. "The only thing keeping the town from going into panic mode is the fact that none of the victims are locals. Of course most are worried how this will affect the tourists." She slowed as they approached Red Canyon Road which would take them to the lower end of Sycamore Canyon. "This is a nice hike through the canyon here," she said. "A lot less crowded then Oak Creek."

"But still used daily?"

"Oh, yes. It's not as remote as the Rim Trail," she said.

"So he wouldn't have been taking a chance that this body would go unnoticed then."

"No. The Dogie Trail gets enough usage, especially up to Taylor Cabin. It's five miles in, then five back. There are a few side trails, if you're looking for solitude." She didn't mention those were the trails she normally took when hiking here. "Parson's Trail goes up to the springs, the only year-round water in the canyon. The creek is seasonal," she added.

"Is that a practiced tour guide speech or are you familiar with the trails firsthand?"

"When I've got the time, I hike here, yes," she said. "I mostly go up Oak Creek though. It's practically at my back door."

She parked her old Jeep at the trailhead next to Joey's new truck. She saw the amused expression on Cameron's face as she cast a dubious glance at the brand-new sheriff's department truck and then at her Jeep, the insignia mostly faded on the doors now.

"Because I like it," she said, answering Cameron's unspoken

question about the old Jeep. She opened the cooler on the back and pulled out two cold water bottles, tossing one at Cameron. "Here. You'll need this."

"How far in?"

"Not too far. About halfway, they said."

"Horses?"

"What? You afraid of hiking?"

"No. I was thinking of the time, that's all."

"Horses aren't allowed on the Dogie Trail," she said, taking the lead.

"Surely we could have made an exception," Cameron said.

Andrea laughed. "It's ninety-five degrees and not a cloud in the sky. Could that have anything to do with your *time* issue?"

"Perhaps."

Andrea walked on, trying to ignore her hiking partner. She hadn't been on this trail since early spring, and she'd forgotten how scenic it was, even following the now dry Sycamore Creek.

"It's pretty down here," Cameron said, as if reading her thoughts.

"Yes. Spring is best. The creek flows then, everything is green."

"This is the kind of place I always imagined sneaking off to when I was a kid."

"Why didn't you actually do it?"

"Because these places didn't exist."

"Where did you grow up?" Andrea asked. "Or is that classified too?"

"I grew up...nowhere. Everywhere."

Andrea stopped, waiting for an explanation.

"Military brat," Cameron said. "Navy. Seems like every few years, we'd move to a new base."

"You hated it?"

"You get used to it," she said.

Andrea continued along the trail, wondering how many questions she could ask before Cameron shut her off. "I figured you grew up in California," she said.

"Why?"

"Blond hair, blue eyes. Tan. Beach bum."

"And all of that just screams California?"

"You could be the poster child, yes. You look like you belong on the beach."

"We spent some time in California. Florida, too. So yeah, I hung around a few beaches."

"Where did you spend your high school years?"

"Washington State."

"Really? What about—"

"Enough. I think you've reached your limit."

Andrea laughed. "I was just getting started."

"Why are you so curious about me?"

"Why not? You're curious about me."

"My curiosity is totally professional," Cameron said.

Andrea stopped abruptly, causing Cameron to bump into her. "And how does checking out my ass fall into that category?"

Cameron raised her eyebrows. "You really want to start *that* conversation up again?" Cameron moved past her. "I'll lead. That way you can check out *my* ass."

Andrea's gaze involuntarily dropped to the ass in question. As usual, Cameron's jeans were loose, faded, comfortable looking. And the rhythmic swaying of her hips as she walked had Andrea mesmerized. That is, until the swaying stopped.

"Are you coming or what?"

Andrea pulled out of her self-induced stupor, embarrassed for not only getting caught looking but also for the blush that covered her face. She ignored the amused and quite satisfied look in Cameron's eyes as she brushed past her. She could not, however, ignore the chuckle she heard.

"Get over yourself already," she muttered, hearing the chuckle turn into an outright laugh.

Thankfully, the rest of the hike was made in blessed silence, most likely because of the fast pace Andrea set. She spotted Joey sitting on a rock under one of the cypress trees, taking advantage of the limited shade.

"How much farther?" she asked.

"Just around the next bend," he said.

She touched his shoulder and squeezed, noting his pale skin and the dread in his eyes. "You okay?"

"I just have never...never seen anything like that," he said, his voice quiet and faraway.

"You didn't disturb anything, did you?" Cameron asked.

"No. No, I didn't," he said. "You want me to wait here?"

"Yeah. Randy's coming with the trailer. I asked him to bring a mule. We'll need to get her out of here, and I didn't think anyone would be up to carrying her that far."

"Okay, yeah, I'll wait for him here."

Andrea glanced at Cameron, motioning with her head up the trail. Joey was obviously shook up and she was afraid Cameron would make mention of it.

"So what happened to your *no horses* rule," Cameron asked.

"I knew this would be quicker," she said. "Besides, we had such a pleasant hike in, didn't we?"

Cameron stopped her with a light touch on her arm. The body lay up ahead, only a few feet from the trail.

"She appears to be laid out like the others," Andrea said.

"Walk a wide berth," Cameron instructed. "See if there are any tracks. I know this is a relatively flat trail, I just have a hard time thinking someone carried a body in."

Andrea nodded, going to the left of the body while Cameron moved to the right. She found nothing out of the ordinary. She stopped, her gaze finally moving to the victim.

"Oh, God," she whispered. It was just a young girl, her throat slashed open just like the others. She watched as Cameron walked carefully toward the body, squatting down beside it.

"Son of a bitch. She's a child. She's just a goddamn kid," Cameron said. She stood quickly, moving away. "Not a college student. Just a kid," she said again.

"The other killings, they were never all college students," Andrea reminded her as she moved closer. She, too, squatted down beside the body, trying to keep her emotions under control as her trained eye took over. Cameron had also slipped into her professional mode, taking her camera and notebook from her bag.

"Maybe not just a kid," Andrea said after studying the girl.

"What do you mean?"

"I mean, I don't think this is someone's baby girl." She stood up. "Cheap makeup. Bright nail polish. Costume jewelry." She pointed at the scuffed shoes. "High heels."

Cameron lowered her camera. "Hooker?"

Andrea nodded. "Possibly a runaway. She's young."

"So maybe he used her services before he killed her."

"And left DNA? He's been so careful not to leave any trace evidence behind. Why would he make things easy by leaving DNA now?"

"Let's assume Patrick doesn't know we've linked these killings to Dallas."

"And he wants to make sure he gets credit for them," Andrea said, following Cameron's train of thought.

"Exactly."

"But why? If he's killed before, if the other cases from years ago turn out to be linked, why does he want credit for it now?"

"I don't know. As far as we know, the Dallas cases were the only time DNA was left behind. We don't know why that differed either. But think about it. Dallas was the first time he was close to getting caught."

"But he didn't."

"Right. So now it's a game. It's much more fun than just killing and moving on. He staged the crime scene in Tucson. It's a game to him."

"And he's winning."

"Sure he is. We don't have a clue as to where he is or when he'll strike next. It's genius," she said. "When the news is filled with warnings to college girls, he shifts gears. He takes out a hooker. We don't know where she's from, what her name is. By the time we find out, he may already have another victim."

"Let's release a sketch of him," Andrea suggested. "We've got pictures of John, his brother. We can just tweak it a bit, based on what the Dallas detectives said."

"It's been my experience that releasing a sketch, rather than an actual photo, causes the opposite reaction than what you hope for."

Andrea nodded. "Neighbor accusing neighbor."

"Right. We'll get thousands of possible sightings and end up chasing our tail as we try to track them down."

"Do you think his MO is still the same? Sleeps during the day, out at night? Changes hair color? Wears a dress?"

"Probably. I think the detectives in Dallas were right on. It's much easier to get close to your victims if you appear to be a harmless woman yourself. In fact, that may have been his MO all along."

Andrea raised her hands in frustration. "I just feel like we're not doing enough. I mean, maybe if we got more information out to the public, more details about the killings then—"

"He'll stop?"

Andrea sighed. "Yeah. He'll stop for a few months, then move on and start all over again."

Cameron came nearer, gently squeezing her hand. "As far away as we are to catching him, we're still closer than anyone's ever been."

Andrea surprised herself—and Cameron too—by letting their fingers link together. "I know." They stood there, their eyes never straying from the other. Andrea felt the gentle pressure of Cameron's fingers, and she returned it. She struggled to get her thoughts in order, struggled to think of something witty to say.

"When we find him, can we throw all professionalism aside and shoot the bastard between the eyes?"

Cameron laughed and stepped away, breaking the tension that was surrounding them. "I think that's an excellent idea. But maybe we should just keep that to ourselves."

CHAPTER FOURTEEN

Andrea wished she'd insisted on having this working dinner out at a restaurant instead of her house, but she knew what they needed to discuss was best said in private. At least Jim would be there. Not, of course, that she was afraid to be alone with Cameron. She would like to think that their relationship would remain professional, although that line had already been crossed. And she wasn't talking about the little hand-holding incident either. It was just, well, there was nothing professional about the way they talked to each other. There never had been.

The hand-holding was a completely different matter altogether. In fact, it was the first time she'd been touched—or touched someone—since Erin died. Not that there was anything intimate about it. It was just...

"It felt nice," she said to her empty room. She glanced at herself in the mirror then quickly looked away. No. Not nice. Strange. It felt strange. She didn't even like Cameron Ross. She found her to be annoying and obnoxious. She smiled. Annoying, yes. Obnoxious? Not really.

"Borderline," she finally conceded as she shed her clothes and stepped into the shower.

Holding hands with an annoying, borderline obnoxious, arrogant and conceited woman...and liking it. She stuck her face into the water.

No, it felt strange, remember?

Cameron knocked on the door with her foot, her hands holding the three pizza boxes and the bag with wine and beer.

"Coming," Andrea called.

"Come faster," she called back.

The door opened and Andrea stood there, eyebrows raised. "Come faster?"

Cameron was thoroughly embarrassed by the flush she felt on her face. "I assure you, there was nothing sexual about that. I just didn't want to drop dinner," she said, moving past Andrea. "Kitchen?"

"To the left."

"You know, when I said I'd pick something up for dinner, I had no idea how hard that would be."

"Small town."

"I refused to settle on burgers or fast food," she said. "But there's only one Chinese restaurant and they don't do takeout. Whoever heard of that? It's probably the only one in the country who doesn't do takeout."

"They have a buffet. Besides, Jim hates Chinese food."

"Well, I didn't know what kind of pizza he liked. I know you like everything on yours. So do I. I got Jim the meat-lovers thing. He looked the type." She handed Andrea a bottle of wine. "I got him a couple of beers."

Andrea laughed. "Jim will love you. I should have warned you he doesn't do wine."

"Where is he, anyway? I thought I was late."

"He'll be along," she said as she turned the corkscrew.

Cameron looked around the kitchen, quickly noting the absence of anything personal. Temporary housing, that's all. She recognized the look. Toward the end, that's how their home always looked. Temporary. Just waiting on the call, telling them they'd be moving to a new base.

"You rent?"

"Is it that obvious?"

"Yeah, it is." Cameron went into the living room, the walls bare. "Are you afraid to put down roots?" she asked.

"I wasn't certain how long I'd be here," Andrea said, handing her a glass of wine. "Now, well, it's home, I guess."

"So when you left LA, you left all of your stuff behind?"

"I sold as much as I could, gave the rest away. I didn't want any reminders. I thought it would be easier."

"Was it?"

Andrea tilted her head. "Why is it, Cameron, that you get to ask questions, but I never can?"

"Oh? You think we should share? Give and take? Quid pro quo?"

"It seems only fair."

Yes, it did. And that's what scared her. But she nodded. "Okay. Ask."

"You went to high school in Washington. When did you join the military?"

"When I turned eighteen."

"And were your parents for or against that decision? I mean, I hear it gets in your blood when you're raised around it."

Cameron turned away and sipped her wine, stalling. Of all the questions Andrea could have asked, she didn't think it would go this way. She wasn't at all ready to answer questions about her parents. But when she looked back at Andrea, there was such an expectant look in her eyes, Cameron surprised herself by her truthful answer.

"Indifferent. Not for or against," she said. "My mother was dead and my father was in a military prison." She shrugged. "Indifferent."

"I'm sorry. I—"

Cameron held up her hand. "Don't apologize. Please."

A knocking on the door ended the questions and Andrea nodded, turning away. But she paused before opening the door.

"I don't know if it was easier or not," she said, answering Cameron's earlier question. "I think maybe there are some memories you're supposed to keep and not leave behind."

"This is my kind of working dinner," Jim said. "Pizza and beer."

"It's pretty good pizza for a local joint," Cameron said.

Andrea rested her chin in her palm, watching them as they both started on their fourth slice. There was not one ounce of awkwardness between them. In fact, their words and gestures indicated a familiarity that Andrea knew shouldn't exist so soon. She envied people like that—those who could make friends so easily. She had always been more guarded, more reserved. More careful.

Cameron looked over at her. "You done?"

"For now. I'm pacing myself," she said.

Cameron put her slice down and wiped her mouth with a napkin. "I heard from Collie. Surprisingly, he concurred with our *hooker* assumption. Sent her picture to the local police in Phoenix, Tucson and Flagstaff. Got a hit in Phoenix. Street name is Cherry. That's all they got."

"He's going to run her through the database?" she asked.

"Missing persons, yeah," Cameron said.

"So this makes two now from Phoenix?" Jim asked.

"Technically, Maggie O'Brien, the first victim, was a student in Tempe," Andrea said. "But we can call it Phoenix if you want," she added. She hated to correct Jim, especially in front of someone, but he took it as good-naturedly as he always did.

"No, you're right. I doubt the good people of Tempe want to be referred to as Phoenix."

"My equations require precise data," Cameron said. "I've been able to get coordinates of where they were last seen, their home address, their work, where they usually parked, that sort of thing."

"And that's going to tell you something? Using that...that *algorithm* thing?" Jim asked.

"Yes. The more data we have, the more likely we are to establish a pattern. Whether it's where he abducts them or where he dumps them, we'll get a better idea of his movements."

"Our last victim probably won't help much," Andrea said. "I doubt we'll be able to get much more information than her name."

"Most likely, yes," Cameron agreed. "But we now have four dump sites. Two in Sycamore Canyon and two in Oak Creek Canyon."

"Twenty, thirty miles apart. Not counting the hike up Rim Trail, of course."

"I think it's safe to assume he used a four-wheeler to transport Maggie O'Brien." Cameron turned to Jim. "Don't know if Andi told you or not, but we found an impression of tire tread up there."

Andrea shook her head, wondering why Cameron's casual use of her name didn't annoy her. "No, I forgot." She met Cameron's curious gaze. "That was the day—"

"Oh, yeah," she said. She smiled quickly at Jim. "Long-ass day," she said as way of explanation.

Andrea nodded, giving her a silent thank you. Jim didn't need to know of their argument.

"Anyway," Cameron continued. "We've been to all four sites. No way a four-wheeler gets up Oak Creek Canyon. Now Sycamore Canyon, yes. Where we found Cherry, it was a pretty level, easy trail," she said.

"But we didn't find anything disturbed. Four-wheelers are destructive to vegetation. Up on the rim, it's mostly rock. But down in the canyon, there's enough plant life—saplings, brush—that we would have seen evidence if a four-wheeler plowed through there."

"I just—" Cameron raised her hands. "I just can't picture a man carrying a body on these trails. Cherry couldn't have weighed more than ninety pounds, but ninety pounds is ninety pounds, especially on a hike. I just don't see it."

"So back to one of our earlier questions," Andrea said. "Does he have help?"

Cameron shook her head. "Research shows that serial killers, for the most part, work alone. I know that's not always the case, but the vast majority of them work alone. The more people who know, the greater the chance for getting caught."

"And Patrick has been doing this for a long time."

"But what about his brother?" Jim asked. "Didn't he help?"

"He may have unwittingly found the victims for Patrick, but I don't think John ever knew what Patrick did," Andrea said. "The Dallas report indicated that he was mentally slow."

Cameron stood, pacing behind them. "But he knew enough to slice Detective Sikes' throat," she said, staring at Andrea. "Son of a bitch." She pulled her phone out of her pocket as she walked into the other room.

"What'd I miss?" Jim asked quietly.

"I'm not sure," she said.

Cameron helped Andrea clean up the kitchen, putting the leftover pizza in the plastic bags she'd handed her. She had intended on leaving with Jim but found she wasn't quite ready for the evening to end.

"Will you let me listen in when you call Dallas tomorrow?" Andrea asked.

"Sure. I was going to do it from the rig, but I can come to your office."

"No. I can come over there. I'm sure you have data and equations to play with."

"Yeah. It's funny, really. I was never very good in math or science," she admitted. "But I found I had an aptitude for computer programs. Not that I used it all that much in my early career. I was out in the field for the most part." As soon as she made the statement, she knew she'd opened herself up for questions.

"Tell me what you did. And don't you dare say it's classified," Andrea said.

Cameron took a deep breath, surprised that she wasn't running and hiding from the question.

"I was a sniper. Mostly."

She was startled by the look Andrea gave her. It wasn't one of condemnation or disbelief. Rather, it was sympathetic.

"I would imagine that's one of the more difficult jobs," she said, her voice soft.

Cameron nodded. "Killing someone in a gun battle is an act of war. But targeting someone and pulling the trigger, that amounts to nothing more than murder," she said.

"I hope you don't really believe that, Cameron. It's all an act of war. Our country has enemies. You signed up to fight the enemy, by whatever means."

"Yes. I keep telling myself that. The alternative makes me a monster."

Andrea watched her for a moment. "Tell me about your parents."

But Cameron shook her head. "No. My turn. Tell me about yours."

"Nothing to say, really."

"You said you had to grieve alone, that you had no one to comfort you. You never mentioned a parent."

Andrea reached for a glass and filled it with ice, taking her time as she added water from the tap.

"My father was a cop. A sergeant. I grew up around cops. It was the life I knew." She paused to take a sip of water. "He was killed. He was at the point in his career where he wasn't out on the streets anymore. Desk duty. But he stopped at a convenience store to pick up cat food because Mom forgot to buy it."

She paused again and Cameron saw the faraway look in her eyes.

"There was a robbery. Dad and the clerk were both killed. My mother, well, she just couldn't deal with it. She blamed herself. She blamed the cat." She put the water glass on the counter and crossed her arms. "And she couldn't deal with me being on the force. I was still in the academy when he died. I think she thought I'd get out, but it made me more determined than ever to make good. But she pulled away. She couldn't handle it." Andrea ran a hand through her hair several times. "She moved to San Diego. We don't really have a relationship anymore." She met Cameron's eyes. "So no, I didn't call her after I got shot."

93

Cameron hated the misting of tears she saw and was sorry she'd asked the question. She knew if she told her own story, there would not be any tears shed. She reached for Andrea, slowly pulling her into a hug. Andrea surprised her by wrapping her arms tightly around Cameron's waist.

"I'm sorry," she said as she gently rubbed her back.

But Andrea just shook her head, burying her face against Cameron's shoulder. It had been awhile since Cameron had offered comfort to someone like this. Actually, it had been awhile since she'd held another woman, period.

She loosened her grip when she felt Andrea move to pull away, but she didn't release her completely. "Would you be angry if I kissed you?"

Andrea leaned her head back. "Yes. Very."

"Why?"

"Why? That's a silly question, isn't it?"

"Is it?" Cameron let her glance fall to Andrea's lips. "Tell me why I shouldn't kiss you."

"I don't want you to should be a good enough reason."

Cameron smiled. "But it's not."

"I don't like you. Not like that."

"You're lying," she said. "I can feel your heart beating fast."

"Perhaps it's from fear."

"And perhaps not. Tell me why."

"I just don't want you to kiss me. That's all."

Cameron loosened her grip a bit more, but Andrea didn't pull away. "You're not the one who died, Andi," she said as gently as possible. "For some reason, however it happened, you were spared. Call it a miracle if you want, but I don't think the reason you were spared was so that you could crawl into a shell and not try to live. You have your whole life still." She leaned closer, hearing the slight shift in Andrea's breathing. "Let me kiss you."

"No," she whispered.

"Why? Is it because you don't want to feel anything? Are you afraid I'll make you want something that you think you shouldn't have? Or maybe you think you don't deserve it," she said, her voice trailing off.

"I—"

Cameron leaned closer still, her lips only an inch from Andrea's. "Kiss me," she whispered.

Their eyes did battle, but Cameron refused to move away. She finally saw Andrea's gaze drop to her lips and knew the battle was won. Just the lightest of pressure on Andrea's back was all that was needed to bring their mouths together, yet she wasn't prepared for just how wonderful the kiss felt. Andrea's lips were soft, moving gently with her own. She should have stopped then, but the subtle moan she heard made her want more. She opened her mouth, deepening the kiss.

She felt Andrea's hands dig in painfully at her waist. She opened to Cameron, taking her tongue inside, no longer trying to hide the moans that now freely escaped. Cameron was on the verge of losing control, knowing they must stop, but Andrea's hands snaked around her waist, their bodies now flush and pressed together tightly.

The magnitude of how deeply she wanted this woman made her slow down. She slid her hands to Andrea's hips, unable to resist one quick, intimate stroke before pulling away.

"God," she murmured, her breathing as labored as Andrea's was. "Shh, shh," she whispered, pulling Andrea into another tight hug. "See? It's okay."

Andrea's hands still clung to her tightly. "I should hate you."

"No. No you shouldn't," she said. "Because I'm good for you." She stepped out of Andrea's arms, away from her. "Now, I'm going to leave before I do something really stupid." She smiled. "Besides, I have a kitten waiting on me."

CHAPTER FIFTEEN

After what happened last night, Andrea was nearly afraid to go to Cameron's motor home this morning. But saying she was afraid to be alone with her was ridiculous. She was a big girl. And it wasn't like Cameron forced herself last night. Not really. Andrea could have stopped it. She *should* have stopped it.

But it felt too good to stop.

She'd spent most of the night beating herself up over her lack of control. She'd tried to convince herself that she didn't even like Cameron, but she knew—as Cameron did—that was a lie.

Okay, so I'm attracted to her. It's not a crime, she told herself. What was a crime was that she didn't *want* to be attracted to her. She didn't want to be attracted to anyone. That was her punishment. For the guilt she carried. She didn't deserve to want someone. Not like that. Not like she was starting to feel with Cameron. And she certainly didn't deserve to have someone *want* her. But she knew Cameron did.

Maybe she should just tell Cameron the truth about Erin. Hell, maybe she should accept the truth herself.

But she couldn't do that. Erin was dead. She wasn't spared. The least Andrea could do was to profess to love her, no matter how good it had felt to have someone hold her...kiss her.

So she parked next to Cameron's truck, trying to put on an appropriately angry mask, one that would tell Cameron she was pissed about what had happened last night. One that would tell Cameron they needed to keep things on a professional level only.

Yeah, good luck with that.

She hesitated before getting too close to the rig, wondering if Cameron's security was off, but she didn't get the warning message as the last time.

"It's safe."

She looked up, trying to spot the hidden speaker and obvious camera.

"It's secret. You'll never find it."

"So I guess you think you can read my mind?" she asked as she walked up the steps. The door opened for her and Cameron stood there in shorts and bare feet. And damn if she didn't have gorgeous legs. She sighed, feeling her angry mask slipping.

"Right on time," Cameron said. "I just got done tracking Tori Hunter down. The FBI is hard to deal with."

"You don't say."

"She's still in Dallas. I talked to Detective O'Connor. Casey. Very friendly. Helpful."

"Yes, she was."

Cameron scooped up the kitten who was playing with a ball. She kissed her quickly, then shoved her at Andrea. "Are you mad at me?"

"Of course," she said, smiling as she nuzzled the kitten's fur.

"I don't believe you."

"Suit yourself," she said. "What have you named her?"

"I told you. Cat."

"And I told you that wasn't going to work. If you don't name her, I will."

"Feel free," Cameron said as she pulled out her laptop and

pointed to the sofa. A few quick keystrokes later and Andrea heard the dial tones as the call was placed.

"Casey gave me Hunter's direct number. She said she'd be pissed but would get over it." She grinned. "Kinda like you, I suppose."

"Hunter."

"Agent Hunter. My name is Cameron Ross," she said.

"Good for you. How did you get my number?"

"You might want to tell her you're FBI," Andrea whispered.

"Sorry. Yeah, listen, I'm *Agent* Ross," she said. "I've got Deputy Sullivan with me. We're working on a case out here in Arizona. Casey O'Connor gave me your number."

"Figures. Okay. What can I do for you? I'm kinda in a hurry, Agent Ross."

"Cameron, please. I wanted to pick your brain about an old case of yours. Patrick Doe."

There was a moment of silence and Cameron and Andrea exchanged glances. "Hunter?"

"Yeah. Just...just one of those names you hope you never hear again."

"I understand. Unfortunately, he's alive and well."

"He's killed again?"

"Yes. Four women."

"Goddamn bastard. Are you sure it's him?"

"We don't have DNA yet, no, but our ME out here has confirmed the knife wounds match those of your case."

"We had him, but the slippery son of a bitch posed as his brother and...well, I suppose you've already read our file."

"Yes. And we've talked with O'Connor. I wanted to run something by you. How certain are you that his brother, John, was mentally slow?"

"He wasn't examined by a doctor, if that's what you mean. I wouldn't say he was retarded or even mildly retarded. He was slow. Childlike. His words were almost that of a ten- or twelve-year-old."

"Could it have been an act?"

"I guess, but he was damn convincing if it was. What are you getting at?"

"Well, everything in the file indicates that John was innocent, that he had no knowledge of what Patrick was doing, that he wasn't involved."

"We don't believe that he was."

"Yet he was able to take a knife and nearly kill your partner in much the same manner as Patrick killed those women," she said.

Andrea heard an audible gasp from Agent Hunter.

"What the hell are you saying?"

"What if it was staged? What if John wasn't really slow and childlike? What if they set you up?"

"Set us up? I don't like what you're insinuating, Agent Ross."

"I'm not insinuating you did anything wrong, Hunter. Hell, all the evidence points to Patrick, not John. I'm just saying it could be a possibility. You were getting too close. Maybe it was staged so that Patrick could get away. Maybe their intention was never to kill your partner. I doubt they would do something to cause John to be jailed or to spend the rest of his life in a mental ward."

Again, there was silence from Agent Hunter. But only for a few seconds.

"It all happened so fast. We were in a dark warehouse. Sikes, my partner, was ahead of me. And John just jumped out at him. It only took a second. But yeah, I see your point. For him to be able to do that..." she said, her voice trailing off.

"Our issue here is that we're wondering if Patrick has a partner. Unlike in Dallas where he killed his victims in their apartments and left the body, he's killing them elsewhere and dumping their bodies in the high desert," Cameron said. "He's leaving them along hiking trails where they're certain to be found, however, we think it's impossible for him to do this alone."

"There was never any evidence that he had a partner. John found his victims for him, but we thought that was just circumstantial. They were homeless. Or at least pretending to be homeless."

"Easy to blend in that way," Andrea said.

"I just don't think I can be of much help on that angle,"

Hunter said. "We went with the premise that he worked alone. If you're saying that John was his partner back then, and now he's had to find a new partner, I think that's reaching," she said. "It would have to be someone he trusted an awful lot to kill with."

"I agree. I was hoping your gut would tell you that there was a third party involved, someone besides John."

"No, I'm sorry, Agent Ross. That just simply wasn't the case."

"I understand."

"I've really got to run. Good luck with your case." She paused. "I'd appreciate you letting me know how this turns out."

"Of course, Agent Hunter. We will. Thanks."

Cameron closed her laptop forcefully. "Well, that was a waste of time."

"I don't think it was," Andrea said. "I think your theory is strong. Just because Dallas didn't find anything to back it up doesn't mean it's wrong. He didn't dump the bodies there. He left them where he killed. Who's to say his partner wasn't a lookout or something?"

"I don't know. Maybe Hunter is right. Maybe I am reaching. I'm just looking for something that makes sense."

"Our killer having help transporting bodies down three miles of trail makes sense," Andrea said. "It's just hard to prove."

"Hell, it's hard to prove Patrick even exists."

Cameron got up, stopping to scratch the kitten who was still sitting in Andrea's lap. "Did you get breakfast?" she asked.

"I had a muffin, thanks."

"Coffee?"

"I'm good. In fact, I should get going," she said, standing. "How about Lola?"

Cameron made a face. "For Cat?" She shook her head. "Nope. Not even close."

"At least I'm trying to find a name," she said. "I'll let you get to work. Call me if you need me."

Cameron wiggled her eyebrows. "Is that a proposition?"

Andrea paused at the door. "You know, you're just annoying enough to be cute. But it's a fine line," she added before walking away.

"Perhaps I should make the same offer," Cameron called as she stuck her head out of the door. "Call if *you* need *me*. I'll be happy to oblige."

"And now you've crossed that line."

But Andrea couldn't wipe the silly grin off her face as she drove away.

CHAPTER SIXTEEN

Cameron paced, loving the wireless headset she'd started using. Waiting, however, for Collie to answer her was pissing her off. It was the third time today she'd tried to call him.

"*Fucker*," she murmured as she disconnected. She immediately called Murdock. He, as it should be, answered on the second ring.

"Agent Ross, to what do I owe the pleasure?"

"Where the hell is Collie?"

"He's in Phoenix."

"Yeah. But I mean *where*? I've been calling him all day. Is he ignoring me again?"

"Would he do that to you, Cameron?"

"Come on, Murdock. I wanted to run something by him."

"I don't know where he is. Hopefully working. You want to run it by me?"

"I have a spot I wanted him to check out. It's not a great

percentage. Forty-two percent. But there's this little coffee shop in Flagstaff, about a block from campus. Forty-two percent is the highest location any of these equations have returned."

"Okay. Send me the info and I'll pass it along to Collie."

"I've already e-mailed him the data. He didn't respond. *Asshole*."

"Let me get in touch with Reynolds, see if he knows where Collie is. I'll let you know."

She didn't know why, but Collie's mere presence on the earth irritated the hell out of her. They were like oil and water.

She looked over when she heard the pitiful meow. The cat—Lola—was sitting by her empty food bowl. "You're getting pretty good with that begging routine."

She scooped the kitten up and held her close, shutting her eyes as she listened to the gentle purring. She always thought that if she got a pet, it would be a dog, not something like this frail little kitten. Of course, looking at the many scratches on her hands, frail didn't exactly describe the cat.

"Lola," she said. "God, I hate that name."

CHAPTER SEVENTEEN

"So? You and Agent Ross? What's up with that?"

Andrea gave as bored an expression as she could muster when she looked up at Randy. "What are you talking about?"

"Sonny Winfield says you've been out to her place twice now. And Joey says she was at your place the other night...late."

"Oh my God. You're just a bunch of gossiping girls. And Sonny Winfield needs to mind his own business."

"Oh? Hit a nerve, did I?"

"No, you did not hit a nerve. As you well know, I'm assisting Agent Ross in her investigation."

"Sure. There's assisting and then there's *assisting*." He leaned closer with a devilish grin. "Does Rosa know?"

Andrea stared at him. "Since when did you decide that it's okay to discuss my private life? I have rules, remember."

Randy laughed, then immediately wiped the grin off his face when the outer door opened. Agent Ross stood looking at them, one eyebrow cocked dangerously. An involuntary smile touched Andrea's face before she could stop it. Cameron hadn't been around yesterday and Andrea noticed her absence.

"Speak of the devil," Randy whispered as he went back to his own desk.

Yes, and apparently you're scared of this devil, Andrea thought. Good. Maybe he would leave her alone. Unfortunately, the indifference she tried to show in Cameron's presence wouldn't come. She found herself watching as Cameron sauntered over with a downright flirtatious look in her eyes.

Cameron bowed slightly. "Deputy Sullivan, a pleasure to see you again."

"Is it now?"

"Absolutely. My day wouldn't be complete without—" she stopped, glancing at Randy who was blatantly listening. "So, Randy, how's it going?"

"Going? It's going fine, ma'am."

Cameron nearly roared with laughter. "Ma'am? Did you just call me *ma'am*?" Her eyes narrowed and her smile disappeared. "You say that to me again, Crawford, and I'll break your neck." She turned back to Andrea with a subtle wink. "Got a second?"

"Sure."

"Is there a private room where we can talk?"

Andrea's eyebrows shot up. "Jim is at lunch. Would you like to use his office?"

"That would be perfect."

Andrea stood, glancing at Randy. "We're just gonna...talk," she said. "Be right back."

"Sure, Andi. I've got things covered while you...*talk*," he said, his voice not loud enough for Cameron to hear.

Andrea closed Jim's door then immediately found herself backed against it as Cameron came closer.

"So? Miss me?"

Andrea hated to admit it, but yes, she'd missed her. Of course, she would never tell Cameron that when she couldn't reach her on her cell, she'd driven out to the rig looking for her. There was a hint of a challenge in Cameron's eyes, and she decided she could play her game. "Did *you* miss *me*?"

"Yes. I should have taken you with me. We could have shared a hotel room last night."

"And where would that have been?"

"Flagstaff."

Cameron's gaze dropped to Andrea's lips and she immediately felt her pulse increase. "Why would I have stayed in a hotel with you?"

"Because you want to." Cameron took another step until their thighs were brushing. "Just like you want me to kiss you now."

Andrea tried to think of a reason why she shouldn't kiss her. There must be a thousand reasons, but none would come to her.

"Don't you?"

Andrea swallowed hard. "Yes," she whispered against the mouth that was already claiming hers. God, what was it about this woman that made her lose all control? But that question was for another time. Her thought process shut down as soon as she felt Cameron's tongue glide across her lips.

Andrea pulled her close, crushing their bodies together, opening to the unexpected kiss. She gasped when she felt fingers brush against her breast, then moaned outright when that same hand closed over her, squeezing gently, a thumb rubbing lightly against her hard nipple. It had been so very long since she'd felt this way, she wanted to just give in to it, she wanted to let Cameron take what she so obviously wanted.

She spread her legs as Cameron's thigh pressed between them. Her head rolled back, eyes shut as Cameron's mouth trailed along her neck, kissing and nibbling, finding all the spots that drove Andrea mad.

But voices sounded—Jim and Randy—and Cameron pulled away. They stood staring at each other, both breathing hard, both flushed with arousal.

"I'm sorry," Cameron said as she ran her hands through her hair. "That was...that wasn't what I intended. I would never—"

"Cameron," she said, stopping her apology. "Yes, I missed you too." She took a deep breath, then squeezed Cameron's arm as she walked past and sat down in one of Jim's visitors' chairs.

She heard Randy stalling and made a mental note to thank him, even if it meant him knowing what had just taken place. She crossed her legs, immediately feeling the tightness between them and she uncrossed them just as quickly. Now was not the time to contemplate how close she'd been to begging Cameron for release.

They heard Jim just outside his door and Cameron launched into a detailed description of one of her algorithms, losing Andrea about two sentences into it.

"So forty-two percent is pretty good," she said, pausing as Jim opened the door. "It's just not great. Hey, Jim," she said. "Hope you don't mind that we borrowed your office."

"Not at all. You got something?"

"I was just telling Andi about a stakeout I did last night. In Flagstaff." She moved easily around Andrea and sat down beside her, no evidence of their earlier indiscretion showing on her face. "Collie is apparently AWOL or else not taking my calls, so I went to check it out myself. There's a little coffee shop near the campus up there."

"You think he might target his victims there?"

"No. I don't think he has a particular place where he watches them. That's what makes him so hard to read. But if we focus on college students—realizing, of course, that Cherry was not one—then we can narrow our search to potential hangouts, like the coffee shop."

"Any luck?" Andrea asked.

"Well, it's a cute little place. Very dark at night. It would be perfect. However, not a huge crowd and those who were there, were usually in groups. I stayed until it closed, and I saw only two single women the whole time."

"So your forty-two percent—"

"Was pretty much a waste of time," she conceded. "I talked to one of the geeks at Quantico. Because the abductions have occurred in several different cities, he thinks it's futile to try to pinpoint where the next victim might come from."

"So you're back to trying to determine a dump site."

"Yes."

"Again, I don't pretend to understand your fancy equations

there," Jim said. "But there's a whole lot of empty space out here. Hundreds of trails. *Miles* of trails."

Cameron stood and moved behind her as Andrea felt the light brush of Cameron's hand on her back. A simple, innocent touch which caused chills to travel across her body. It was hard to believe that just minutes earlier that same hand was touching her breast, making Andrea want something she'd vowed she couldn't have. She blinked several times, trying to focus, trying to pull in her thoughts.

"You're right, Jim. I get that it's vast out here. But why does he pick the sites he does? I mean, two are on the main trail in Oak Creek Canyon."

"Because he wants to ensure that they're found," Andrea said. "Hundreds of miles of backcountry trails, but if he dumped them back there, they may go weeks or months without being found."

"Exactly." Cameron sat down again, her voice animated and excited. "He can't pick an obscure trail or he'll have the same issue as he had with Maggie O'Brien. No one found her."

Jim leaned back in his chair and took the toothpick out of his mouth, flipping it between his fingers. Andrea felt him studying her, studying *them*, and she felt a blush on her face. Could he tell what had happened just before he walked in? Did he know they'd blurred the line between professional and personal?

"So, it still looks like we're looking for a needle in a haystack," he said. "Unless you can give me a more precise location, that is. I mean, I've got six deputies. We can disperse along the trails if need be."

"We assume he dumps his victims at night. And if he wanted to be really safe, he may even dump them between two and four a.m.," Cameron said.

"The darkest hours," Andrea murmured.

"Statistically, the least traveled hours, yes." Cameron stood again. "Jim, this is a serial killer who has killed many times before. I just need to make sure your guys can handle that, if they encounter him."

"I understand what you're saying. Truth is, my guys have had limited training. I'm not a hundred percent certain that they could handle the situation." Jim popped his toothpick back in, his mouth working it. "Or worse, some backpacker is coming down the trail at dawn and they mistake him for our guy."

"Well, staking out trails might be a last resort anyway. Because not only do we have to pinpoint location, we also have to have a date. And so far, the pattern is simply that there is no pattern."

"In other words, we haven't really made any progress other than we have another body," Jim said.

"I wouldn't say no progress," Andrea said, feeling the need to defend Cameron. "We know that he dumped Maggie O'Brien with a four-wheeler. We...we," she stammered, glancing at Cameron.

"And we've speculated a whole lot more," she finished for her. "Unfortunately, it is what it is. There is no evidence. We have nothing to go on but speculation. Speculation and past history." Cameron looked at her watch. "Listen, I need to head back to the rig. I'm expecting a call." She glanced at Andrea. "I'll...I'll be in touch."

"Okay."

Andrea watched her leave, wishing they could have a moment alone to talk. She turned when she felt Jim's eyes on her.

"So? Everything okay?" he asked.

She nodded. "Yes. Why?"

"Just checking. You and Cameron getting along okay?"

"There are moments where I still want to strangle her."

Jim smiled at her, a smile that indicated he knew *exactly* what was going on between them. She stood, not wanting to take the conversation any further. For one, she didn't have a clue as to what was happening between them—other than Cameron Ross seemed to set her on fire. That, however, wasn't something she cared to share with Jim.

"I'm going to...get back to work," she said as she backed out of his office.

"Yep. Sure," he said, that same knowing smile on his face.

She let out a relieved breath as she walked away, only to have Randy waiting for her. He crossed his arms and raised his eyebrows.

She went to her desk, unable to look at him.

"Well?"

"Well, what?"

"Do I at least get a thank you?"

"I don't know what you're talking about."

He squatted down beside her desk. "You know, if you ask me nicely, I'll keep it to myself."

"If you *don't* keep it to yourself, Randy, then I will have to ask Agent Ross to shoot you." She smiled. "How will that work for you?"

He stood back up. "So, you want to play dirty, huh?"

"Yes. Now leave me alone."

CHAPTER EIGHTEEN

Cameron paced across her kitchen, her headset on and ready. Murdock was to call at six sharp. It was now two minutes after. She wanted to be done with business by the time Andrea got there.

She closed her eyes for a second, acknowledging the gentle wave of affection that hit at just the thought of her. She liked her. She liked her a lot, in fact.

And I want to sleep with her.

That was obvious. She hoped Andrea felt the same. But she didn't want to make the evening about that. She'd stopped in town at Juanita's Café and brought back a huge order of fajitas and their homemade tortillas for dinner. As an afterthought, she stopped at a liquor store and picked up two bottles of sangria wine which were now chilling in the fridge. They'd have a nice dinner, they'd share wine, they'd talk.

And if things moved in the direction of the bedroom, so be it. If not, it wouldn't be the first time someone had turned her down. Truth was, she wasn't certain Andrea was ready. Oh, her body definitely was. Andrea was like liquid fire in her arms. But there was still Erin, her late lover, who had a hold on her. She doubted these two weeks had changed that.

Or maybe it had. Andrea no longer got angry when Cameron brought up her past. Perhaps it had done her good to talk about it. Maybe she might finally be able to let go of the guilt that she'd carried for so long.

And if not, well then she'd made a new friend, nothing more. Besides, she would be leaving as soon as this case was over. If she did some good by getting Andrea over the hump, that would be a plus.

A soft beeping in her ear indicated Murdock was calling and she hit the remote, letting the call through.

"Well? Anything?" she asked immediately.

"Hell, Cameron, I'd almost think you had a soft spot for Collie the way you've been hounding me to find him."

"Yeah, right."

"But, no. I haven't talked to him."

"What the hell, Murdock? It's not like him to go missing."

"Well, there was that time in Mexico," he reminded her.

"That was after the case was over and if I recall, that cute señorita he was with would have made *me* go AWOL."

"Yeah, well, I'm concerned. Reynolds said they all had dinner at the hotel, then Collie planned to make a run by the homeless shelter."

"You're kidding? You mean he actually believed the homeless story from Dallas? I thought he said it was crap?"

Murdock ignored her comment. "My contention with Reynolds is why would Collie go alone? He knows better."

"Had he already been there before? Did he have a contact he was meeting?"

"Reynolds didn't know."

"That's because Collie just goes off in whatever direction he wants, not following leads, not following the progression of the case, hell, not following protocol."

At this, Murdock laughed. "Protocol? What the hell do you know about protocol, Ross?"

"I'm just saying, it would be like Collie to finally use the homeless angle because it makes sense. He just doesn't want anyone to *know* he decided to pursue that angle. That would make him look like he's taking advice from me, now wouldn't it?"

"Why can't the two of you get along, Cameron? What's up with that?"

"He pisses me off. He intentionally does the opposite of what I suggest, just because I'm the one who suggested it."

"Right. And why is that?"

"You'd have to ask him."

"I'm asking you."

She took a swallow of her water, thinking back to when she'd first met Collie. They were both still military at the time. They were at a little dive of a bar in Greece and the ouzo and *mezedes* were plentiful. The thing with Greek *cafeneons*, the locals never met a stranger and the ouzo never stopped flowing. She smiled as she remembered the raven-haired beauty who came by their table, flirting shamelessly with all of them. Collie fell in love on the spot. When the evening ended however, Collie wasn't the lucky one.

"There was a woman," she said.

"Figured as much."

"It was a long time ago, Murdock."

"Military days?"

"Yeah."

"You stole his woman or what?"

"Me? No. We were at a bar in Greece. And when the evening was over, she picked me. I didn't even know Collie. That was the first time I'd met him. Apparently, he hasn't forgotten."

Murdock laughed again. "I see now why he disappeared in Mexico that time. He was afraid you'd steal the señorita."

"Maybe. But back to this. What's Reynolds doing to find him? How can the team leader on a case go missing?"

"We've got a trace on his phone. There's been no activity. Reynolds is pulling security tapes from everywhere he can find them—traffic cams, ATMs, businesses around the hotel. They showed his picture around the homeless shelter, but no one remembered seeing him."

"He can't just disappear, Murdock. FBI agents don't just disappear."

"I know that, Agent Ross, I'm not stupid. Until we find him, Reynolds is in charge down there. The team's first priority is this case. I've got another agent on his way down there to see if he can find out what the hell happened to Collie."

"Do you want me to go down there?"

"No. You stay put. I don't want to take resources away from this investigation. If we don't catch this guy soon, it's going to become a media circus and a public relations nightmare."

"It's actually been quiet down here. Sheriff Baker said the paper in Phoenix came out for a story after the second victim was found but not since."

"Well, that's because Collie has been giving them daily briefings. Jesus, Cameron, do you not watch the news? Collie's pretty face has been a fixture on CNN."

"Sorry I've missed that. And yes, I have a satellite, I just haven't turned the TV on since I've been here. Kinda busy, you know."

"I know. Listen, Reynolds said he filled you in on the semen match."

"Yeah. At least we can now be one hundred percent sure it's Patrick Doe. It didn't appear that there was sexual trauma, just the semen left on the body, so that also matches the cases in Dallas."

"Yes. I talked to Jason at Quantico. He said you talked to him about the algorithms. He said he advised you to focus on the dump sites rather than where he gets his victims."

"That's right."

"Do you concur?"

"Yes. There are too many variables. If he was targeting one city, possible. But not when he's hopping all over the damn state. At least this is constant, here where he dumps them."

"Okay. See if you can narrow it down. I can bring in a team of agents if we need to."

"Yeah? All your pretty boys in their suits and ties. You going to have them crawling over these rocks looking for our killer?"

"I'm sure if I gave them the order to dress down, they could get to your level, Ross."

"Doubtful. I'm pretty low on the clothing chain, you know."

"I'm well aware. Why do you think I've got you stuck in a motor home, away from the public? You think we picked you for your skills?"

"Careful, Murdock. You don't want to go too far with your insults. I may decide to leave this glamorous life behind and retire after all."

"Oh, Cameron, we both know you love this job. Don't threaten to walk out on me again."

She grinned. "Well, it does have its perks," she said.

"Okay, I gotta run. I'll be in touch tomorrow."

As usual, the call disconnected without a "goodbye." She neatly folded the headset and put it on her desk. She closed the office door but didn't lock it, as was her habit. She thought maybe she'd give Andrea a tour of the rig. Not that it would take long, of course.

Andrea stopped on the side of the road, giving herself a few minutes before she took the little service lane that would lead to Cameron's rig. She was feeling nervous and maybe even a little scared. When Cameron had called and invited her to dinner, she'd made it plain that it wasn't a working dinner. It was, well, a date. Which, considering how things had gone in Jim's office, it wasn't *just* a date.

On one hand, that was a good thing. If she was ever going to let go of the past, let go of her guilt over how things had ended with Erin, then a brief affair with Cameron Ross seemed like the perfect antidote. Lord knows her body was willing. And it was obvious Cameron was willing.

But was she ready for that? Was she ready to open herself up like that? Maybe she should tell Cameron the real reason for her guilt. She hadn't ever told anyone, not even her shrink. She was too ashamed. She was afraid it would make her appear selfish—uncaring—and that just wasn't the case.

She took several deep breaths then turned the Jeep toward Cameron's. She wanted to talk. For the first time since it happened, she was ready to talk. She only hoped Cameron was willing to listen.

She parked next to Cameron's truck and again she hesitated, not knowing what type of security system Cameron had running. And as before, her voice on the speaker sounded.

"It's safe. Come on in."

Andrea opened the door, the wonderful smell of fajitas hitting her. Cameron stood near the small table, folding napkins and placing them next to the plates.

"How do you know when I'm here?" Andrea asked.

"There are cameras on all sides of the rig. There's also a silent alarm if I happen to not be watching. And at night, it's an audible alarm."

"And the shotgun?"

"Just for my amusement. Actually, there's an electric current that protects the rig. It's low voltage but enough to knock you back on your ass." Cameron grinned. "Your very lovely ass, of course."

Andrea returned her smile then went to pick up the kitten. "Hi, Lola," she murmured.

"We will not name her Lola," Cameron said.

"Then what name have *we* come up with?"

"We're still working on it."

Andrea went into the kitchen area, trying to find the source of the enticing smell. "If I had to guess, I'd say Juanita made us dinner," she said, opening the oven and finding the platter covered in foil. "Fajitas?"

"Yes. So tell me, is there really a Juanita?"

"I have no idea. I just know it's the best Mexican food in town."

"Well, I'm actually starving. Is it too early for dinner or can you manage?"

"Oh, I can always manage fajitas," she said. "Do you need help with something?"

"There's a bottle of sangria in the fridge. You can open that," Cameron said as she placed utensils on the table.

116

Andrea found the corkscrew in the first drawer she tried, noting the large variety of spatulas and spoons there. "Do you cook?"

"Some. I enjoy cooking. This current job is really the first time I've had the time to cook." She shrugged. "Unfortunately, old habits are hard to break."

"Meaning it's easier to eat out?"

"Yeah. But now that I've got Lola here—and she's not keeping that name—I'll probably spend more time at the rig, so I'll most likely cook more," she said as she opened the oven door and took out the foil-wrapped platter of fajita meat.

Andrea pulled the cork out of the wine bottle, inwardly smiling at Cameron's insistence that she didn't like *Lola*. She suspected the poor cat was stuck with the name now.

"Excuse me," Cameron said as she pressed against Andrea in the small space, reaching around her to the refrigerator to get the sour cream and guacamole dish Juanita's had supplied.

Andrea felt her pulse quicken immediately at the contact, and she moved to the side, giving Cameron room.

"Let me get the tortillas, and we're all set."

Andrea filled their wineglasses and sat down, waiting for Cameron to join her. When she settled across from her, she picked up her glass and held it up. Andrea did the same, lightly touching hers to Cameron's in a silent toast.

"Thank you for coming," Cameron said before taking a sip.

"Thank you for inviting me."

Cameron handed Andrea a tortilla, then took one for herself. "Should I apologize for what happened earlier today?" she asked unexpectedly.

"You mean in Jim's office?"

"Yes."

"I don't think you have anything to apologize for. I seemed to be a willing participant," she admitted.

"Does that scare you? Or upset you?"

"No. Well, a little, yes."

Cameron nodded, but thankfully didn't continue with her questions or pursue any more answers. Instead, she piled her tortilla high with both chicken and beef then lathered on sour cream and guacamole. Andrea looked at her more modest fajita and added another strip of chicken.

Cameron gave an audible moan of pleasure after her first bite, her cheeks puffed out as she chewed. "This is fabulous," she said around a mouthful.

"Mmm," Andrea agreed.

Cameron put her fajita down and picked up her wineglass instead. "So, tell me about—"

"No, no," Andrea said, interrupting her. "It's my turn."

"Your turn? Are you sure?"

"Quite sure."

"Okay. Go for it," Cameron said as she returned to her fajita.

Andrea took a sip of wine first, flirting with a number of questions. She settled on perhaps the most dangerous, but it was one she was dying to know the answer to.

"How many times have you been in love?"

"Well, there's love and then there's love," Cameron said. "The...I-thought-I-was-in-love-but-it-was-only-lust-kind. And the real stuff—the madly, deeply in love."

"The latter."

Cameron seemed to consider the question and Andrea saw a hint of sadness in her eyes.

"Once," she said.

Andrea debated the merits of asking more questions and decided she would. Cameron could always decline to answer.

"Tell me."

"Another tragic ending, I'm afraid," Cameron said. "I've suddenly realized I have a lot of those in my life."

"I'm sorry. We can talk about something else then," Andrea suggested.

"No. It's okay. I've asked you tough questions. I think we had an agreement," she said as she pushed her plate aside and took her wineglass, twirling it aimlessly in her fingers. "Laurie. I met her in Australia. We had been doing some exercises around the islands there and had a couple of days of shore leave in Sydney." She nodded when Andrea offered her more wine. "She was a water nymph and full of vigor," Cameron said with a smile. "She owned a small sailboat and whisked me away thirty minutes after meeting her. We returned to shore just in time for me to head back out with my team."

"So your shore leave wasn't really shore leave."

"No. But I left that day with a lovesick heart," she said. "Over the next two years, we got together whenever we could, sometimes for only a quick couple of days, sometimes longer."

"How long ago?"

"A while. I was twenty-five."

"When you told me you lost a partner and a lover, this—"

"No. Laurie wasn't in the military." She paused before continuing. "We were sailing. The boat capsized. I was the only one wearing a vest. We had been swimming when a squall blew in. We hurried with the boat, trying to get her turned around and back to shore. Laurie didn't take the time to put her vest on."

"I'm sorry. I shouldn't have—"

"No, Andrea. There's nothing to apologize for. It's a story from my past, that's all. I loved her. Deeply. It had a tragic ending and it took me a long time to get over it, but it was one of those lessons that you learn—live life to its fullest. Laurie did that. She never slowed down. And she died doing something she loved. It's like a mountain climber dying on the summit of a peak he had finally conquered. Tragic, yes, but he died doing what was most passionate to him." Cameron smiled slightly. "I hope we are all that lucky," she said. "It beats slowly dying in a hospital bed." Cameron stood, pointing at Andrea's plate. "You done?"

"Yes." Andrea got up too, helping to clear the table. "Lola doesn't seem interested in our food. She hasn't learned to beg yet?"

"No, thankfully. She only begs at her own bowl. But you know, I do need to get her to a vet."

"She hasn't had shots?"

"No. I just found her a few days before I got here. And you know, I wasn't sure I was going to keep her."

"There are two vets in town. I don't know them, but I can ask. Jim has dogs. I'll see who he uses."

"Thanks."

After they'd cleaned up from their dinner, Cameron brought

the bottle of wine with her to the sofa, ignoring her normal spot in the recliner.

"My turn," Cameron said, after filling both their glasses. "How many times have you been madly, deeply in love?"

It was a question Andrea knew was coming, and she still didn't have an answer for it. Well, other than the truth.

"None," she said.

Cameron cocked an eyebrow. "None? But Erin—"

"My guilt over Erin's death is completely different." She met Cameron's eyes, seeing them filled with questions. She often thought her therapist never understood why she clung to the guilt like she did. They'd talked about it, and Andrea understood that she should let it go, she just was never able to actually do it. "I have this vision in my head—in my heart—of what it should feel like to be in love. I told myself it would come, but I didn't feel that with Erin. I knew I would *never* feel that with her. So, that morning, the morning of the ambush, I broke up with her." She ran her fingers through her hair, remembering the terrible fight they'd had. "It didn't go well," she said. "In fact, after it was over with, we both said some horrible things to each other. I agreed to talk about it. We were going to get together the next day." She paused. "Stupid, I know. But I couldn't handle the tears, and that was the easiest way to get past it."

"Andrea, you can't—"

"I know, Cameron. I know I *shouldn't*," she said. "I wanted to love her that way. She said she loved me. She begged me to stay with her. I want to grieve for her like I loved her." She took a deep breath, trying to keep tears away. "But it's my fault. She was upset. She was the lead, the first one in. Because of me, she was upset, she probably wasn't totally focused on the job. She was distracted." Andrea closed her eyes, feeling her composure slipping. "And my team died and I grieve for them, I grieve for...for Mark," she said, the name of her best friend finally causing the damn to break. Cameron reached for her but she shook her off. "He was...he was my buddy, he was the brother I never had," she said, sobbing. "I grieve for him, and I feel guilty that I don't grieve for Erin that way." She stood, needing some space from Cameron. "I told Mark I was going to break up with her, and he said I should wait until the weekend, that I shouldn't jack with our team right now." She wiped at her nose, hating the tears that wouldn't stop. "I meant to wait, I really did. But Erin was talking about taking a trip together. She wanted us to go to San Francisco. She had the phone. She was calling to make reservations, and I just couldn't take it. I couldn't let her make those plans, knowing I wasn't going with her. I...I just couldn't wait until the weekend," she finished. "So I try to pretend that I loved her, and I hold on to my guilt because I didn't love her. Not that way."

She closed her eyes, remembering the horrible scene that ensued, the yelling, the accusations. She heard Cameron move, felt her approach. This time, she didn't pull away when Cameron touched her. This time, she let herself be comforted. Cameron didn't say anything, perhaps knowing that any words she spoke would be hollow. Andrea had heard them all before. So she slipped deeper into the embrace, feeling safe, feeling a little of the weight lifted from her aching shoulders. When Cameron finally spoke, her voice was soft, soothing.

"No one can tell you how you should feel, Andi. No one can judge your guilt or your grief. Only you. And I think you're still judging yourself pretty harshly." Her arms tightened, pulling Andrea even closer. "When you're ready to let it go, you will. Whether it's next month or next year, only you know. But eventually you'll let it go." She loosened her grip and Andrea pulled away, meeting her eyes. "I've been there. I know how heavy the feelings can be. I know the toll they take." Cameron touched her cheek, and Andrea's eyes slipped closed again. "But it will pass. I promise," she whispered.

Andrea often felt like she hung on to the guilt as punishment for living. She felt she didn't deserve to be happy, she didn't deserve to get her life back. They were gone. Erin, the woman who professed to love her. And Mark, her best friend and confidant. And here she was, still hanging on to her guilt and her grief, nearly three years later.

She cleared her throat. "Bathroom?"

"Of course." Cameron pointed just past the kitchen area. "First door on the right."

Andrea closed the door behind her, then immediately splashed water on her face, washing the traces of tears away. She reached for a tissue and blew her nose, feeling somewhat back to normal. She was surprised by what she was able to confess to Cameron, but then again, should she be? Since the day they'd met, Cameron had been able to pull things from her, willingly or unwillingly. She did admit that it felt good to purge herself. Maybe Cameron was right. Maybe it would pass. Eventually.

She returned, trying to salvage what was left of the evening. She gave a tentative smile. "I'm sorry."

"Please don't apologize," Cameron said. "If you ever need to talk, I'll listen."

"Thank you." Andrea took a deep breath, letting it out slowly, feeling some of the awkwardness dissipate. "The bathroom was quite roomy," she said. "It's like a real-sized bathroom."

"Most of the bigger rigs have nearly full-sized ones. Did you peek into the bedroom?"

"No. Should I have?"

Cameron gave a quick smile. "Only if you're curious."

Andrea was. "Okay. May I?"

"Of course."

And again, Andrea was surprised at the roominess, the slide-outs giving nearly eight more feet of floor space. The bed was large and neatly made, the room tidy. One wall consisted entirely of drawers. The back of the room was obviously the wardrobe, with two full-length mirrors for doors, giving a more wide-open look.

"It's huge," she called.

"I wouldn't say huge but more than enough room for me," Cameron said when Andrea joined her again. "I don't even use half of the drawer space in there."

"So you live in this full time?"

"Yes. It suits me. I've never really put down roots. Not as a kid, certainly not in the military."

It was the opportunity Andrea had been waiting for. Cameron seemed to know it as well. The new bottle of wine sat on the small table next to the sofa. She filled both of their glasses, waiting for the eventual question.

"Tell me about your parents."

"It's not a happy story," Cameron warned. "But I don't dwell on it anymore."

"If you don't want to talk about it, it's okay. I won't ask again."

"No. We had a deal. Share."

"Quid pro quo."

Cameron nodded. "My father was a pilot. Helicopters. It was during the first Gulf War. His missions were classified. We didn't really even know where he was. My mom and I, we weren't real close, so I didn't hang around the house much."

"How old were you?"

"Sixteen, nearly seventeen. I just kinda did my own thing and she did too. Anyway, my father came home unexpectedly. He picked me up at school. He had two backpacks. He said we were going on a survival training exercise."

Andrea wondered how often Cameron told this story. Her sentences were short, to the point. Just the facts and little else. "Did you know he was back?"

"No. He'd been gone a couple months, I guess. He just showed up at school. But I went with him. I thought it was cool. I got to miss school and hang with my dad for a few days. Only a few days turned into a few weeks. We went into Canada and ditched the car and went up in the mountains."

"Oh, no. Like you were kidnapped?"

"Well, yeah, only I didn't know it at the time."

"What about your mother? Did she know?"

Cameron glanced at her quickly, then away. "My mother... no, she didn't know," she said, her voice thick. "I started asking him how long we were going to be gone, what about Mom, my school. He got crazy. Mean. It was no longer a game. No longer fun. I was afraid, actually," she said.

"How long?"

"It was a month by that time. I will say I learned an awful lot about surviving on your own. But I noticed anytime we'd see evidence of people, he'd head in the opposite direction. Anytime I mentioned going back down for supplies, he would freak out. He turned into this monster, really. He quit bathing. He didn't

123

shave. His eyes were that of a crazy man." She took a deep breath. "I stopped asking questions. I stopped talking. I knew I had to get away from him. I didn't know what was going on with him. I didn't know if something had happened on his last mission that sent him over the edge or what."

"He didn't abuse you, did he?" Andrea asked softly.

"No. No, he didn't. Not like that."

"I'm sorry."

Cameron shrugged. "Just part of the things in life that shape you, I guess. Anyway, where we were camped, I could hear highway noise off in the distance. I didn't know how far it was, but I thought that was my only opportunity. We moved every three days or so, and I was afraid he'd take us farther back into the mountains."

"You were in tents?"

"Yes. We each had one. That night, after I was sure he was asleep, I left. The moon was high, so I had some light." She smiled. "And thankfully I didn't run into a grizzly or a pack of wolves. I just kept heading in the direction of where I thought the highway was."

"Oh, Cameron, that was so dangerous. You were just a kid."

"That wasn't my first survival training exercise, Andrea. He used to take me out once a year, at least, but only for a weekend. That's one reason I knew something was wrong. That, and the fact that we'd crossed into Canada. I mean, obviously, he was AWOL."

"So you found the highway?"

"Yes. Took me four hours at a fast pace. I flagged down a trucker. I started telling him my story and he stopped me and said, 'Wait, are you the kid of that army dude who's on the run?'" Cameron pulled the sleeping Lola into her lap. "Apparently, we had been on the news for weeks. There was a manhunt." Cameron met her gaze head on. "He'd killed my mother and her lover, a navy lieutenant."

"Oh, no."

"He shot the navy officer, but he stabbed my mother twenty-something times. I guess he wanted to make sure she knew what was happening."

"Okay, stop. Enough. I'm sorry. I had no idea—"

"Andrea, you've got to quit apologizing. If I didn't want to tell you the story, I wouldn't have."

"But I'm still sorry. Did you have to go through that alone or did you have any siblings?"

"I had an older brother. He was in the Marines at the time, but he wasn't deployed." She absently rubbed Lola's ear, her fingers moving back and forth slowly. "He hung around for the funeral, then left. I went to live with my grandmother and finished high school, then enlisted."

Had. She *had* an older brother. Their eyes held, Andrea silently asking the question.

"He was killed in Afghanistan," she finally said. "I have a grandfather still living, but we don't speak."

"Your dad's father?" she guessed.

"Yes. He thinks I should forgive my father, that I should go visit him in prison." She gave a quick smile. "Like hell I will."

"No, I don't blame you." Andrea hesitated before asking her next question. "How long have you been alone? I mean, since your brother—"

"He was killed eight years ago. Andrea, it's hard to explain, but when you're both on assignments, there's not really time to have a relationship. There are so many normal things you miss out on. When we were younger, at home, we were brother and sister. But once we went our separate ways in life, we just lost touch, you know. A year would go by and we hadn't spoken. I hate that he was killed, of course, but he wasn't really a part of my life, other than he was my brother. We didn't really even know each other anymore."

"So you're just used to being on your own? Used to being alone?"

"Yes. I try not to become dependent on anyone. Besides, when you have to pack and leave on a moment's notice, you really never have time to get dependent on anyone." She shrugged. "The people in my life that I've let get close to me are gone. My parents, my brother. Lovers. Teams. It's always a tragic ending. I think I'd rather be alone than suffer through any more of those. Any adventures I have now, I prefer to do them alone."

Andrea watched as she continued to stroke the kitten, wondering if Cameron really believed her own words. She supposed Cameron did believe them, but it made Andrea realize she was living pretty much the same way. Alone. Since the ambush, she'd shunned nearly all contact, leaving behind good friends in Los Angeles without even bothering with goodbyes. She'd settled here in Sedona, but she still kept to herself, trying not to get too involved in anyone's life—and keeping them out of hers. But were they both sacrificing too much? Were they merely existing in life and not really living? Yes, Andrea knew that was the case for her. For some reason, the thought that Cameron had been doing the same disturbed her. Cameron was a beautiful woman with—once you got to know her—a charming personality. She suspected the arrogant and conceited sides of her were mostly for show. And mostly to keep people away. A lonely existence, but one which Andrea could definitely relate to.

Tonight though, she decided she didn't want to be alone. She reached over, stilling Cameron's hand as it moved across Lola's soft fur. When Cameron looked up, meeting her eyes, Andrea leaned closer. Their kiss was soft, lips barely touching. Then Cameron shifted, bringing her closer. Andrea moaned at the contact, opening to her, the lingering taste of wine still on Cameron's tongue.

"You want to stay with me tonight?" Cameron whispered, her lips still hovering over Andrea's.

"Yes." Then, "Do you want me to?"

As if reading her thoughts, Cameron nodded. "I don't want to be alone tonight either."

There wasn't any preamble as Cameron led her through the motor home and into her bedroom. Andrea stood still as Cameron slowly unbuttoned her blouse. Silly, but Andrea was thankful she'd worn the tiny red bra when she saw Cameron's eyes travel across her bared torso. When Cameron's fingers went to remove the bra, Andrea stopped her, tugging at Cameron's T-shirt instead. Cameron lifted her arms, letting Andrea remove it. She would have expected nothing other than the sleek black sports bra that greeted her, but her gaze was fixed on the nasty scar slashed across Cameron's shoulder as it disappeared under her bra. She raised her eyes, meeting Cameron's, but Cameron shook her head, leaning closer for a light kiss.

"A story for another time," she said, letting her lips linger.

Andrea pushed the thought of the scar away, giving in to her desires. They'd had enough stories for one night. Now, she just wanted to lose herself in Cameron's arms and forget about everything. She suspected Cameron wanted the same.

She didn't protest when Cameron's fingers unsnapped her bra. Their eyes held as Cameron's touch moved across her skin, slowly pushing the garment aside. Despite knowing where those fingers would end up, Andrea gasped when they touched her. Involuntarily, her eyes closed and she moaned, loving the way her body responded to Cameron's hands on her breasts. Her nipples were rock hard from Cameron's touch, aching for more. Again, as if reading her mind, Cameron ducked her head, her warm breath fluttering across Andrea's skin. Andrea leaned her head back, offering herself to Cameron.

She groaned loudly when that hot mouth finally settled over her, Cameron's tongue snaking out to twirl around her nipple.

"Feels so good, Cameron," she murmured, letting her hands thread into Cameron's hair as she held her tight against her breast. "So good."

And, oh, so long since she'd made love with anyone, her body was on fire. Cameron's hands slipped down to her hips, pulling Andrea against her body and Andrea let herself be molded to Cameron, again moaning at the intimate contact. She could feel wetness between her legs and she welcomed it, having gone so long without this kind of touch.

Cameron's lips left her breast, returning to her mouth. Their kisses were fiery hot now, wet and hard as hands moved freely across the other's skin. Andrea impatiently shoved Cameron's bra up, exposing her breasts. Cameron pulled away enough to slip it over her head and Andrea's hands cupped her. Cameron's breasts were small and responsive to her touch, the nipples cutting into her palms. Her eyes were glued to the nasty scar that stopped an inch from her nipple. She wanted to touch it with her mouth, but Cameron had other ideas as fingers fought with the button and zipper of Andrea's jeans, loosening them enough to allow her hand inside.

They were within feet of the bed, but Cameron couldn't wait. Andrea spread her legs, feeling Cameron's hand inside the protective layer of her panties. She clung to her, accepting Cameron's tongue into her mouth at the same instant long fingers slipped into her wetness. She pressed hard against those fingers as they filled her. It had been so long, she'd nearly forgotten the sensation of having someone inside her.

"You're so wet," Cameron whispered, her mouth nibbling at her neck, causing Andrea to moan with pleasure.

"Yes. Are you?" Andrea gasped as her hips jerked, meeting Cameron's thrust.

"Yes. I can't wait for you to touch me."

Andrea bit down against her shoulder as Cameron's fingers slipped out of her, moving over her aching clit instead. Andrea moved wildly against her fingers, panting against Cameron's skin, feeling the first signs of her approaching orgasm. Yes, it had been so long and she wanted to draw it out, savor it, make it last. But her body—apparently starving for release—wouldn't prolong her pleasure. Her breath caught, held tight within her as she climaxed. She covered Cameron's hand with her own, pressing fingers hard against her, pulling out every last ounce of pleasure as her hips slowed their movements, rocking gently now against Cameron's hand, finally stilling altogether.

"Cameron," she said quietly, her mouth moving, finding lips waiting. Soft, slow, gentle kisses now, nothing hurried about them. "That was wonderful," she murmured.

"We've got all night, if you want."

Andrea's hands found Cameron's jeans, slowly sliding the zipper down. "Let me make love to you," she whispered, guiding Cameron to the bed. "I so want to touch you, be inside you." She paused. "It's been so long since—"

"I know." Cameron smiled gently against her lips. "And we've got all night."

CHAPTER NINETEEN

"Are you sure this has a high probability?" Andrea asked as they stood at the trailhead. "The trail is brutal after the first mile. Rocks. Boulders. The trail is hardly visible."

Cameron stared at her, letting her eyes travel freely now. After the way they'd spent the night—and morning—Cameron thought she had the right. Andrea turned, catching her watching. She cocked an eyebrow, waiting.

"Yes," she said, clearing her throat. "Yes, high probability."

Andrea walked slowly toward her, their eyes locked together. "Seriously? You have the energy to check out my ass?" Andrea asked.

Cameron grinned. "I have the energy to do much more than just look."

"How can you possibly?"

"Want me to show you?"

Andrea smiled, reaching out to touch her arm. "Surprisingly, even in my exhausted state, that thought is alluring," she admitted. "But no. Let's climb some boulders in the heat of the day. We'll try to kill ourselves that way instead."

Cameron laughed and followed her along the trail. "I told you we should have come out at daybreak."

"Don't start with me. It was *you* who wouldn't get out of bed."

Cameron didn't contradict that, but they both knew it was Andrea whose hands and mouth wouldn't stay still this morning. Not that Cameron had minded, of course. The night had been far too enjoyable to bring it to a close. And as much as she'd professed to enjoy her solitude, it was nice waking up with Andrea in her arms, nice having her there as they showered and then shared muffins and coffee.

The algorithm she'd set to run before dinner the night before had returned some results. Devil's Rock Trail ranking a whopping seventy percent. As soon as she mentioned the trail name, Andrea told her that her algorithm "sucks." No way would he use Devil's Rock Trail, she said. But results are results and Cameron didn't even pretend to be smarter than the guys who'd written the programs in the first place. She'd talked Andrea into at least taking a look.

Now here they were, the trail taking them up the edge of Coyote Canyon. As Andrea had warned, after the first mile—which wasn't easy in itself—the trail deteriorated drastically. Cameron was having a hard time keeping up as Andrea scampered over the rocks like a mountain goat.

"Come on, Agent Ross, you're lagging behind," Andrea called.

Cameron stopped and looked up, finding Andrea standing proudly on a huge boulder some fifty feet above her. "Show off," she muttered. She struggled over the rocks, finally reaching Andrea. She rested her hands on her hips, taking in big gulps of air. "I guess you're right," she said. "This trail sucks."

"I'm sorry. Perhaps your algorithm didn't account for the difficulty of the terrain."

"No, it should have. I entered all that data. Elevation gain, trail rating, altitude, everything."

"Well, then maybe the coordinates are off. This trail doesn't dead end. If we follow it long enough, it goes into Coyote Canyon where the rock slab—Devil's Rock—is. Maybe we should have started on that end, near Oak Creek," she suggested.

"No. The program accounts for that."

"Okay, then—" Andrea stopped, looking past her, her eyes to the sky.

"What is it?" Cameron asked, turning.

"Vultures. Maybe your algorithm wasn't that far off." Andrea climbed higher. "Let me have your binoculars."

Cameron pulled them out of her pack, handing them up to Andrea.

"That's the Devil's Playground over there," she said. "Even though it's close to this, the trailhead starts on the east side of the canyon." She lowered the glasses. "Maybe that's why your algorithm picked this trail. It's closest to the target."

"Just because there are vultures, that doesn't mean there's a body," Cameron said.

"No. That trail is pretty popular. Especially in the mornings. The rocks make a great backdrop for the sunrise."

Cameron held her hand out to Andrea. "Okay, come on. Let's go take a look."

Andrea took her hand, sliding off of the boulder beside her. Totally unprofessional, yes, but Cameron couldn't help it. She tugged on Andrea's hand, pulling her closer. She didn't ask. She simply lowered her head, kissing Andrea hard on the lips. That proved to be a mistake as one kiss brought back all the desire, the arousal, from last night. Andrea moaned, deepening the kiss. Before Cameron knew what was happening, they were locked in a tight embrace, hands moving freely, tongues battling.

Andrea boldly cupped her hips, pulling their lower bodies together. Cameron groaned at the contact, all of her senses coming alive again. She wanted to rip Andrea's clothes off right then and there and make love to her. She didn't care that they were standing in the middle of a rock pile, the midday sun blazing down on them.

Andrea must have sensed her intentions and she pulled away, her breath coming fast, as was Cameron's. "Damn."

"Sorry." Cameron took a step back, away from her. "Way unprofessional. It's just—"

"I know. Me too." Andrea took a deep breath then motioned down the trail. "Shall we?"

Andrea had a bad feeling as they took the more moderate trail to Devil's Playground. It was easy hiking, the trail wooded, not exposed like Devil's Rock. But she was having a hard time keeping focused. She could feel Cameron's eyes on her, and it made her heart beat just a little faster. She had to admit that she was the one who kept them in bed that morning, not Cameron. Andrea didn't know if it was just the fact that she'd gone three years without intimacy or what, but she simply could not get enough of Cameron Ross. Even earlier, on the trail, she wanted so badly to slip her hands under Cameron's shirt and touch flesh. She could imagine her wetness and in her mind, she remembered the way it felt to go inside her, feeling Cameron tighten around her fingers. She remembered the hardness of Cameron's nipples and how they felt in her mouth. And she remembered the taste of Cameron as she went down on her, the glorious sounds Cameron made as Andrea had feasted.

She nearly stumbled as her vision blurred, her mind's eye seeing them as they'd been in Cameron's bed—naked and uninhibited.

"You okay?"

Andrea nodded but didn't dare turn around. She knew Cameron would read her thoughts in an instant. "This trail is about four miles in," she said, trying to stay focused on the case.

"Easy walking?"

"Yes."

"Andrea?"

"Yes?"

"Can we stop a second?"

"No."

"Please?"

Andrea stopped but still didn't turn around. Cameron walked in front of her, meeting her eyes.

"It's okay what we did, Andrea," Cameron said, her voice quiet. "You're not...you're not regretting it, are you? You're not feeling guilty over it, right?"

Andrea smiled. "No. But thank you." She took a deep breath. "Quite the opposite, actually. I'm trying to stay focused on the case and not on the fact that I want to make love with you all over again." She was surprised by the relief Cameron showed.

"Oh. Good. Because, earlier, I was out of line. And I didn't want you to think—"

"Cameron, last night, I needed that. I think we *both* needed that. I just didn't realize I would enjoy it so much," she admitted with a quick smile. "Or that I might want to do it again."

"Okay. I'm glad you feel that way. But I just want us to be able to work together too. I don't want this to be a distraction."

"Then quit kissing me in the middle of a rock field," Andrea teased. "Now come on. Let's see what the vultures have found."

They walked on in silence, side-by-side, stopping occasionally for a sip of water. When they were nearly three miles in, Andrea pointed across the ravine.

"That's where we were earlier," she said, spotting the rock pile off in the distance.

"That is close. But that trail doesn't hook up with this one?"

"No. That one goes up the side of the canyon then drops down into it. Great views, but it's rated difficult, especially from this end. Where the trailhead starts on the other end of the canyon, it's a lot easier hiking. This one dead-ends," she said. "It goes to the base of the canyon. Its lure is the Playground with all the different rock formations. Devil's Kitchen, Devil's Piano, Devil's Bridge," she explained. "But it's an easy hike all the way in."

As they got closer, the smell of rotting flesh hit them. She glanced at Cameron, who nodded.

"Decomp," she said.

The vultures took flight as they approached and Andrea's gaze landed on Devil's Bridge. A body was laid out on the rock slab.

"There," she said.

They hurried, climbing over the fallen rocks of the ages-old arch that had fallen, making the bridge. Cameron stopped up short, her gasp loud, the sound hanging around them in the still air.

"Oh, my God," she murmured.

She turned around quickly, away from the body, and Andrea noticed the color had faded from her face. She was ghostly white.

"Cameron? What is it?"

Cameron just shook her head, moving farther away. She took her cell phone out, then paused before connecting, her eyes squeezed closed.

Andrea glanced at the body, finally realizing that it was a man, not the young college student they were expecting.

"Murdock? We found Collie," Cameron said, her voice thick with emotion.

Andrea jerked her head around, finally understanding Cameron's reaction to the body.

"He's...Christ, Murdock, he's out here like the others. We found him. The goddamn son of a bitch killed him."

Andrea stared at the body, seeing the now-familiar gaping hole where his throat had been sliced, just like the others. It was shredded, as the vultures had started in on it. She took a deep breath, her eyes still glued to the body. This was intentional. Surely it wasn't just a coincidence that Agent Collie was a victim.

She walked closer to Cameron, the sound of her voice agitated now as she explained how they'd found him. Andrea noticed the tight grip Cameron had on the phone, the furrowed brow, the clenching of her jaw. She was about to reach out a comforting hand when her own cell rang. She took a step away, answering quickly.

"Sullivan."

"Andi, it's Joey. Got a couple of hikers here. They said they saw a body out at—"

"Devil's Playground," Andrea finished for him. "We're here now."

"How did you know?"

"I'll explain later. Listen, get Randy. Bring the rack and evidence bags. We've got to process the scene."

"We'll carry her out or bring the mule?"

"Mule and horses. The body is up on the outcroppings so we'll have to carry him down a little ways."

"Him? Not a—"

"No. Him. Agent Collie. He was working this case in Phoenix."

"Holy shit."

"Yeah. Make it quick, Joey. And bring someone else with you. We'll need to close off this trail."

"I'm on my way."

Cameron was off the phone, but she was still visibly shaken. Her arms were folded tightly across her chest, her normally smiling mouth was tense, the blue, laughing eyes were shrouded—troubled.

Andrea was about to say "I'm sorry" but stopped herself. Cameron had told her often enough to quit apologizing for things that weren't hers to control. Instead, Andrea kept it all business. She held her hand out.

"Let me have your camera and the GPS gadget you use."

Cameron looked at her, blinking several times before answering. "No. That's my job."

"Let me do it, Cameron."

"I should be able to process the goddamn scene," she said loudly. "I've had team members die. I've lost partners." She ran her hands through her hair. "Christ, you know he wasn't careful. Patrick was probably in a dress and Collie thought some chick was coming on to him."

"Cameron, you've lost people before in the name of war, in the line of duty. This is different. This man was murdered. And you knew him."

"It doesn't matter." Cameron stared at her. "How could this happen? He's a goddamn FBI agent. He should have been more aware of his surroundings. Hell, he never believed the Patrick angle. He probably never even read the damn file. He probably didn't *know* Patrick dressed up as a woman."

"Look, let me process the scene. You're in no shape." She moved closer, her voice softer now. "Cameron, let me do this for you. Please."

The war of wills ensued for long seconds. Cameron finally conceded. She reached in her shoulder pack, pulling out the camera first, then the GPS finder. She kept the digital notebook.

"Here. Tell me what you find. I'll log it," she said.

"Okay. Thank you."

Andrea moved away, then glanced back at Cameron. She'd found a spot on a rock under one of the small junipers. Andrea went to the body, noticing that, unlike the others, Agent Collie's arms weren't folded neatly across his stomach. They were out by his sides, one stretched out wide, the other against his body. It was almost like the killer had dropped him, leaving him to land as he may and not placed specifically like the others had been. Perhaps because Agent Collie was close to two hundred pounds and not like the slight frames of the young girls.

"What do you guess he weighs?"

"Two-twenty."

"If Patrick looked like his brother, then he was a small man."

Cameron stood up. "More evidence that he's got help."

"Why don't you check the perimeter and see if he was dragged or not."

Cameron walked in a circle around the area and Andrea went back to her work. She took several pictures from each angle, along with the surrounding areas, trying to determine from which direction he had been carried. Then she held the GPS out, waiting to get a reading.

"Don't forget to mark elevation too," Cameron called.

Andrea nodded, saving the information like she'd seen Cameron do. She walked closer, careful not to disturb the scene. She squatted down beside him and picked up one hand, noticing blood under the nails.

"Do you have any evidence bags?"

"Not with me. I didn't think we'd be processing a scene. Why?"

"Trace under his nails. Blood."

Cameron slowed her pace, bending down to inspect some rocks, Andrea supposed. "How good are your guys? Do we need to request CSI from Phoenix?"

"This isn't a scene, it's a dump site," Andrea reminded her. "And my guys don't process, I do," she said.

"Okay. Just make sure you get pictures of everything. I don't want to miss something."

"I won't." She went back to inspecting the body, her eyes avoiding the bloody wound at his neck.

"Andrea? Come here for a second."

She looked up. "What is it?"

"These rocks are disturbed. Looks like a drag pattern," she said, pointing. "Bring the camera."

"Why would he drag him from up there?" she asked as she joined Cameron on the rocks. Her gaze traveled through the junipers. "Unless..."

"Unless what?"

Andrea looked back at the body. "He's been dead a couple of days." She met Cameron's eyes. "You don't think he killed him up here in the trees, stashed the body for a few days, then came back to display him, do you?"

"We've never found any of the murder scenes."

"What if the desert has been the murder scene all along?"

Andrea followed the drag pattern into the junipers, ducking under the branches as she moved higher on the rocks. She stopped when she saw the dark pool of dried blood.

"Son of a bitch," Cameron murmured from behind her.

"He didn't have to carry him."

"He made him walk," they said in unison.

Andrea turned, clutching Cameron's arm. "That means he's been right under our noses all along. The others, we scanned the immediate area, but we didn't do a thorough perimeter search. We assumed it was a dump site only."

"As he meant for it to appear. The blood left in Tucson was just to confuse us."

"And to play with us," Andrea added. "I'm sorry. Do you want to call Phoenix in to process the scene?"

"No. We can do it. A three-day old scene, out in the elements, any kind of trace is sure to be gone."

Andrea nodded. "Let me call Sheriff Baker and let him know what's going on."

"Okay. And I'll—" But her cell interrupted and she answered, turning away from Andrea. "Yeah, Reynolds, I know."

Andrea moved away, giving her some privacy, but she kept her attention on Cameron as she called Jim.

"I can process the goddamn scene, Reynolds."

Andrea's eyebrows shot up at Cameron's raised voice.

"She knows what she's doing, so don't call her a yahoo country bumpkin."

That would be me, Andrea assumed. But she didn't blame them. One of their own was down. Stood to reason they'd want to be thorough and send in experts.

"Blame who you want, but the blame still lies with Collie. He refused to see the connection, refused to believe the serial killer angle. Hell, even when the knife wounds matched, he was still skeptical." She paused. "I'm not. I worked with the man too, you know. Let me do my job. How about you guys find some answers instead of just sitting around with your heads up your asses waiting for the next goddamn press conference."

Andrea was about to end her call when Jim's voice sounded. "Jim, sorry. Let me get back with you."

"Joey filled me in."

"Yeah. Okay. I'll call you right back."

Andrea moved to Cameron who stood with her back to the scene, her shoulders tense. Her head was raised skyward but her eyes were closed.

"Cameron?" She reached out, gently touching her arm, then wrapping her fingers around her, squeezing lightly. "You want to talk?"

Cameron shook her head. "No. We have work to do. Just give me a minute."

"I won't be offended if they send in a CSI team."

"You can do the job." She turned then. "Right?"

Andrea nodded. "I have some experience in it, yes. I spent a year in forensics." She raised her hands, palms up. "We just don't have all the fancy equipment."

"We already have DNA of the killer. What we're looking for is trace evidence, fibers, something to give a clue as to where the bastard lives, where he stays, where he hides. And I'm fairly certain we're not going to find that."

Their eyes met and Andrea was shocked by the depth of sadness in Cameron's. As far as she could tell, there was no love lost between Cameron and Agent Collie. In fact, she would have sworn their relationship bordered on hatred. But Cameron's eyes told her how terribly wrong she was. Without thinking, she pulled Cameron into a quick, hard embrace, realizing, for Cameron, it was another chapter in her life with a tragic ending.

It took a few seconds before Cameron relaxed, accepting Andrea's comfort for what it was. When she stepped back, Cameron nodded.

"Thank you."

Andrea didn't say anything. She just watched as Cameron's expression changed, her professional mask slipping back into place.

"Let's process this first," Andrea suggested, following suit. "We'll wait until the guys get here with the equipment before we start on...the body."

"You want the recorder?"

"Yes. I'll let you handle the camera, if that's okay."

"I can manage that."

Andrea took her cap off and brushed her damp hair off of her forehead. She pulled the cap back on as Cameron handed her the digital recorder. She turned it on, her gaze immediately finding the blood pool under the juniper where Agent Collie had been killed.

"Blood splatter on the limb here," she said, pointing it out to Cameron. "He was standing," she said, moving closer to the spot, "here. The killer came from behind him." She followed the scenario in her mind, turning. She reached out, fingering the limp juniper branch. "Broken branch here. Overturned rocks. Blood is contained. He fell here. It doesn't appear the body was moved." She looked up. "Until it was placed on Devil's Bridge," she added. "We'll need a blood sample, just to make sure he didn't stage this like he did the apartment in Tucson."

She moved in a circle, looking for anything out of place. There were no torn shards of cloths, no strange fibers. There were more displaced rocks opposite the others. She frowned, her head tilting as she saw it in her mind.

"He covered him," she said.

"What?"

"Look," she said, pointing to the rocks. "Here. These rocks

are flipped over." She moved to the other imaginary corner of a square. "And here. He covered him with something, then weighted it down with rocks in each corner."

"Like a tarp or something."

"Camouflage. He didn't want someone finding the body before he was ready."

"He could have snatched him the night he went to the homeless shelter. Brought him up here and killed him that night."

"Covered the body and left."

"Came back two days later to display it."

Andrea nodded. "Which means he's probably done that with all of them. He doesn't abduct them and hold them. He abducts them, kills them and hides them."

"It's like you said, he's been under our noses all along."

"Why Collie? Why deviate from his pattern?"

"Probably saw him giving his press conferences, knew he was the one looking for him. What better way to say fuck you to the FBI?"

"But Cameron, that's taking a huge risk. How would Patrick have known that Collie was alone? For that matter, how would Patrick have known Collie would show up at the homeless shelter?"

"Maybe he didn't know. Maybe he saw him, recognized his face from TV and panicked. Maybe he thought Collie was on to him."

"Okay." Andrea paced now as her mind jumped from scene to scene. "But, it doesn't make sense. If Patrick is as smart as we all make him out to be, why would he even be at the shelter in the first place? He has to know we've connected him to Dallas. Surely he wouldn't follow the same pattern and try to blend in with the homeless. He has to know we'd look there."

"So what's your thought? That he was following Collie?"

"Maybe. If you're the hunted, don't you want to keep the hunter in your sights?"

"Dangerous," Cameron said. "If the FBI is looking for you, you're not going to be following them around. That's crazy."

"Okay. So maybe it was planned. He watches the news, sees

Collie at the press conference, then targets him as his next victim. Conveniently, Collie leaves the hotel alone, giving Patrick his chance."

"Follows him to the homeless shelter and nabs him? Come on, Patrick is a thin, small man. Collie is over two hundred pounds, a trained FBI agent. No way Patrick abducts him."

Andrea put her hands on her hips, facing Cameron. "Well, obviously he did. We have a body to prove it."

CHAPTER TWENTY

Cameron watched as Andrea slipped on latex gloves before beginning her exam of the body. The other victims, as Andrea had told her, were assumed dumped. The scenes were processed superficially only. This one, she would go over methodically, looking for any foreign material that might help them find Patrick Doe.

She stood maybe twenty feet away from Andrea, Randy and Joey beside her. All three were fixed on Andrea's movements. Cameron noted that Andrea's gaze seemed to avoid Collie's face. Who could blame her? Cameron had been able to do nothing more than give him a quick glance before looking away. Andrea was right. She'd lost team members in the name of war. Never like this. Never intentionally murdered, their throat slashed open in such a horrific manner.

"Got blood under the nails," she said, looking at Cameron. "Epithelial."

Cameron nodded.

"Epi what?" Randy asked quietly.

Cameron glanced at him. "Skin cells."

"Oh."

Andrea carefully bagged his hands, then placed them by his side. She looked up again. "Where would he keep his FBI credentials?"

"I think upper coat pocket," she said, trying to remember Collie's habit.

Andrea opened the coat, patting each pocket. She then slightly rolled him over, feeling his backside. She shook her head. "Nothing. How did he carry his weapon?"

Christ. Cameron hadn't even thought about his weapon. She pointed to her hip where her own holster was clipped. "Like mine. He should also have a secondary weapon strapped to his leg." Should being the key word. A lot of agents, when out in the field, used different means to conceal their backup weapon.

"Nothing. He's clean. No ID, no wallet, no weapons."

"Follows the others. They had nothing on them either." She stepped away from the guys and pulled out her cell. "I need to notify Murdock that his service weapon and credentials are missing."

"Fine. There's nothing here. Nothing out of place. No smudges, no tracks. Nothing," Andrea said.

"Like the others," Cameron said, then turned her attention to Murdock. "It's me. Just finished processing the scenes up here. There's nothing—"

"Do you want me to request CSI from Phoenix?" he asked, interrupting her. "Reynolds thinks—"

"Look, Murdock, she's had training in forensics. I've had training. There's nothing here."

"Just want to cover all the bases, Agent Ross."

"*Special* Agent Murdock, are we going to get all formal now? Reynolds been complaining about me already?"

"Of course. I'm sorry, Cameron. I just don't want anything to slip through."

"Well, we have a different angle, that's for sure. We found where he was killed."

"What? He wasn't dumped like the others?"

"He was laid out like the others, but when we were doing a perimeter check, we found drag marks. We followed them up a ravine about fifty yards. He was killed there, under some small trees." She turned, seeing Randy and Joey helping Andrea lift Collie onto the rack. She quickly averted her eyes. "Judging by the overturned rocks, Deputy Sullivan thinks—and I agree— that he was killed two days ago, then covered with something to camouflage him. The killer then came back and dragged him down to the trail, where he'd be found."

"So you think they all may have been killed there?"

"Possible. Probable, even, since there's been no other discovery of a murder scene."

"Jesus, Cameron, we were going on the assumption that they weren't killed there. The initial reports from the sheriff's office were that the bodies were dumped."

"They *were* dumped. Christ, this isn't a fucking city street here, Murdock. It's a remote wilderness. A high mountain desert. Have you bothered to look at any of the photos I included in my reports?" Her voice was raised and she glanced quickly at Andrea, seeing a sympathetic look in her eyes. "It was quite by accident we found the drag marks, and it's probably because Collie weighed over two hundred pounds and the killer couldn't carry him. The girls, they were all small. He could have killed them anywhere up here and moved them. Nothing to drag."

"Okay, okay. So now what? Do you want to move the whole team out there?"

"No. I don't think that's a good idea. In fact, it's probably futile. There are dozens of trails and hundreds of miles of them. Besides, if we move the focus of the investigation here, we might just send him under again. He'll move on and resurface in another place a year from now."

"So you're still going with the theory of the ten-year killing spree that Patrick's been on?"

"Just because Collie didn't agree with it, doesn't mean I don't. It's plausible. In fact, quite probable."

"I agree. I've got the geeks in Quantico going over Sullivan's report. They're going to pull in the ME records from all the cases and compare them—strangulation patterns, knife wounds, everything."

"Good. But let's stay focused here. First of all, Reynolds needs to find where the hell Collie was abducted from. Any luck with the surveillance tapes?"

"They're still going over them. I need to set up a meeting with Reynolds. I want you there. I've got a meeting in Washington tomorrow so I'll have to video-feed in, but I want you and Reynolds in the same room. You need to talk this out, share everything you've found so far and come up with a plan of action. We need to nail this bastard and soon."

"Okay. What time?"

"I'll let you know in the morning. You're just a few hours away, right?"

"Yeah. I'll hang around the rig, play with the algorithms."

"Good. And I know we're all stressed, Cameron, but let's try to keep our cool."

"So what's up? Reynolds tattled on me already? Did he learn that from Collie?"

"You're naïve if you think Collie is the only one who tattles on you, Ross. Everyone who works with you has a complaint."

She smiled. "Great. Then my reputation is still intact." She watched as Andrea zipped the bag closed, finally hiding Collie's face from her view. "Oh, forgot to tell you. Collie's badge and weapon are missing. He had no ID or personal effects on him."

"Wonderful," he said dryly. "So this lunatic now has FBI credentials and a gun. Always full of good news, Ross."

As always, the call ended without pleasantries, although under the circumstances, it was enough. She slipped her phone into her pocket and hurried over to the others, helping to carry the rack across the rocks that littered Devil's Bridge. She stood back as Randy and Joey lifted him onto the mule, then waited while Andrea strapped him down.

"Take him to Cutty's," Andrea said. "The ME is bringing their van from Phoenix to pick him up there."

"Okay."

"What's Cutty's?" Cameron asked.

"Funeral home. James Cutty. He's been kind enough to

house all the victims until they come for them."

"Hell of a name," she said.

"You want to ride out with Randy?" Andrea offered.

Cameron spied the two horses that Randy and Joey had rode in on, guiding the mule behind them. She thought maybe the least she could do was to take Collie out of here. She'd avoided him enough already. Besides, she needed to get this new data loaded.

"Yeah. I think so." She glanced at Joey. "Okay with you, man?"

"Sure. I'll walk out with Andi."

She nodded, taking the reins of his horse. She turned to Andrea, silently thanking her before climbing in the saddle. She let Randy take the lead, her horse side by side with the mule... and Collie.

CHAPTER TWENTY-ONE

After much debate with herself, Andrea set out to do what she'd intended all along. She drove to Cameron's rig. She'd not heard a word from her since she'd left the canyon. When she and Joey made it back to the office, the medical examiner had already collected Collie's body and was heading back to Phoenix. She'd placed a call to them, letting them know she'd e-mail her preliminary field report. She spent the next hour completing it, making sure she'd not left anything out. She still had Cameron's digital recorder, but Cameron had the data for the coordinates. She noted that in her report.

She spent another hour going over everything with Jim, bouncing ideas off him. She wanted to go back to the other scenes and do a more thorough search of the perimeter. They'd initially checked twenty, thirty feet out in all directions. If Collie, who weighed two hundred pounds, was left more than fifty feet away, chances were the young college students were killed even farther away from where their bodies were placed.

She had ideas—theories—that she wanted to discuss with Cameron, but she'd hesitated going to her. She thought perhaps Cameron wanted to be alone or that she had work to do, the case becoming more urgent now. So she'd waited, hoping Cameron would call. As the dinner hour came and went, Andrea half-heartedly ate a cold sandwich she'd thrown together. Finally, as the clock ticked past eight, she could stand it no more. She grabbed a bottle of water from her fridge and the keys to her Jeep and sped away. If Cameron didn't want to see her, she'd just have to send her away.

Now, as she parked next to Cameron's truck, she had second thoughts. The rig appeared dark. Although there was still enough light in the summer sky, Cameron may not have turned hers on yet. She got out of the Jeep, hesitating. Maybe she should have called first. Maybe she should—

"Security is off. Come in."

She took a deep breath, letting it out slowly before moving closer. Cameron's voice sounded strained, tired. She opened the door, taking the two steps to get inside. It was indeed dark, not a light turned on. Cameron was sprawled on the tiny loveseat, the black kitten curled in her lap. Her computer sat on the small table beside her, a view of the outside and Andrea's Jeep on her screen.

"I should have called, I guess," she said, moving inside and closing the door behind her. "I thought maybe you would need to talk."

"Not a whole lot to talk about, really." Cameron looked at her for the first time and Andrea wondered if she'd been crying. "I'm sorry. I won't be very good company I'm afraid."

"I didn't really come for the company," she said. "I just thought you might want to talk." She nudged Cameron's legs out of the way and sat down beside her. Cameron's normal jeans were replaced with shorts and Andrea noted her hair was still damp from an earlier shower. "Have you had dinner?" Andrea asked, knowing it was a silly question that she didn't need an answer to.

"Not hungry."

Andrea leaned back, saying nothing, just watching as Cameron continued to stroke Lola's fur. The kitten's loud purring was the only sound.

"I didn't really like the man," Cameron said finally. "In fact, most days, if you'd asked me, I'd have said I hated him."

"Did you really?"

"No. But he liked to push my buttons. He knew which ones to push, and I let him. He drove me crazy."

"Maybe it was just a game that you both played," Andrea guessed. "You still respected him and he you."

Cameron gave a bitter laugh. "No. I'd be lying. There wasn't any mutual respect between us. I just...well, he was someone I loved to hate. It went both ways. But you're right. It was a game to see who could piss off the other more." She pushed Lola onto Andrea's lap as she stood. "And now I goddamn feel guilty," she said. "I hate myself. All the times I called him an asshole, a *fucker*," she said loudly. "Now he's dead. He let himself get abducted, for God's sake...and now he's dead."

"Cameron—"

"Don't tell me I shouldn't feel guilty," she said. "You know all about feeling guilty, don't you?"

Andrea didn't say anything as Cameron paced. Yes, she knew all about feeling guilty. She was the queen of guilt.

"So many people have come and gone in my life. Why are there so many tragic endings? Why?" She held her hand wide, touching a finger. "Gloria. She was ten years older than me, a British agent. We were on a joint assignment. We became lovers. I let my guard down, they got past me. She was killed." Cameron touched another finger. "Ten members of my team. Roadside bomb. I survived. They didn't." Another finger. "Max Caldwell, sniper. He taught me everything he knew. Took a knife to the back when he thought he'd scored an easy lay. She was a spy." She closed her eyes. "Laurie. Swallowed by the sea at the age of twenty-eight." She opened her eyes again, her stare cold as she looked at Andrea. "My mother. My brother. Dirk Walker, my best friend in high school. He jumped off a fucking bridge and killed himself."

"Cameron, stop," Andrea said.

"No, I don't want to stop. There are so many more. So many dead. Yet I go on. I keep going on, just waiting my turn." She met Andrea's eyes in the lengthening darkness. "I sometimes wish it would hurry up and get here already, you know."

Andrea stood then, going to her. "Stop it. You don't mean that."

"Don't I? What good is it all, Andrea? What good has come of any of it?" She pulled away when Andrea reached for her. "No. Don't," she said as she jerked her arm from Andrea's grasp. "I told you I wasn't going to be very good company." She plunged both hands into her hair. "I need to get out of here. I need to take a drive, clear my mind."

"No."

"No? You're not really in a position to stop me."

"Cameron, please. You're scaring me. You're scaring Lola," she said, pointing to the kitten who was huddled in the corner of the sofa, her eyes wide with fright at Cameron's loud voice. Cameron's intense stare finally left Andrea as she glanced at the kitten. Andrea saw her expression soften immediately.

Cameron closed her eyes again and tucked her head. "I'm sorry, Andi. God, I'm so sorry." She moved then, scooping up the kitten and bringing it to her chest. "Hey, furball. I didn't mean to scare you." She looked at Andrea, her eyes gentle now, asking for forgiveness.

Andrea nodded. "It's okay."

"I'm sorry," Cameron said again, then sighed. "I hate the name Lola, you know."

"So what do you want to call her?"

Cameron tilted her head, her gaze lingering on the kitten. "I was thinking I'd name her Sedona. That way, when I leave here, I'll have something to remind me."

"Will you need something?" Andrea asked quietly.

The rig was nearly surrounded by darkness, but Andrea could still make out Cameron's thoughtful expression. She slowly returned Lola to the loveseat then reached for Andrea.

"No. I won't need a reminder." She paused, lightly touching Andrea's face with both hands. "I need to be with you tonight," she whispered, her mouth inches from Andrea's. "Will you please stay with me?"

Andrea closed the distance, accepting Cameron's hard kiss. Cameron pulled her into a tight embrace and just as quickly pushed her away, leading her through the darkness and into her bedroom.

CHAPTER TWENTY-TWO

Andrea sat at her desk, knowing she had several things she could be doing—should be doing—but she couldn't seem to focus. Her mind, her body, was still filled with Cameron. Never in her life had she made love with the intensity that Cameron had demanded last night. Each touch, each kiss, took her breath away. Cameron had been insatiable and Andrea had given her what she needed, to the point of pure exhaustion. She'd collapsed on top of Cameron finally, her fingers still inside her. She couldn't remember Cameron's mumbled words as she pulled the covers over both of them, but she remembered feeling completely safe as Cameron's arms wound around her as she slept.

She'd left without waking Cameron, pausing only to feed Lola before escaping to her Jeep, thankful the security wasn't on. Apparently, Cameron—in her haste—had forgotten to arm it.

Now, exhausted as she was, she wished she'd stayed. Her body came alive at just the thought of waking up with Cameron. She was delightfully sore, her muscles aching, but she could still feel the remnants of her arousal, could still picture—with intimate detail—Cameron's mouth as it left her breasts only to travel much lower, Cameron's loud moan was so sensual as she claimed Andrea, her tongue slicing through her wetness, raking over her swollen clit, bringing her to orgasm yet again.

Andrea squeezed her legs together tightly, nearly moaning out loud at the sweet tightness that ached to be touched. She stood quickly, heading to the bathroom to perhaps do just that when she saw Cameron's truck pull up outside. She had a sudden, wicked thought, wondering how much she'd have to beg Cameron to slip into the bathroom with her and give her the release her body suddenly craved.

She shook that thought away, trying in vain to appear somewhat professional when Cameron walked in. Randy and Joey were already eyeing her suspiciously. But her professional mask slipped away when she met Cameron's eyes. Their gazes locked for long seconds before she finally pulled hers away, embarrassed as surely Randy and Joey knew exactly where her thoughts had been.

"Good morning, Deputy Sullivan," Cameron said. "I'm wondering if I can have a word?"

"Of course." She looked around, but Jim was in his office and the guys showed no interest in leaving. That left the somewhat exposed break room in the back. She motioned with her head and Cameron followed.

"I missed you this morning," Cameron said quietly. "You should have woken me up before you left."

"If I did, it wouldn't have been to say goodbye," she admitted, her voice just as quiet as they stood mere feet apart.

Cameron smiled, but her eyes belied how tired she was. "I... well, thank you for staying last night. I'm sorry that I freaked out and got a little crazy. I didn't mean to scare you. It just, well, everything got to me at once."

"I understand. I've been there."

Cameron took a deep breath then moved away, clearing her throat. "I have to go to Phoenix. I've got to meet with Reynolds. He's taking over for Collie. Murdock is going to do a video feed so we can all meet and talk this out."

Andrea had a moment of panic. "You're leaving?" Of course she knew Cameron would be leaving eventually, but she thought—

"No, no. I'm leaving the rig here. But I was hoping maybe you'd stay there." She looked around them quickly, seeing Randy and Joey blatantly watching them. "Take care of Lola for me," she said.

"Oh, okay. Sure. Will you be long?"

"I should be back tomorrow, I'd think." She pulled out her remote. "Listen, this is easy. To arm it, you push this," she said, pointing to the "program" button. "Punch in the code—I've written them down for you—and hit 'enable.' Simple as that."

"And to disarm?"

"Hit 'program,' do the code, and 'disable'." Cameron handed her the remote. "You can use this from the inside too. There's a keypad and the controls for the cameras in my office, but it's too complicated to try to explain, so just use this. Now, I drove the rig to the campground this morning and dumped the holding tanks and filled her up with fresh water, so she's ready to go."

"But it's back where you normally park it?"

"Her," Cameron corrected with a smile. "Yes. And thank you for doing this."

"Of course."

"You might want to change the sheets on the bed," she said, her voice again quiet, teasing.

"I'm thinking that's probably a good idea."

"Feel free to snoop around. The sheets are in one of the pull-out drawers under the bed."

"Okay." Andrea held her ground as Cameron took a step closer.

"I wish I could kiss you," she whispered.

"Yes. So do I."

Cameron's gaze dropped to Andrea's mouth and Andrea took a step back, afraid she would really do it. "Don't you dare."

Cameron smiled. "No, I wouldn't dare." She glanced at her watch. "I need to get going. I'll call you tomorrow and let you know when I'll be back."

Andrea almost said something foolish, like "I'll miss you,"

but thankfully came to her senses before the words tumbled out. She simply nodded, squeezing the remote tightly in her hands as she watched Cameron saunter out of the office.

"Damn, but she's hot," Joey said as he stretched his neck to the side, watching as Cameron got in her truck.

"I'll say. She looks so buff. Wonder what she looks like naked," Randy murmured.

They both turned and looked at Andrea, eyebrows raised. She felt a blush cover her face.

"How the hell should I know?" she said as she sat back down at her desk, making a show of straightening the clutter.

Randy laughed loudly. "I have never seen you blush before, Andi. What's up with that?"

Andrea ignored them, not wanting to get into a teasing battle with either of them. The fact that she and Cameron were sleeping together was completely unprofessional. The fact that they were partners on this case made it even more so. The last thing she wanted was for someone to question her ability or dedication to the case. So far, she and Cameron had been able to work together fine, despite the intimacy between them. She hoped they could keep it that way.

CHAPTER TWENTY-THREE

"I've already explained about the dump sites, Reynolds. What is it you don't get?" She pierced him with her best glare, pleased to see some unease in his eyes. Then he flashed a fake smile, his teeth white against his ebony skin.

"We've been searching in vain for the murder scenes, that's what I don't get."

"And we've been looking too. As I explained to Murdock, it was quite by accident we found this one."

"Then maybe we should send the team up there to go over the other sites again."

Cameron leaned back in her chair, taking in his fancy suit and tie, his shiny, polished shoes, his perfectly manicured hands, the pristine white shirt beneath his black coat. She gave a lazy smile. "Sure, Reynolds, you come on out to the desert. Bring your friends."

"You don't think we can handle it?"

"You wouldn't last half a day."

"I'll have you know—"

"Agents, can we not have one discussion without testosterone getting in the way?" Murdock's voice sounded through the speakers.

"About time you get here," Cameron said as the monitor sprang to life and Murdock's somewhat hazy image appeared. She frowned. "You've lost weight," she said.

"Yes. Thanks for noticing. I've also gotten gray. Working with you does that to me."

She also noticed how tired he looked. This case was obviously as stressful for him as anyone. Particularly because of Collie. Whereas Cameron and Collie never saw eye-to-eye, Murdock and Collie usually did. Being the go-between must have taken its toll on him.

"I've already given her what little we have," Reynolds said. "We're still going over the security tapes. We managed to find his car on one of the traffic cams, but it's only for a block. It never shows back up, so we don't know what street he took."

"Possible that he was on the way to the shelter?" Cameron asked.

"Possible, yes. We assume he never made it there. Or if he did, he never made it inside. None of the workers recognized his photo."

"Have they done the post on Collie?"

"Yes. Results aren't back. Of course, we all know cause of death," Reynolds said, his voice quiet with emotion.

"I'm still wondering how he could have been abducted," Cameron said. "He was a large man. From what we know of Patrick, he's small, has a slight frame. How does someone like that take control of Collie?"

"Gunpoint?" Murdock suggested.

"You have to assume it was in a somewhat public place," she said. "Why not use your training and disarm him? That's what most agents would have done."

"We can only guess what happened," Reynolds said.

"Yeah. That's because your team can't seem to find out where the hell he was taken."

"Agent Ross," Murdock warned. "We're here to share facts and come up with a plan of action. Now, what's going on with you?"

"I e-mailed Jason about his algorithm. He's going to tweak it." She looked at Reynolds. "His program pretty much pinpointed the dump site," she explained, "but was off on naming the right trail. The trail it named was only a few hundred feet from where Collie was found, however, it was across the canyon wall."

"Good," Murdock said. "Have you filled Reynolds in on your theory?"

She gave a crooked smile. "We didn't actually get that far," she said.

"Well let's try to go over it without getting into an argument, shall we."

"I'll assume then that Reynolds will be more receptive to my ideas than Collie ever was." She stood, pacing slowly in front of Reynolds. "Our main issue has been how the hell he carries the bodies to these dump sites. While they've been close to the trails—close enough to be spotted, obviously—it's still not an easy hike. The first one killed, second found—Maggie O'Brien—was up on the rim of the canyon, a two-hour trip on horseback. How did he get her up there?" She stopped, looking at Reynolds. "When we found Collie, it all made sense. He didn't carry them. He made them walk. Were they bound and gagged?" She shrugged. "Don't know. Collie never shared the ME's results with me, thinking it was out of my domain. Did any have ligature marks?"

"I don't know. I haven't read them either."

Cameron glanced at Murdock on the screen, eyebrows raised.

"Collie briefed me on the reports. I think he was mostly looking at tox to see if they were drugged. That was negative."

"I'll read through them," Reynolds said, making a note. "Do you want me to forward them to you?"

Cameron sat back down. "No, I'll let you do the dirty work. Not that it will help us. But my theory is he makes them hike up the trail at night where he kills them. He then hides the body, covers it. Leaves it for a few days, then returns—again at night—to move the body to the trail where he displays it."

"Why would he do that? What's the point?" Reynolds asked.

"Who knows? To confuse us? It's worked so far. To screw with the timeline? To skew the time of death? Could be any number of reasons."

"And what about these programs you're running?" he asked.

"The more data we have, the more likely they are to be accurate. As far as when he kills, the time in between each one, that's varied so far. If we can nail a dump site, then we would stake it out, hope to catch him as he's taking his victim up the trail."

"Well, that sounds promising."

She laughed. "Yeah. But we're talking hundreds of miles of trails, Reynolds. On foot. At night."

He nodded. "What about the other murder sites?"

"Haven't found them. Collie was about fifty yards from where he was killed." She paused, amazed that they were talking about Collie so casually, almost as if he wasn't a colleague. "Collie was a big man. Patrick knew he wouldn't be able to move him far. He was killed uphill from where he was found. Patrick dragged him down the hill. That's the only way we found it. The others, we assume Patrick carried them. They were all small women." She looked at Murdock. "That just clicked with me. He targets women who are small. Ones he can carry. I wonder if that was the pattern all along. The ones he kills and leaves in the apartments, he doesn't care about size. The others, the ones who've been found in rural areas, have they all been small?"

"I'll make a note to check with the guys researching that," Murdock said.

"What are you talking about? What apartments?"

"Jesus, Reynolds, did Collie totally keep you in the dark or what? In Dallas, Patrick murdered his women in their apartments. He didn't move the body."

"Oh. The serial killer theory. Collie didn't put much credence in that."

"Obviously not."

"Okay. I've got a meeting. You two can continue without me," Murdock said. "Reynolds? Are you okay with the press briefings?"

"I can handle it, yes."

"Let's tighten up on it a bit," Murdock suggested. "We have to give some information, but because we have an agent down, they'll understand the need to keep some data from the public."

"Not too tight," Cameron said. "The last thing I need is to have the media crawling all over Sedona."

"Since the first body, we've stopped giving location," Reynolds said. "We've been very vague as to where they've been found."

"Good. But we all know if a reporter wants to know, they can find out."

"Yes, of course, but they're cooperating. In fact, the longer this drags on, the less crowded our press conferences have been," Reynolds said.

"Old news already?"

"Apparently. Arizona media is still hot with it, but nationally, not as much."

"Let's not release COD on Collie," Murdock said. "I don't want him linked to these killings," he said. "We'll discuss that later, Reynolds. Agent Ross, thank you for making the trip down. I'll be in touch."

The screen went dark before she could comment. She turned in her chair, facing Reynolds. "Now what?"

"We haven't found Collie's car. We didn't put an APB out. We didn't want the locals getting too involved. Our guys are taking block by block from where he disappeared off of the traffic cam. You want to join us?"

"Sure. Then you can treat me to dinner later."

CHAPTER TWENTY-FOUR

Andrea filled Lola's food bowl, then scooped up the kitten, holding her close as she kissed her furry face. She hated leaving her alone again and had a sudden thought.

"You need your shots," she said. "Wonder if your mommy would get mad if I took you along with me?"

She put Lola back down, watching as she munched on her food. She stepped back, making sure she'd left everything the way Cameron had it. She'd actually enjoyed herself last night, especially after she figured out how to work the TV and satellite. She had been transfixed as she channel surfed through the more than four hundred choices.

She'd been a bit disappointed that Cameron hadn't called, but she reminded herself that they were working, not dating. The fact that she was having a sexual affair with Cameron in the first place—knowing that Cameron would be leaving as soon as the case was finished—was out of character for her. Oh, sure, she'd had a few casual encounters in the past, usually one-night stands that were agreeable to both parties. But for the most part, her sexual partners were women she was seriously dating.

Like Erin.

Her eyes widened. For the past three years, Erin—and the others—had been on her mind, in her thoughts, constantly. She rarely went hours without thinking of her, much less days. Yet, since her confession to Cameron the other night, Erin hadn't made an appearance. Was Cameron just a distraction for her? Or did her confession actually chase the guilt away? Could it just leave so suddenly that she hadn't even noticed?

And would it return when Cameron left her?

Andrea took in a deep, heavy breath, now almost feeling guilty because she no longer felt the guilt. That thought, at least, brought a smile to her face.

She glanced at Lola, now methodically cleaning herself. She supposed she'd save the vet for another day. She wasn't certain how she'd transport her in the Jeep anyway.

"Okay, girl, I gotta go."

She grabbed her small backpack and the remote, taking one last look around before leaving.

Cameron had every intention of heading straight to the rig, but an hour after she left Phoenix, her thoughts were less and less on the case and more on Andrea. If she were honest with herself, she'd admit that she was getting much too involved with her. Brief, sexual affairs were common in her line of work. Very common, in fact. She wanted to believe that's all this was—a brief affair that would end as soon as she left the city limits of Sedona. The fact that Andrea invaded her thoughts more than she should didn't have any bearing.

Why, then, was she heading into town instead of the Red Rocks Park and the rig? Why was she going to Andrea instead of her computers? She hadn't been able to add Collie's data to her programs. That night after they found him, she just didn't have the heart for it. Then, of course, Andrea had showed up and had been her salvation, taking her mind off of the pitiful trip through her life's tragedies. She'd needed Andrea that night, and Andrea gave willingly, offering herself up to Cameron's desires.

And Cameron had taken it, ridding herself of the memories that snuck up on her sometimes, the scars that reopened, the wounds that festered. Andrea took all of that away, giving herself instead.

So here she was, ignoring the practical side of her brain that said she needed to work. Instead, her emotional side was telling her she needed to see Andrea. That fact alone should have been alarming to her, but it wasn't. She was simply satisfying a need.

This time when she walked into the office, she gave a cursory nod in the direction of the receptionist. Her eyes found Andrea immediately, ignoring the other two deputies. The smile Andrea flashed her was matched by one of her own.

"Deputy Sullivan," she said, her mouth still flirting with a grin. "How's my cat?"

"Lola survived the night without you."

Cameron walked closer and just couldn't resist the most obvious retort. "And did you?" she asked, her voice low.

"I see you're as conceited as ever," Andrea said, but the blush on her face was telling enough.

"True." She took a step back. "If you've got a minute, I'll fill you in. Is Jim available?"

"Yes. He's in his office."

Cameron followed her down the short hallway, her eyes inappropriately glued to her backside.

"Jim, Agent Ross is here," Andrea said. "You have a minute?"

"Of course, Andi."

He stood, offering his hand to Cameron. "I'm sorry about your colleague, Cameron. That had to have been a blow."

Cameron nodded as she shook his hand. "Yes. You work a case, the last thing you believe is that you'll be a victim yourself." She sat down next to Andrea in the visitor's chair.

"Well, Andi said you were off to Phoenix yesterday. Any news?"

"They found his car about midnight last night. They processed it this morning. I left before they were finished."

"Where did they find it?" Andrea asked.

"It was in a paid parking garage," she said. "They're pulling the security tapes. It was nowhere near the homeless shelter so we have to believe it was driven there by someone else or he was under duress."

"Are they going to relocate the operation here?" Jim asked.

"No. You don't want all those guys in their fancy suits running around out here," she said. "They're going to focus on where and how he was abducted. Hopefully the security tape of the parking garage will give up a face."

"You gotta believe that Patrick would know about the security cameras," Andrea said.

"True. But maybe, at this point, he doesn't care. Or maybe he thought it would be days before the car was found." She shrugged. "And it was."

Andrea nodded. "Well, there's something I wanted to discuss with you. We don't know how he chooses his trails. He could use a map—a trail map—but that doesn't really give you a true picture of the trail."

"What are you getting at?"

"I think he checks them out first. In the daylight."

She stood, her brow drawn tight. "That never occurred to me. You think he does reconnaissance?"

"I do, especially if he's hiding the body for a couple of days. You can't do that at night and know what's visible and what's not during the day. In Collie's case, he had to know he wouldn't be able to carry him, so he didn't hide him as far."

"And he made sure the body was uphill of the dump site," Cameron said, nodding. "It makes perfect sense." She grinned. "Good job."

"But does it help us?"

"I haven't entered the latest data yet. I'll do that and run the algorithm again tonight. We can take the top two hits, do our own reconnaissance." She turned to Jim. "If we find a suitable trail, then we can do a stakeout."

"My guys?"

"Or me and Andi," she said. "No vehicles. On foot, hiding off the trail."

Jim looked at Andrea. "Any of the guys fit that bill?"

She shook her head. "Randy would be no help. He's terrified of mountain lions."

"Mountain lions? You have mountain lions here?"

"Of course."

"Now you tell me."

"They prefer deer and elk. You would be a third choice," Andrea teased.

Cameron returned her smile then realized Jim was watching them with interest. She motioned out the door. "What about those two guys? I didn't recognize them."

"Michael has been on vacation, back yesterday. Antonio, well, he's new. Haven't got a good feel for him yet," Jim said. "Now, I don't want you to get the impression that my guys are inferior, Cameron. They're not. But they're sheriff's deputies in a small town. They're not trained for the kind of stuff you're needing." He looked at Andrea. "She is."

"I understand. I would need a couple of them to be on standby, at least. If we're going to stake out a trail and happen to get lucky, we'll need backup."

"That we can do."

"Well, I should—" The beeping of her phone interrupted her and she glanced at the caller, seeing Reynolds' ID come up. "I need to get this," she said. "Ross," she answered, moving out into the hallway.

"Got DNA back. It doesn't match."

"What the hell? Doesn't match what?"

"Doesn't match the semen."

"Hang on." She moved back into Jim's office, switching the phone to the speaker mode. "I put you on speaker, Reynolds. I've got Sheriff Baker and Deputy Sullivan with me." She turned to Andrea. "The DNA under Collie's nails didn't match the semen."

"You're joking?"

"No, ma'am," Reynolds said. "That's not to say we didn't get a hit on it."

"What'd you get?" Cameron asked.

"It matched the DNA belonging to John Doe."

"John Doe?"

"As in John Doe from the Dallas case," he said.

Cameron shook her head. "Not possible. He's dead."

"I realize that."

"Oh, my God," Andrea said. "Do you know what that means?"

"Holy shit. You're right," Cameron said. "Are you sure, Reynolds?"

"Just passing on the report, Ross. Tox came back clean, but you were right on the ligature marks. His wrists were bound. I went back on the other reports. All had evidence of ligatures except the hooker."

"Okay, I gotta call Dallas. I'll be in touch." She snatched up her phone, her eyes meeting Andrea. "I can't believe this."

"Me, either," she said, her fingers flipping through speed dial on her own phone.

"What's going on?" Jim asked.

"We think—hang on," she said. "I need to speak with Agent Hunter. This is Agent Ross."

"Casey O'Connor, please," Andrea said as she paced across the room with her phone.

"Will someone tell me what the hell is going on?" Jim demanded.

"I'm sorry, Agent Hunter is unavailable," the voice sounded in her ear.

"I'll try her later. Thanks," she said, disconnecting. She looked at Andrea. "Any luck?"

She shook her head. "Please ask her to call Andrea Sullivan. I'm the deputy who called her about the Patrick Doe case," she said. "She has my number." She glanced at Cameron. "She's doing an interrogation."

"What the hell is going on?" Jim asked again.

Andrea looked at him. "They're twins."

"Identical twins," Cameron said.

"There's a third person," Andrea said.

Jim looked from one to the other. "What are you talking about? I thought you already knew they were twins."

"Not identical. The semen found in Dallas, when it didn't match John's, was assumed to be that of Patrick, his brother."

"When we got the same semen match here," Cameron said. "It pointed to Patrick."

"But now we have DNA that matches John Doe. That can't be, of course, since John is dead," Andrea said. "The only possible way would be because Patrick has the same DNA."

"Identical twins share the same identical DNA," Cameron explained.

Jim's brow furrowed. "So you're saying Patrick is not the killer?"

"We're saying there's a third person involved."

"With similar DNA to be a relative. Or a sibling," Andrea said. "Wait a minute. Do you think there's another brother?"

"I want to read the Dallas file more thoroughly. And I'd like to speak with them again."

"Detective O'Connor sent me a very detailed file, more than the FBI database had. You want that?"

"Yes. E-mail that to me." She looked at her watch—it was now well past one. "I need to get to the rig, plug this data in. I'll call Reynolds and let him know our thoughts." She turned to Jim. "Sorry. I'll keep you up-to-date as well as I can."

"Just so Andi's up-to-date," he said, plucking a toothpick into his mouth. "I'll try to stay out of your way."

She glanced at Andrea. "I'll call you."

"Okay."

She hurried back to her truck, her mind racing with this new information. She tapped the console, bringing it to life. She typed in her code, then put a call into Murdock.

"That was kinda fun to watch," Jim said.

"What?"

"You two."

"What do you mean?"

He took his toothpick out of his mouth. "I've been in law enforcement over forty years, Andi. Even though the last twenty-five have been spent right here in Sedona, I've been around the block a time or two," he said. "And you two have got a connection."

She felt a blush immediately cover her face and she looked away, only to hear him laugh.

"I don't mean *that* kind of connection, although that's quite obvious too."

She bit her lip. "It is?"

"Quite. But I was talking about you working together. You communicate without words, you anticipate the other's train of thought. All signs of a good partner. I'm just saying, you work well together."

She nodded. "After the first couple of days—when I wanted to strangle her—I never would have thought so, but yeah, we do."

He smiled gently. "And the other?"

She sighed. "It just sort of happened. I'm sorry. I know—"

"Oh, hell, don't apologize, Andi. I'm just happy to see some life in you, that's all. You've kept yourself so closed off since you've been here, I was afraid that was going to be a lifelong habit."

She swallowed then cleared her throat. "For whatever reason, she's been able to ease my guilt somewhat." She met his eyes. "Over what happened in LA and all," she said.

He leaned back in his chair, watching her. She knew he had something on his mind and she waited.

"Over the last year, you've told me some of what happened. I think it's only fair that I tell you...well, I ran a background check on you when you applied for the job," he said.

His words took her breath away, making her chest feel heavy. "You knew?" she whispered. "All along?"

"I'm sorry. But a man doesn't just hire a deputy without knowing what the hell kind of baggage they've got."

"You know all of it?"

"I know you pulled your weapon on your captain, that's for sure."

"And you still hired me?"

"Common sense said I shouldn't have, no, but there was just

something in your eyes that day. A bit of desperation, I think, Andi."

She nodded. "Yes. I couldn't find a job. No one would hire me. You were my last option."

"You've told me about your father and what that loss meant to you. Who did you lose that day? What caused such profound sadness? What caused the guilt you talk of, the guilt that Cameron took away from you?"

"I felt responsible for what happened, Jim. Indirectly. I lost my best friend. Mark. And I lost...my lover. Erin. She was my partner." She closed her eyes. "It was a relationship coming to an end, an end she wasn't ready for. I should have waited to tell her. But I didn't. And that night," she paused. "Well, that night my world ended."

"And you carried the guilt of that with you?"

"Yes."

"As punishment?"

"I'm not sure it started out that way. As punishment, I mean," she clarified. "It evolved into that. Every week, every month that went by, it got worse. That first year, I honestly didn't think I was going to make it." She folded her arms across her chest. "So many days I just wanted to give up," she admitted. "I let the guilt just eat at me and eat at me until there wasn't anything left inside. I was just a shell. Just existing."

"You still carried it with you when you came here," he said.

"Yes. But I was managing. You know my morning routine by now," she said. "I go up there on the rocks and greet the day. It's a form of meditation," she said, not wanting to go into the whole Tai Chi ritual she'd started. "I thought that was keeping me going. Obviously, the last couple of weeks, I've not been able to keep to my practice."

He smiled. "Something else took its place?"

She blushed again. "She's been an outlet," she admitted. "I can talk to her about it. She understands. She's been where I am." His eyes held questions, but she didn't feel she was at liberty to share any of Cameron's secrets with him. "She's been good for me."

"And when she leaves?"

Yes, Andrea, then what? She shrugged. "I'll be okay. I feel like I've purged myself, you know? I feel like I've put that part of me in the past now. Finally."

He twirled his toothpick thoughtfully between his fingers then tossed it expertly into the trashcan beside his desk. She knew he'd reach into his shirt pocket and get a fresh one from the never-ending supply. He did, pulling out a new one. He popped it into his mouth, chewing it a bit before tucking it against his cheek.

"You know what, Andi? Hiring you was the best thing I ever did. You've been good for us. You've taught everybody, including me." He smiled. "Common sense told me you'd be nothing but trouble. But my gut said you'd be the best thing that could happen to this department." He nodded. "I went with my gut. And you have been."

"Thank you."

He settled back in his chair. "Now, you keep me informed, okay. I don't want to be totally out in left field when you catch this bastard."

She smiled, then went to him, bending down to lightly kiss his cheek. It was the first time she'd shown him that much affection.

"Thank you, Jim. Your words mean a lot to me."

She could tell he was touched and she left quickly, not wanting to embarrass either of them further.

CHAPTER TWENTY-FIVE

Cameron walked back and forth in her tiny kitchen, Lola tucked protectively in her arms. She could almost hear the inner workings of her computer as the algorithm did its thing, the data scrolling across the screen in nothing more than gibberish to her. Once it finished, she would take the data and load it into the conversion file, as Jason called it, dummying it down for her. There, the data would be sorted into a readable language that she could interpret. The whole process took hours, and she wished now that she'd loaded Collie's data the other night when she had it.

"But I was in no shape, was I, Lola?" she kissed the kitten's tiny head, loving the sound of the constant purring. She smiled, still amazed at how quickly she'd fallen in love with the furry little thing. She made a mental note—again—to take her to a vet for shots.

She looked up, hearing Andrea's Jeep before her alarm

signaled her arrival. Soon, the silent flashing light indicated the perimeter had been breached. She recognized her involuntary smile for what it was and left it at that. No harm in feeling happy that Andrea was here.

She punched the speaker key on the laptop. "Security is clear. Come on in."

Andrea walked in and their eyes met, the first time they'd been alone in two days. She waited, realizing she was still holding Lola under her chin. Normally, she would have been embarrassed at the display of affection she was showing the cat, but with Andrea, she felt none of that.

"Did she miss you?"

"Yes. Did you?"

Andrea came closer. "Yes, I missed you."

Cameron was surprised that she felt a bit nervous in Andrea's presence. She shrugged it off, smiling instead. "Well, then it seems we all missed someone."

Andrea reached out, taking Lola from her, immediately nuzzling the fur as her eyes closed. "I've missed having a cat," she said. "We always had a cat or two when I was at home. When I moved out, I just never got around to getting one," she said.

Cameron watched them, feeling a surge of...what? She couldn't put her finger on it, but it felt good.

"I never had a pet before," she admitted.

Andrea looked up. "Never?"

She shook her head. "We moved around so much, it just never came up."

Andrea kissed Lola then put her on the floor. "Well, I'm glad you have one now. They're great company."

"Yes." She laughed quickly. "I'd started talking to Clair, so that was worrying me."

"Clair?"

"The GPS voice."

Andrea grinned. "You named her Clair? That's sweet."

"I don't know about sweet," she said. She moved finally, opening the oven. "Did you know they delivered pizza out here?"

"I'm not surprised. Is that our dinner?"

"Is that okay?"

"Wine?"

"Of course."

"Then it's okay."

Cameron took the pizza out and glanced at the wine bottle. "Why don't you open it? I think you know where I keep everything." She dished out two slices each as Andrea pulled out the side drawer and retrieved the corkscrew, quickly opening the bottle.

They settled on the loveseat as had become their habit. Cameron noted that she seldom ever sat on the thing until Lola and Andrea came into her life. Now, she'd practically abandoned her comfortable recliner.

Lola surprised them both by jumping up and sniffing their pizza. Cameron gently put her back on the floor.

"I guess she's at the age where she's curious," Andrea said. "They say if you don't ever feed them people food they won't beg."

"Is that true?"

"I don't know. We were never able to hold out. Our cats always begged."

They ate in silence for a moment before Andrea brought the conversation back to the case.

"Is your algorithm running?"

"Yes. In fact, it may be finished. Then I need to import that data into another program Jason wrote. That's the one that feeds out English instead of gibberish," she said.

"Jason is your computer geek?"

"Yeah. Most of the time he talks way over my head. I have to remind him I'm just a dumb agent sometimes."

Andrea sipped from her wine, holding the glass out to Cameron. "You have excellent taste in wine, by the way. This is very good."

"You like wine, don't you?"

"Yes. I'll have a beer out occasionally but rarely anything else."

"I never used to drink wine," she said. "My parents never had it. They had beer and cheap bourbon. When I was a teenager and most of the dads were deployed, we'd have a party," she said, remembering the fun they'd had. "We'd all sneak liquor and meet up at someone's house when their mother would be out." She shook her head. "Warm beer and cheap bourbon. Recipe for a hangover."

"When did you start drinking wine?"

"I had an assignment in France. My cover was an American socialite," she said. "And I hated wine. I had to take a crash course, learning to order it by name. I was there for three weeks. Unfortunately, my taste while undercover was far too expensive for me when I came out," she said with a smile. "But I adapted."

"Can you speak French?"

Cameron shook her head. "I can get you to a restaurant and a bathroom, that's about it."

Andrea set her empty plate aside, turning to Cameron. "I never really drank it either. My mother never touched alcohol. My father would have a beer occasionally, but he wasn't a drinker. We didn't have it around the house at all," she said. "When I joined the force, well, alcohol flows freely, as you know."

"Yeah."

"I never developed a taste for hard liquor, so I always ordered wine." She shrugged. "Erin...Erin loved wine." She smiled. "She thought she was a connoisseur, but she refused to pay anything more than ten bucks a bottle."

Cameron watched her, noting that her expression didn't change when she'd mentioned Erin's name. Amazing how a few weeks could change someone. She'd like to think she had a part in that.

"What?"

Cameron blinked, unaware that she had been staring. "What?"

Andrea held her eyes for the longest moment then leaned closer. "Can I have that kiss now?"

Cameron was surprised by the sudden jolt of arousal she felt at such a simple question. "You can have anything you want," she said, leaning back as Andrea's mouth met hers. Her kiss was soft, her lips nibbling, teasing her, so different than the last time they'd been together. Cameron had been in an emotional state and had needed Andrea in the worst way. Tonight, however, those raw emotions were missing and instead, it was just a mutual attraction they shared...and a desire to please.

Cameron let Andrea take the lead, leaning back farther to give her room. Andrea continued to tease her, slowly moving her hand up, cupping her breast as her mouth played with Cameron's lips. Her breathing changed, her senses alive and pulsing.

"Does this feel good?" Andrea whispered, her hand slipping between Cameron's legs.

"Oh, yeah," she murmured, her eyes closed.

Andrea cupped her, putting pressure between her thighs. "I can feel how wet you are, even through your jeans."

Cameron could no longer speak as Andrea's mouth moved to her breast, her teeth lightly grazing the nipple through her shirt and bra. She was moaning, and she didn't care, her breath coming fast now as her lips parted. Then Andrea's fingers pushed hard against her, making Cameron jerk her hips, the seam of her jeans pressing against her clit. Two strokes, three, and Cameron's hips lifted off the sofa, her orgasm sneaking up on her as she tried to stifle her cry.

Andrea lifted her head from Cameron's breast, apparently as surprised as Cameron was. "I didn't know you were that ready," she said as her lips moved to Cameron's mouth again.

Embarrassed, Cameron stood quickly, her legs wobbly, and she nearly dumped Andrea on the floor. "I'm sorry," she said. Damn, she felt as clumsy as a fifteen-year-old boy on his first date. Andrea had an incredulous look on her face, a slight smile teasing her lips.

"I rather enjoyed it."

Cameron met her eyes, and it suddenly became so clear to her. She took several steps back as realization dawned on her. She hadn't had these feelings since Laurie, nearly ten years before.

"Jesus," she murmured, pulling her eyes from Andrea and hurrying away. She ripped open her office doors, standing there taking deep breaths.

You're not supposed to fall in love with her. That wasn't part of the plan.

"Cameron? What's wrong?"

Cameron turned, finding Andrea standing there watching her. She couldn't believe how nervous she was, and she didn't have a clue as to what to say. She ran her hands through her hair impatiently, trying to think.

"I...I need to...uh...I need to get this loaded here," she said, pointing to the computers. "It's finished...so...I need to...uh... *Christ*...I need to start the conversion process."

Andrea stared at her. "You're as white as a sheet. What is wrong with you?"

"Nothing. Nothing. I'm sorry. I just—"

"Cameron, are you embarrassed?"

Cameron looked away. "Maybe."

"Why on earth?"

Yeah, Cameron, why?

"I just feel like a damn teenaged boy who can't hold his—"

Andrea touched her stomach, stopping her with a light rubbing motion. "Oh, Cameron. Don't be embarrassed. I mean, wasn't that kinda the point of it all? For you to climax?"

Cameron didn't say anything, unsure of how to explain herself without, well, without making a fool of herself.

Andrea finally shrugged. "Okay, so you want me to just leave?"

Those words nudged Cameron out of her stupor and she shook her head. "No, no." She pulled Andrea into a tight hug, letting her eyes slip closed. "I don't want you to leave. I'm sorry." She took a deep breath, inhaling Andrea's scent, admitting, at least to herself, how right it felt to hold her, how perfect their bodies fit together. "I want you to stay with me tonight." She pulled back. "I'm sorry. I'm just not used to being so out of control like that."

Andrea smiled, leaning closer and giving Cameron the softest, gentlest kiss she could ever remember receiving. "I kinda like it when you lose control," she whispered as her lips left Cameron's mouth.

Cameron closed her eyes, feeling it start again, feeling her body respond to Andrea in a way it hadn't responded to another woman in ten years. And it felt so good. She cleared her throat, taking a conscious step away from Andrea.

"Tell you what. If you'll put the pizza up for me, I'll get this program going so it can run while we sleep."

Andrea nodded, but didn't move. Cameron tried to read her eyes but all she saw was desire. Desire for her. She stood still as Andrea took a step toward her. Her kiss this time wasn't gentle. It was hard and demanding, her tongue sliding past Cameron's lips with ease. Cameron lost the little resolve she still had, giving in to Andrea, cupping her hips and pulling her close. Before she knew what was happening, she had Andrea pressed against the wall, their hips rocking together, trying to find purchase. She covered both of Andrea's breasts with her hands, catching Andrea's moan in her mouth.

Andrea's hands tugged at her shirt, shoving it up, her warm fingers gliding across her skin. Her own hands went to Andrea's jeans, quickly unzipping them, giving her room.

"You make me crazy," she whispered against Andrea's mouth. "It's like fire when I touch you."

"Then touch me already," Andrea begged, taking Cameron's hand and shoving it inside her jeans.

Cameron's hand slipped past the thin barrier of her panties, drenched by her wetness. She groaned as the silky smoothness coated her fingers. She found Andrea's mouth blindly, kissing her hard, her tongue mimicking her fingers as she entered her. Andrea's thighs parted, taking her inside. But it wasn't enough.

Cameron dropped to her knees, jerking Andrea's jeans and panties down in one motion. She grabbed Andrea's hips, bringing her forward to her waiting mouth, her tongue slipping between her slick folds, finding what she wanted.

Andrea thrust against her, her hands supporting herself on Cameron's shoulders, crying out when Cameron's mouth closed over her clit, sucking it hard and fast. They were both groaning, Cameron nearly delirious from the taste of her. She heard Andrea panting, felt her fingers digging into her shoulders, her hips grinding against Cameron's face, increasing the pressure between them.

Andrea grabbed Cameron's head as she climaxed, her sharp cries loud in the tiny hallway of the motor home. Cameron's mouth slowed, moving now with gentle pressure, prolonging

Andrea's pleasure as much as she could. She felt Andrea relax, tense muscles releasing, her breath slowing.

"God, I love when you do that to me," she murmured, her hand still threading through Cameron's hair.

Cameron slowly got to her feet, pulling Andrea into her arms. Yes, she loved *doing* that to her. They stood together for long, quiet minutes, just holding each other, their bodies relaxed against the other.

It was nice. It was almost too nice.

CHAPTER TWENTY-SIX

Andrea leaned on her elbow, her fingers lazily trailing across Cameron's breast, smiling as her nipple hardened yet again.

"Are you enjoying yourself?"

"Mmm." Andrea watched as Cameron's eyes fluttered open. "Did you sleep well?"

Cameron stretched her legs out beside her. "Did we sleep?"

"Not much, no." Andrea's fingertips moved to the scar that slashed across Cameron's body, the edge of which marred her beautiful breast. "Does it hurt?"

"No. In fact, it's pretty numb. Probably always will be."

Andrea leaned closer, her lips touching the surface of it. She pulled back, finding Cameron's eyes in the muted light. "What happened?"

Cameron was still, her eyes never leaving Andrea's. "Are you sure you want to know?"

"Yes."

Cameron's gaze left hers and Andrea noted her expression changed, her eyes now had a faraway look as if she were rewinding a movie, trying to find the right scene. Finally, she turned back to Andrea.

"I was captured. In Pakistan. I was to be executed." She paused. "Beheaded."

Andrea gasped, feeling her heart jump into her throat. She suddenly didn't want to know. She didn't want to know the horrors that Cameron had endured.

"The rescue team got there right when the sword was in the air. It was in motion when they shot him, but the force of it... well, I managed to roll away a bit. Saved my neck, at least."

"Oh, Cameron," she whispered.

"Please don't say you're sorry, Andi. That was just my life back then."

Andrea's fingers lightly ran across the length of the scar, trying to imagine what Cameron's thoughts had been that day. "You weren't really just Special Ops, were you?"

Cameron rolled to her side, facing Andrea, her own hand sliding over Andrea's skin. "Officially I was, yes. Technically, no."

"Classified?" she asked, her voice only slightly teasing.

"I was part of an elite unit, of which there are several," she said. "And that's classified," she added, "so you'll have to keep it to yourself or else."

Andrea smiled, waiting for Cameron to continue.

"We were trained in various means of warfare. Highly trained. We were trained physically, mentally...emotionally." She took a deep breath. "I became nothing more than an assassin," she said, her voice low. "And I couldn't do it anymore."

Andrea stopped Cameron's hand as it moved over her hip. She brought it to her lips, kissing her fingers gently.

"I wanted out, but I was only thirty-three and they'd invested a lot of time and money. They offered me a position with the FBI." Cameron rolled onto her back again. "Murdock has four teams assembled under him. All are ex-military, like me. Like Collie. We're not exactly your traditional FBI teams. We're more of an experimental group, a little unconventional."

"Like this motor home?"

"Yeah. This is the only one. We'll reevaluate after a year," Cameron said. "When you think of the FBI, you think of Washington, New York, LA—the big cities. But the logistics for rural assignments pose a problem. Like here. If we didn't have the rig, we'd operate out of Phoenix. Or send a team back and forth. We wouldn't be able to hang out here for weeks, like I've been able to."

"I'm glad you're able to *hang out*," she said.

"Yeah. We got off to a bit of a bad start," Cameron admitted. "I was, you know, that arrogant, conceited person that you hated."

"It just threw me when you started asking about LA. I wasn't prepared for it."

"And now?"

"You were right. You're good for me. It helped to talk it out. I don't know whether it was just time for me to let go or if it's the distraction of the case." She paused. "Or you."

And it was true. She didn't know. When Cameron left, would it all return? The guilt she'd harbored for so long had become second nature to her. Was she foolish to think it was really gone? That it had just disappeared without a fight? Or had she actually accepted that the guilt was unfounded. She lost her team, her best friend, her lover. That was the reality of it all. Nothing she did would change that. She could do as Cameron had said, wallow in her guilt...or she could choose to live. Because it was indeed a miracle that she survived the attack. A miracle that she'd carelessly tossed aside because she felt it was her punishment to carry the weight of their deaths on her shoulders. A weight that Cameron had taken away from her.

Cameron pulled her down for a lingering kiss. "I'll be happy to be a distraction," she said.

Andrea was tempted to let go and give in to her desires again, but the morning was upon them. They didn't have the luxury of a lazy day in bed. She eased back from Cameron, leaving her with a quick kiss on her nipple. "Don't start," she said when Cameron tried to pull her back. "The sun's already up."

Cameron sighed. "I know. Time to work."

"What's on the agenda?"

Cameron got out of bed, and Andrea stared, seeing her naked for the first time in the light of day. Her body was exquisite and she wasn't ashamed to watch as Cameron rummaged in her drawers for clothes.

"I'll have to process the results of the algorithm. Hopefully we'll get a hit on something." She turned, raising her eyebrows as Andrea still laid there watching.

"You have a beautiful body."

"With all these scars?"

"I'm looking past the scars. Besides, the scars are you. I just meant, your body is so...well, the guys say you're hot. Joey is infatuated."

Cameron laughed. "What's he, like, barely twenty-five?"

"Yes. Barely."

Cameron stood in front of her, still naked head to toe. "We had a lot of physical training," she said. "Lots of running, weights, martial arts. I don't do nearly what I used to. Jump rope, mostly, or I'll take a run a couple times a week." She paused at the door. "I'm going to take a quick shower."

Andrea nodded. "I'll start coffee."

"So you haven't heard back from Dallas?"

Andrea shook her head, taking a bite of muffin. "I'm going to e-mail Casey O'Connor today."

"And I'll try Hunter again." She got up, taking her coffee cup with her to her tiny office. "Let me check on the process."

She'd taken the conversion file and loaded it into the "dummy box," as she called it. Jason had some fancy name for it as it took his results and put them into simple English for her. This part of the process took only a few minutes.

"Finished?"

"Yeah." She moved to the side, letting Andrea see the monitor. "Tower Ridge Trail. What do you think?"

Andrea shook her head. "Not likely. It's at the edge of Sycamore Canyon. Only the first few hundred feet or so has brush cover, then it crosses a ridge and goes along Coyote Canyon. It's a mostly exposed trail, lots of rock. Great views, though. Remember when we hiked Devil's Rock? Tower Ridge would be those cliffs above it."

"Yeah. But eighty-four percent," Cameron said. "Quite high."

"Maybe it's missing again, like it did with Devil's Rock."

"No. Jason fixed that. Or so he thought."

Andrea stood back. "Show me the trail map. Let's double-check."

Cameron pulled it up, letting Andrea have the mouse so she could maneuver as she wanted. She quickly scrolled across the map, slowly shaking her head.

"Rim Trail wasn't exactly concealed," Cameron reminded her.

"Yeah. And the body wasn't discovered either."

"Is this a well-traveled route?"

"Not so much this time of year. It's blistering hot on the south-facing side. You would mostly get people wanting to catch either the sunrise or sunset. It has great views of both. It's advertised that way so tourists would know that." Andrea picked up her coffee cup again and took a sip. "The locals would take the hike on the weekends, if at all. There's a great sunrise spot up Oak Creek Canyon that would be closer than this one."

"Well, the next best hit is only thirty-three percent."

"Okay, then let's take Tower Ridge and have a look," Andrea said. "It's been awhile since I've been out there. Maybe I'm missing something."

"Thanks. I know you and Jim don't think much of this program, but Jason swears by it. And I've used it before," she said. "Not on this large of a scale, but it's usually right on."

"I'm sorry. I didn't mean to come across as being smarter than your computer," Andrea said with a smile. "I just know the trail."

"Fair enough."

"I've got to run by my place," Andrea said as they returned to the kitchen. "You want to meet where?"

"I'll swing by and pick you up," Cameron said. "Do you need to let Jim know?"

"Yes. I'll call him on my way." She paused to scratch Lola's ear. "Don't be too long," she said. "Let's try to do the climb up while it's still relatively cool."

"Okay. I need to make a call to Murdock. And I want to try Hunter again," she said.

Andrea opened the door then closed it again, smiling as she turned back around, coming closer. "Thank you for last night. For dinner and everything," she said as she kissed her.

Cameron had been doing a nice job—she thought—of reining in her feelings, of telling herself that her burst of emotion last night was a fluke. But as soon as Andrea kissed her, a kiss that was sweet and soft, not one derived from passion but one that only hinted at the intimacy between them, she lost what was left of her resistance. She pulled Andrea into her arms and held her, a hug not meant to ignite a fire between them—it was meant to convey her growing affection for Andrea.

Their eyes held as they stepped apart, and she wondered if Andrea guessed the direction of her thoughts. Or worse—that Cameron's feelings were teetering between a casual affair and full-fledged falling in love.

Andrea left without another word and Cameron scooped up Lola, holding her close. She took a deep breath, letting her eyes slip closed as she simply embraced the feelings Andrea brought to the surface. It had been so long, she was surprised she'd even recognized them. In the years since Laurie, she'd had her share of bedmates, but she was never once tempted by love. They were just casual, sexual encounters that satisfied needs—both their needs. She assumed her affair with Andrea would be lumped in with the others. But she hadn't counted on becoming so involved with her. They'd both shared emotional secrets that by their own nature brought them closer together, an invisible bond linking them. No, she hadn't counted on that. And she certainly hadn't counted on falling in love with her.

"Now what are we going to do?" she asked Lola, the constant purring her only reply.

CHAPTER TWENTY-SEVEN

Andrea led the way up the rocky portion of Tower Ridge trail, the sun scorching the already parched earth. A slight breeze helped cool her skin and she looked up, a lone raven following their progress as he landed atop a juniper, his sharp eyes never leaving them.

"Once upon a midnight dreary," Cameron quoted, her gaze lingering on the raven as well. "Since the raven is a symbol of death, do you think this is a sign?"

Andrea smiled and shook her head. "You'll find a raven on every trail. I hope it's not a sign."

"You think this is a waste of time?"

"I don't know. Who knows how the mind of a killer works? If your program says this trail is his next stop, then who am I to argue?"

They emerged from the brush-covered lower section of the trail, now walking on bare ground. There were outcroppings of rocks and a few standing spiral formations, but no junipers, mesquites or scrubs in sight, just handfuls of thorny cactus and the smooth yet jagged edges of the red rock that symbolized Sedona—the red rock that was now baking in the midday sun.

"It's hot as hell up here," Cameron noted as she paused to take a drink of water.

"You need a cap," she said, removing her own to run her fingers through her damp hair.

Cameron smiled at her. "Then my hair would look like yours."

"Yeah? So who are you trying to impress with your perfect hair?"

"Just you."

Amused—and flattered—Andrea put her cap back on, covering her hair again. She knew exactly how messy her hair looked after wearing a ball cap all day. "So you'll take your chances with heat stroke to impress me, huh?"

Cameron fell into step beside her as they hiked on. "Never been one for caps, really. You know, beach bum and all, wind blowing through my hair all natural and everything."

Andrea's mind conjured up an image of a natural and *naked* Cameron Ross as she played on the beach, her skin still wet, tiny granules of sand clinging to her. And of course that thought conjured up many, many others, and she stopped, unable to deny herself what she wanted. She turned Cameron with a quick touch to her arm, leaning closer and kissing her hard, surprising Cameron.

"What was that for?"

Andrea walked on. "I had an urge," she tossed over her shoulder.

"An urge?" Cameron caught up with her, her voice amused. "An urge to kiss me?"

"That was part of it, yes."

Cameron laughed. "Out here, the sun beating down on us, we're hot and sweaty, and you get the urge to kiss me?"

"It was the beach bum thing."

"Huh?"

"Never mind. Let's just say you were wet and naked." She grinned. "Or naked and wet."

"Why Deputy Sullivan, whatever is on your mind?"

"Must be the heat, Agent Ross."

"Must be."

Andrea wasn't sure who saw him first, but they both stopped. As if sensing their presence, he turned, and they watched each other cautiously across the expanse of rock. His hair was light brown, not the jet black as described by the Dallas detectives. Andrea's mind flashed to the photo Detective O'Connor had faxed them, the photo of John Doe. That man—or his twin—stood before them.

Then as quick as lightning, he ran. They followed, Cameron showing off her running skills by leaving Andrea several paces behind her, struggling to catch up. Patrick was swift and agile, making Andrea think he knew the trail better than she did as he maneuvered around the rocks and cactus with ease, seemingly unphased by their chase.

The path he took ended, the rocks giving way to a drop into the canyon. He paused, flashing them a cocky grin, then turned and jumped. Andrea stopped, panting, then her eyes widened in disbelief as Cameron followed him over the cliff without breaking stride.

"Oh...my *God*."

She ran to the edge, skidding to a halt as she peered over the side, her fear mixed with relief as she saw the drop wasn't into the canyon at all, but to another ledge. Her relief was short-lived, however, as she spied Cameron lying in a heap on the rocks, barely two feet from a thorny cactus.

"Oh, God, *no*," she groaned. She retraced her steps, trying to find a route to the ledge without having to jump herself. She found a crevice, sliding down on her ass as she carefully avoided the sharp edges of the rocks.

"She's an idiot," she murmured. "She's insane." She jumped the last five feet, landing squarely, then ran to Cameron, relieved when she saw movement. She fell to her knees beside her, touching her shoulder.

"Don't move," she said.

"Am I dead?" Cameron mumbled, her face still buried in the rocks.

"Not unless I shoot you," Andrea said. "Which is still an option. Just what the *hell* were you thinking?" Cameron tried to roll over and Andrea stopped her. "I said don't move. Something could be broken."

"I've got to move, Andi. Or do you want to call an ambulance and have them pick me up on the street corner over there?"

She did have a point. They were more than an hour away from the trailhead, closer to two. Andrea helped her roll to her back, seeing blood on Cameron's face. "You are insane," she whispered. "You could have killed yourself."

"Oh, it was barely twenty feet."

"It's twenty-five, nearly thirty," she countered as she poured water into her hand to wipe the blood from Cameron's mouth. "Besides, you didn't know how far it was. Jesus, Cameron, that could have been one of the cliffs that drop into the canyon." That thought shook her and she sat down, trying not to picture Cameron's broken body after a fall into Sycamore Canyon. Or worse—the rocky bottom of Coyote Canyon. She met her eyes. "Please don't do that again."

"I knew it wasn't into the canyon," Cameron said. "He wouldn't have ever ended things that way. Anticlimactic."

"Oh, so you're trusting that a crazed serial killer knew it wasn't a fall into the canyon?"

"Well, when you put it that way," Cameron said as she sat up, flexing her shoulders. "Maybe it wasn't one of my better decisions."

"Can you stand?"

"What's my alternative? A helicopter rescue?"

Andrea got up, helping Cameron to her feet. She noticed the grimace that Cameron tried to hide.

"What hurts?"

"Everything." She looked past Andrea and sighed. "We had the bastard. Why didn't we just shoot him and be done with it?"

"Oh, yeah. That was going to be our plan, wasn't it."

"So, the algorithm was right on." Cameron grinned. "Can you believe it?"

"Not really, no. I would never have guessed this trail."

"But you were right. He does do reconnaissance. I'll assume, since we surprised him, that he won't use this as a drop now."

"If he's scouting locations—"

"Then he's going to kill again," Cameron finished for her. "Let's get out of here. I need to call Reynolds, and we need to talk with Jim and have some sort of a plan. I don't want to just sit around and wait for the next body to be found."

"You hit your head. You may have a concussion or something," Andrea said. "Are you sure you want—"

"I'm sure. And I don't have a damn concussion."

"Of course you don't," Andrea said. "With that hard head? What was I thinking?"

"Funny, *Deputy* Sullivan."

Andrea gripped Cameron's arm, helping her, noticing her limp as she walked. "It's going to take us a good two hours to get out of here, *Agent* Ross," she said, wondering if perhaps Cameron hadn't sprained her ankle in the fall.

"I can make it."

"I just meant it's after noon already. Why don't you head to the rig, and I'll get with Jim," she offered.

"Yeah. Okay. See how he feels about staking out some trails tonight."

"He'll defer to you," Andrea said, guiding Cameron to the crevice in the rocks.

"That's fine, but I want his input. I don't want him to feel like I've just come in here and taken over."

"We invited the FBI in, remember," she said. "Can you make it up?"

"No choice."

"Maybe there's another route."

"No time, Andi. But I'll go first. In case I fall, you can catch me," she said, her smile trying to hide her pain.

"Let's just don't fall, okay? Because we both know I can't catch you."

Cameron reached out, wincing as she gripped the rock's edge.

"How bad is it?" Andrea asked.

"What?"

"Your shoulder."

"Just jammed it a bit. It'll be fine." She paused. "Maybe you could give me a shove?"

Andrea knew not to argue. The quickest way out was back along the trail they'd come in on. Finding an alternate route that didn't involve Cameron having to climb up through a crevice might take longer than the entire hike back. So she cupped Cameron's hips, giving her a boost up. She pretended she didn't hear the painful groan as Cameron pulled herself along the rocks.

True to her word, Cameron made it up, although it was excruciating for Andrea to watch—and listen—as she fought through her pain. Cameron lay down flat on the rocks, her right hand massaging her injured left shoulder.

"Is it separated?" Andrea asked.

"No." She turned her head, an almost lazy smile on her face. "Know why I fell?"

Andrea shook her head.

"I was heading right for that damn cactus," she said. "I did a quite graceful midair twist to avoid it."

Andrea nearly laughed, picturing Cameron wrapped around the large prickly pear cactus. A separated shoulder would have been the least of her worries. They would have spent hours trying to pick the thorny spines out of her.

"I know. Funny, right?"

"Could have been a yucca," Andrea said. "Those things will cut like a knife. But I think you may have made the right decision." She stood, offering her hand to Cameron. "Of course, jumping off in the first place leads me to question your sanity."

"I sometimes forget how old I am."

Andrea paused, eyebrows raised. Cameron's age was something she never speculated on. She assumed she was near her own.

"Thirty-five," she said. "For a few more months," she added.

Andrea nodded. "You have me beat by a year."

Cameron flexed her shoulder several times then motioned for Andrea to lead the way. "I can keep up. Don't go slow on my account."

"What about the ankle?"

"Damn, you saw that too?"

"Is it sprained?"

"Let's call it strained," Cameron said.

Andrea laughed. "Let's call it stubborn."

CHAPTER TWENTY-EIGHT

"Give me a break, Reynolds. You're dreaming if you think your team could have done better." Cameron opened the cabinet in the bathroom, surveying her options. "They'd have landed on the damn cactus," she murmured, wishing she could take something stronger than the ibuprofen she found.

"What cactus?"

"Never mind. I'm just saying, there was nothing else we could have done."

"I'm coming up there."

"No. The hell you are."

"No?"

"No. We don't need your suits and ties up here," she said. "We're close. As I told Murdock, I don't want to send him under by having FBI crawling all over the place."

"Well, you obviously can't catch him, Ross."

She laughed. "And you're doing a hell of job at it too,

Reynolds. Have you found out where Collie was taken from yet? Surveillance cameras? Anything?"

"We have the tapes from the parking garage. Collie wasn't with the car when it was dumped. And we can't get a facial. He knew where every camera was and avoided them."

"So you have nothing?"

"I got about what you have."

"I, at least, had a visual on the bastard," she countered.

"Yeah. Did you a lot of good, didn't it?"

"Jesus Christ, Reynolds, you learn your bedside manner from Collie or what? Last I checked, we were on the same goddamn team," she said, having the satisfaction of ending the call first. For some reason, it lacked the gratification that she used to get when she hung up on Collie.

She poured a handful of pills from the bottle, counting out four before putting the rest back. She popped them in her mouth, chasing them down with a swig of water. Her ankle was killing her, but the pain in her shoulder had subsided. The icepack she'd put on it earlier had helped. She was surprised it wasn't separated. After she'd landed awkwardly, twisting her ankle, her shoulder had taken the brunt of her weight. She wouldn't tell Andrea, but she'd actually blacked out for a moment when her head hit the rocks.

All in all, if she had to do it over again, she'd have just shot the bastard. Not exactly following the rules, but then in her line of work, rules were ambiguous, to say the least.

She migrated back to the main room, sitting down gingerly in her recliner, easing the pressure on her ankle by propping it up. Lola found her lap and she leaned back, eyes closed as she stroked the kitten. The loud, constant purring lulled her into a relaxed state. If she allowed it, she knew she would fall asleep, but she couldn't. There was work to do, new data to store and feed into the program. And they needed a game plan. She could only hold Murdock off for so long. He was already pushing her to move in Reynolds and the team.

But her gut told her if they dropped a load of agents in Sedona, Patrick would disappear. And they were close, she could feel it. If they missed this opportunity and he dropped off the radar again for a year or more, then he'd have won another round and they'd just have to wait for the next killing spree to start. Unless, of course, Reynolds could dig up something in Phoenix, and that was looking to be unlikely.

"She jumped off the ledge? What is she, crazy?"

Andrea cocked an eyebrow at Randy. "You think?"

"So you had him? I mean, you had him, and he just jumped and she followed him?" He grinned. "Now that's hot."

"That's *so* hot," Joey added. "God, I'd have loved to see that. She's amazing."

Andrea glared at them. "You're missing the point. She blindly jumped off a cliff, not knowing whether it was a hundred-foot drop or a ten foot. She could have killed herself."

Jim, who had been listening silently, took the toothpick out of his mouth, his brows drawn together thoughtfully. "You sure it was him?"

"Yes," she said.

"So how'd he know it wasn't a hundred-foot drop?"

"We assumed he did recon on the trails. Apparently he's very thorough in his research."

"Either that or damn lucky." He plopped the toothpick back in. "Now what?"

"How do you feel about staking out the trails?"

"At night?" Randy asked, his eyes wide.

"Yes, at night," she said, glancing at Jim for approval.

"Is that what Cameron thinks we should do?"

Andrea nodded. "Yes. But she wanted to run it by you first."

Jim smiled. "Andi, we can stop pretending I have a say in any of this. We lost that opportunity when we invited the FBI in."

Again, Andrea felt the need to defend Cameron. "She's always asked our opinion on things. I wouldn't say we've lost our voice. At least, she's not made it appear that way."

"No. She's been quite good at keeping us informed and including you in this search. That's not what I meant." He moved toward his office. "Tell her we'll do whatever she thinks is best."

Andrea glanced at Randy. "You and Joey be ready."

"Tonight?"

"Yes." Of course, she was only speculating, but she assumed Cameron would want to stake out the trails tonight. That is, if she could walk.

"But...mountain lions," he said, his voice shaky. "And...and rattlesnakes."

"Yeah. And?"

"I just think maybe that's not such a good idea."

"You've been here ten years. When's the last time you've heard of someone getting attacked by a mountain lion?"

"You hear about it all the time," he said.

"But here. I'm talking here in Sedona. You hear about it where cities encroach on wilderness, yes. But here?"

"Look, I'm a city boy, born and raised. And being out on the trails at night is not my idea of fun."

"Not mine either," she said. "But it's our job, so suck it up. I'll call you later with a time and place."

She turned to go, but Joey stopped her.

"Wait. Casey O'Connor called," he said, looking at a piece of paper in his hand. "From Dallas. She got your e-mail and wanted to discuss it with you, but she said she'd just write you back instead."

"Okay." Andrea eyed her computer on her desk, but decided to wait on the e-mail. She was anxious to get back to Cameron. She was limping noticeably by the time they'd made it back, even though she'd tried to hide her discomfort. "I'll get in touch with her later. I need to go check on Cameron."

Randy winked at her. "Check on her, huh?"

"Yes, check on her. She really should have seen a doctor," she said, ignoring his blatant insinuation. "And we need to decide about tonight." She pointed her finger at him. "Be ready."

195

CHAPTER TWENTY-NINE

Andrea paused at the door, waiting for Cameron's familiar voice telling her the security was off, but the speakers remained silent. She debated whether to trust that it was off or to be safe and call. She decided on the latter. A sleepy voice answered her call.

"Sorry. I'm outside," she said. "I didn't know if it was safe to come in."

"I fell asleep," Cameron said unnecessarily. "But yeah, come on in."

Andrea opened the door, finding Cameron sprawled out in her recliner, Lola sitting on her chest as if protecting her. Without thinking, Andrea held her phone out, capturing the sight. Not that she would need memories of them when they left, but Lola's pose and Cameron's sleepy eyes were too much to resist.

"A picture?"

"Yes." Andrea put her phone away. "How do you feel?"

"If it were anyone other than you asking me that, I'd lie and say I felt fine."

"Okay. And the truth?"

"I feel like hell."

Andrea noticed the ice pack strapped to her ankle. "Swollen?"

"A little."

Andrea put her hands on her hips. "You need to see a doctor."

"No."

"We could go—"

"No," Cameron said. "I've had my share of doctors. It's just twisted a little. It'll be fine. I can tape it up."

"Did you take anything? Do you have pain meds?"

"I took ibuprofen. I have pain meds, but they knock me out. I need to be focused."

"Okay. You know best," she said, not wanting to push it. "Are you hungry?"

"Starving."

Andrea glanced at the kitchen. "Do you have anything I could cook?"

"Not really, no." Cameron raised her eyebrows. "Pizza?"

"Again?"

"Well, they deliver. And I've got them on speed dial."

Andrea nodded. "Pizza is fine." She went to help as Cameron tried to stand.

"Thanks. I need to update the data in the algorithm. It'll take a little while to run."

"Okay. And Detective O'Connor called me back while we were out. She sent me an e-mail, but I haven't checked it yet."

Cameron's limp was noticeable as she shuffled in bare feet toward her office. She pointed to her laptop on the loveseat. "You can use that, if you want. I'll call in the pizza and update the program. It'll take me a few minutes."

Andrea plopped down on the loveseat, bringing the laptop to life. Lola jumped from the recliner to her lap in one giant leap, purring loudly as she looked at Andrea.

"Yes, you know you're cute, don't you," she cooed, scratching under her chin affectionately.

She was about to open up a browser when she spotted two folders in the upper right corner of the monitor. Her name was attached to both. One was titled LAPD. The other, Personal. She stared at them, knowing they were from the background check Cameron had done on her. She knew what the LAPD one would contain, that was no secret. But her personal file? What could the FBI possibly dig up on her that it warranted them sending it to Cameron?

She wanted to ignore the files. She really did. In fact, she opened up a browser to check her e-mail. But curiosity simply got the best of her. She quickly closed the browser and again stared at the two files. She bit her lower lip, chancing a glance down the hall, but Cameron was nowhere in sight. A quick double click opened the file and she scanned it, her eyes moving swiftly across the words.

Erin Rogers...lover killed...dating five women...Sullivan in the dark.

"What the hell?" she murmured. Her eyes widened as she read on. *Jena Sommers? She was sleeping with Jena?*

Her chest felt tight as her heart raced, her breath difficult to catch as the words sunk in. Erin had been seeing four other women. Not just seeing them. Sleeping with them. Having sex. She closed her eyes tightly. Having sex with four other women— including Jena Sommers, Andrea's closest friend on the force besides Mark—yet Erin vowed she loved Andrea. Erin's last words came rushing back to her—Erin crying, begging her not to end their relationship, saying Andrea was killing her, breaking her heart. Erin vowed love and devotion, saying they could work things out. And Andrea gave in, saying they'd talk about it. And then the guilt, because they never got that chance to talk about it. The guilt, because Andrea knew she wasn't in love with Erin. And more guilt, thinking she *should* have been in love with her. After all, Erin had said that Andrea was her life. A life cut so short.

Andrea looked up as Cameron came out of her office. Cameron raised an eyebrow questioningly.

"What's wrong?"

"You knew? All along you knew?"

"Knew what?"

Andrea tossed the laptop and Lola aside, standing quickly, pacing in the small space of the motor home. "Erin. You knew about Erin," she said.

Cameron's gaze left her face, locking in on the laptop. "The files," she said quietly. "You read them?"

"I read one of them, yes. Why the hell didn't you tell me?"

"Andrea—"

"You knew what I was going through, yet you didn't tell me." Andrea turned quickly, rushing out the door. She had to get away. She needed some time, some space, to absorb this. She didn't know what hurt more—Erin cheating on her or Cameron keeping it from her.

"Andrea, wait," Cameron called from the steps of the motor home.

"No. Leave me alone," she said as she hurried to her Jeep.

"I didn't read the files, Andi. I told you I wouldn't."

Andrea jerked the door open then turned, seeing Cameron—her feet still bare—limping after her. The sight of Cameron struggling to reach her caused her heart to tighten, making her feel light-headed.

"Please don't go, Andi."

Andrea stood there, one hand still clutching the Jeep door, Cameron's words causing all sorts of emotions inside of her. Their eyes met and Andrea lost her anger almost immediately. "But you knew? You knew about Erin?"

Cameron nodded. "Murdock gave me the short version, yes. But I didn't read the file."

"I had been struggling with my guilt for so long," Andrea said. "Why didn't you tell me?"

"Because you needed to let go of your guilt on your own. You needed to get past it without having a crutch to rely on. If I had told you the truth, your guilt would have been replaced by anger. But it would have been an anger you could never get past because she wasn't here to confront."

Andrea knew it was the truth, but it still hurt that Cameron had kept it from her.

"You've already let go of your guilt, haven't you?"

Andrea nodded.

"So now you can be angry with her, but it won't be an anger that consumes you, like the guilt did."

"Yes. Yes, I am angry. I can't believe she did that. I mean, I knew it wasn't working for us. I knew I wasn't in love with her. So I tried to do the right thing. I tried to end it. And she begged me not to leave her. Begged me, Cameron." Andrea closed the door on the Jeep, walking away, again pacing. "Why? Why would she do that if she's already seeing others? Why would she do that to me?"

"I don't know. Maybe ego. Maybe she couldn't stand the thought of getting dumped."

"I've beaten myself up for this for three long years. I mean, she said she loved me. She said I was killing her. That morning, she said I was killing her by leaving. So I didn't. And that night, I believed it to be true. I had killed her."

"No, Andi. You didn't kill her."

Andrea stared at her, their eyes holding as her anger dissipated. She had finally let go of her guilt. She'd wasted enough time and energy holding on to it. She wouldn't let anger take its place, so she let it go. She sighed, her eyes traveling over Cameron's body, landing on her feet.

"God, Cameron, you can't go out in the desert without shoes. What were you thinking?"

"I didn't want you to leave."

Again, those words touched a spot deep inside her, causing a swell of affection to rise. She went to Cameron, wrapping her arms around her and pulling her into a tight hug, feeling completely secure as Cameron's arms slipped around her waist. They stood there for long moments holding each other in silence. Words weren't necessary, she knew. She pulled away slightly, brushing her lips across Cameron's.

"Come on, let's get you inside. You don't want to step on a scorpion."

"Scorpions? There are scorpions?"

"Of course. They say the sting will drop you to your knees."

"Great," Cameron murmured, leaning on Andrea as they made their way back to the motor home.

At the steps, Andrea paused. She touched Cameron's face, gently brushing the hair out of her eyes. "I'm sorry I read the file," she said. "It was your laptop. I should have respected your privacy and not opened it."

"I would have done the same thing. You had a right to know."

After Andrea helped her up the steps and to the recliner, Lola joined her, her purr as loud as always. Cameron stroked her, feeling comforted by the tiny cat.

"Can I get you something?"

"I'd love something to drink. Something with a little substance," she said.

Andrea raised an eyebrow.

"The cabinet above the pantry," she said. "Scotch."

Andrea found it and paused before pouring. "Ice or straight up?"

"On the rocks."

Cameron watched as she poured a generous amount in a glass, then, as if debating with herself, Andrea got a second glass for herself. She went back to the loveseat, eyeing the laptop she'd tossed aside earlier.

"Maybe I'll try this again," Andrea said, pulling it onto her lap.

Cameron nodded, watching her. "What did Jim say about the stakeout?"

"He deferred to you. I've got Randy and Joey lined up. I didn't think we'd need more than that since your programs only target one, maybe two with high probabilities." Andrea studied her. "Will you even be up for it? I mean, your ankle—"

"It'll be fine," Cameron said. At least she hoped it would be. To prove her point, she got up without assistance, although she was sure Andrea saw the pained look on her face. It still hurt to put much weight on it. "I need to check the algorithm, see if it's ready to convert. Although I can't imagine him going out tonight, not after our little chase today."

"He's arrogant that way," Andrea said. "Did you see that smile on his face right before he jumped?"

"Yeah. I think—" But the ringing of her phone interrupted her. "Ross," she answered, her eyes still watching Andrea.

"It's Reynolds. I got a missing persons report. Not official, it's only been since this morning, but it's a college student. It threw up a red flag."

"From where?"

"Flagstaff. Last seen at a little coffee joint at the edge of campus."

Cameron met Andrea's eyes. "The coffee shop."

"What are you talking about?" Reynolds asked.

"Nothing. Doesn't matter. What else?"

"She didn't show up for any classes today. Her roommate called campus police when she didn't turn up for their study group."

"Okay, what's her name?" Cameron asked as she shuffled into her office.

"Tiffany Eisenhower. Nineteen."

"Background check? Are we sure she's not just hanging out with a boyfriend or something?"

"It's too soon to label as a missing person, I know, Ross, but with all that's going on," he said. "But yeah, we're doing a check."

"Okay, Reynolds, we'll be out on the trails tonight. Maybe we'll get lucky and catch the bastard."

She ended the call then checked the algorithm. It wasn't through running and she watched the data stream across the screen, the code nothing but gibberish to her.

"What's up?" Andrea asked from behind her.

"Missing girl," she said. "Last seen at the coffee shop I staked out the other week."

"So Flagstaff. You think he'll do it tonight?"

"That's been the pattern. Kill them, then let them lay for a couple of days."

Andrea motioned to the computer. "How much longer?"

"Shouldn't be long."

"And then the conversion?"

"Forty-five minutes or so. We have time. I wouldn't anticipate him coming out here until after midnight."

"Right. I should let Jim and the guys know," Andrea said. "Should I tell them we'll meet them at the office?"

"Yeah. We've got to get our plan together first. What's the moon phase? Will we have light?"

Andrea shook her head. "Don't think so. New moon."

"Great. I don't suppose your department is stocked with night vision goggles, huh?"

"Sweetheart, we're lucky to even know what night vision goggles are." She held up her phone. "I'm going to call Jim."

Cameron nodded, feeling a strange fluttering in her stomach at Andrea's casual use of the endearment. *Sweetheart.* She closed her eyes for a second, wondering when was the last time someone had called her sweetheart. Of course, as casually as it was tossed out, surely Andrea didn't mean anything by it. Surprisingly, she wanted it to mean something.

"Don't go there," she whispered. She would be leaving soon. Leaving Sedona and Andrea behind. Leaving Andrea—even though she knew she was falling in love with her, could be full-fledged in love with her if she let herself be.

No! She had a job to do. Christ, she couldn't let her feelings get in the way of the job. So she pushed any thoughts of Andrea away, staring at the computer, willing it to finish its run.

CHAPTER THIRTY

Cameron listened while Andrea went over the plan with the guys. The algorithm had turned up an eighty-eight percent probability that he would hit Devil's Lookout. Next highest was Cathedral Rock Trail with fifty-two percent, although Andrea didn't think that was likely. She said Cathedral Rock was only about a mile and a half long, hiking straight up the rock. The trail was a photographer's paradise, the only spot where there was a three hundred and sixty degree view of the Verde Valley and Sedona. Andrea thought they'd be wasting their time staking it out, but Cameron didn't want to leave anything to chance. But something was nagging at her, and she couldn't put her finger on it. It was almost like she'd forgotten something.

"Agent Ross?"

She turned, seeing Andrea's expectant expression. "Sorry. What?"

"Communication?"

"Yes."

Andrea cocked an eyebrow. "Right. Hand radio or trust our cells?"

"Oh. Sorry. What do you think?"

"Take the radios," Jim said. "The range is good. That way, I can monitor what's going on from here."

Cameron nodded. "Okay. But do you have earpieces? We've got to be exceptionally quiet."

Jim looked at Andrea, who shook her head. Cameron sighed, thinking it shouldn't be this difficult to formulate a plan and put it in action.

"We'll take the radios, but our communication has got to be minimal. Don't radio in unless you've got something. Use your cell for anything else." She looked at the guys. "And don't forget to put it on vibrate, please."

"So, Cathedral Rock, I mean, that's just straight up," Randy said. "Do we hide out at the beginning of the trail or what?"

Cameron glanced at Andrea. Cameron didn't have a clue as to what this trail looked like.

"The only cover you'll have is the first few hundred feet," Andrea said. "After that, nothing but scrub brush, so you don't want to go too far up."

"And Devil's Lookout?" Cameron asked.

"The trailhead is off of Bear Creek Road, so most of the climbing will be done by vehicle. We'll have junipers and hardwoods for a good part of it, before it opens up on the rim."

"Jim? You're good to drop us all off?"

"Yep. I'll drop you off, then head back here to wait. And call Phoenix if need be."

"I know it'll be a long night, especially if he's a no-show, but we have to wait it out until daybreak."

"We're good," Joey said. "Unless we hear a mountain lion scream. Then I'd guess Randy would be heading back down the trail in a fast run," he said with a laugh.

"Yeah. And you right behind me, no doubt."

"Will you forget about the damn mountain lions," Andrea said. "They'll take one whiff of you and run the other way."

"I would keep an eye out for rattlesnakes though," Jim said

with a slight smile. He took his toothpick out of his mouth and pointed it at Randy. "They like Cathedral Rock."

Cameron nearly laughed as the color faded from Randy's face.

"Just kiddin'," Jim said. "That hunk of rock is too damn hot for rattlers. You'll be fine."

"Thanks a lot," Joey said. "I'm the one who'll have to be with him all night."

Cameron glanced at her watch. "Okay, it's nearly ten. I'd like to head out and be settled in before midnight. Remember, no radio unless it's absolutely necessary."

All five of them were crammed into Jim's truck, Andrea and Cameron sharing the backseat with Joey. Andrea noticed Cameron's lightly twitching leg and the nervous tapping of her fingers against her thigh. She leaned closer.

"What's wrong?" she whispered.

"This doesn't feel right."

Andrea raised her eyebrows in a silent question.

"Tower Ridge."

"But—"

"He would assume we'd dismiss that trail now, right?"

"Yeah. But your program says Devil's Lookout."

"That's because the program thinks Tower Ridge was the last dump site. It wasn't."

Andrea looked up at the rearview mirror, meeting Jim's eyes, wondering how much of their conversation the others could hear. It didn't matter. If Cameron had doubts, they needed to talk about it.

"Tell me what you're thinking," she said quietly.

"He would assume we wouldn't target the same trail, since we nearly caught him on it. And that's exactly what we're doing. We're assuming he'll pick a different spot. It's the logical thing to do. That's what our program tells us." Cameron tapped Andrea's leg, as if making a point. "But what if he's thinking the same thing? He knows we won't come back to this trail. Why would we? We spooked him. So he does the opposite, thinking he'll be safe. He takes the same Tower Ridge Trail, assuming we'll be looking for him elsewhere."

It made sense, but Andrea was hesitant to go with Cameron's gut versus what the algorithm was telling them. The truck slowed and Andrea again met Jim's eyes. He was pulling over to the side of the road. Apparently he *had* been listening to them.

"I tend to agree with Agent Ross on this one," he said as he turned in the seat. "So make up your minds. Cathedral Rock trailhead is just up ahead."

Randy turned too. "What are you talking about?"

Cameron looked at Andrea. "What do you think?"

Andrea took a deep breath. "Okay. Let's go with it."

Cameron squeezed her hand quickly, then turned to the guys. "Change of plan. You two take Devil's Lookout. We're going back to Tower Ridge."

"But—"

"Just a gut feeling, Randy, but I think he's going back there."

"Okay. But if your gut is wrong, then me and Joey are stuck with eighty-eight percent probability he'll hit Devil's Lookout," he said, his panicky voice revealing his apprehension.

"You're a cop. You should be able to handle it."

"Yeah, but—"

"Randy, you'll be fine," Andrea said, feeling the need to reassure him. "You've had training. Go with your instinct."

"Don't shoot anyone," Jim added.

"Okay. Yeah. We'll be fine then," Randy said with a quick, nervous glance at Joey.

Andrea understood his fear. He hadn't been in law enforcement all that long and all of it was spent here in sleepy little Sedona. Now they were asking him to possibly apprehend a vicious serial killer. This, after dealing with nothing more than rowdy campers or the occasional domestic violence call for most of his career.

"Yes, you'll be fine," she said again.

They were all silent for the rest of the short trip to Devil's Lookout. Jim pulled in at the trailhead, then turned in the

207

seat, casting an anxious glance at her. Andrea nodded, hoping to reassure him as well. As Cameron had said, they were cops. They should be able to handle this.

Joey was the first out and Andrea noted how his hands kept touching his weapon as if he was double—and triple—checking that he was armed. The evening was cool and he slipped on a light jacket then shoved water bottles in each pocket. Randy stood beside him, an uneasy smile on his face. He, too, took a couple of water bottles.

"Remember, quiet," Cameron said. "If you think you spot him, call Andi's cell. If you're certain it's him, use the radio. We won't need to worry about quiet on our end then."

"Got it."

"This guy uses knives as his weapon of choice. That doesn't mean he won't be armed though," Andrea added, handing them one of the high-powered flashlights.

"We'll be fine," Joey said. "See you in the morning."

"Keep a look out for those mountain lions now, boys," Jim said with a wink, trying to lighten the mood. He tossed Randy a small canister and Randy laughed.

"If I'm close enough to one to use mace, I'm in big trouble," he said, but he dutifully slipped it in his pocket.

"Watch your back," Jim said, then slowly pulled away. "You know he's going to piss all over himself if this Patrick Doe shows up, don't you?"

"I would imagine so," Cameron said. "Let's hope I'm right about Tower Ridge."

CHAPTER THIRTY-ONE

As soon as Jim left them, they wasted no time in hiking up the trail. Cameron wanted to get into the brush cover before turning on the flashlight. As Andrea had said, there was no moonlight and the footing was awful, especially for her bum ankle.

"This is far enough," she said.

Andrea immediately turned on the flashlight, guiding the way through the brush and into the trees.

"Shine here," Cameron instructed as she took off her backpack. She quickly assembled the digital microphone. It was small and compact, not nearly the range as the ones she was used to using, but it would be enough for their purpose. She took a tiny earpiece and held it up. "Turn," she said. Andrea did and Cameron fitted it into her ear, then slipped one inside her own ear. She motioned for Andrea to step away. "Testing," she said quietly, the microphone held behind her. Andrea nodded.

Cameron then took out a pair of night vision goggles, which were simply night vision binoculars and a head gear set. She held them up. "I only have the one pair."

"You lead, I'll follow."

She took out her digital notebook and GPS locator, marking their position. She quickly pulled up the trail map, turning to face north so they could get their bearings.

"I want to go up the trail at least as far as we did this morning," she said.

Andrea shook her head. "There'll be no cover. Besides, he doesn't kill them in the open. He hides them."

"Okay, I'll let you judge how far up we go." She secured her pack again, then motioned to the light. "Kill it."

With her night vision goggles on, Cameron was able to make out the path with little difficulty. However, the microphone was picking up their footsteps and little else. She turned it off, knowing it would do them no good until they were stopped and silent. For thirty minutes they picked their way along the trail, her ankle throbbing constantly with each step she took. She could make out the cliffs up ahead and she felt Andrea tug on her sleeve.

"Here."

Cameron stopped, looking around and trying to find cover. Two juniper trees close together offered that and she carefully led them off the trail. Once they were settled out of sight, she again set up the microphone, holding it away from them and pointing it down the trail from where they'd just hiked. They were both silent—listening—and Cameron smiled as the soft sound of an owl echoed in her ear. Other sounds filtered through, rustling noises in the rocks, night birds. She relegated all of that to background noise and let her training take over, listening for the sound of a car door, footsteps, snapping of limbs or conversation.

After forty-five minutes she began to get restless, constantly glancing at her watch. She felt Andrea move close beside her, and she closed her eyes as she felt warm breath on her ear.

"Why don't we sit? It would be more comfortable."

She nodded, finding a clear rock with no close cactus to

worry about. She pointed it out to Andrea silently, then sat down beside her. She stretched her legs out, trying to flex her ankle. She had it tightly wrapped, but it still ached. If they did find Patrick and there was any kind of chase, Andrea would have to take the lead.

When another hour passed with no activity, Cameron began to question their whole plan. Worse, she was afraid that the algorithm was right and he would choose Devil's Lookout, leaving Randy and Joey to try to stop him.

As if reading her mind, Andrea leaned closer. "It's only midnight."

"What if I'm wrong?"

"It's only midnight," Andrea said again.

She leaned closer, touching Andrea's ear with her mouth. "Patience has never been my strong suit."

Andrea's hand squeezed hers hard. "Be quiet."

Cameron tried to relax, but thirty minutes later, she was visibly twitching as her fingers tapped an unnamed song on her thigh. She finally stood, her legs feeling cramped from sitting so long. She winced as she tested her ankle, the pain shooting up her leg causing her to grab a branch for support. She stopped suddenly as the microphone picked up the sound of a car door slamming, then another. She reached for Andrea, pulling her up beside her. Again, she put her mouth directly on Andrea's ear.

"We must be extremely quiet," she whispered.

Andrea nodded.

Cameron adjusted her goggles, then held the microphone out farther away from her body. She could make out the sounds of footsteps on the rocks down below them. Before long, the faint glow of a flashlight could be seen through the trees, and finally, muffled conversation.

"Keep her moving."

"She's moving. Aren't you, little girl? We're not going to hurt you."

Hearing two male voices confirmed what they already knew—Patrick had a partner. But hearing the faint whimper of the girl brought everything into perspective. Patrick was bringing his next victim to Tower Ridge.

"Yeah, Charles. She probably thinks we're coming up here to party," he said with a laugh.

The whimper was clearer, yet muffled. Most likely gagged, Cameron thought. The footsteps were louder now and the beam of the light was easily seen as they climbed higher. Cameron felt her adrenaline increase, causing her heart to beat faster. She took deep, even breaths, telling herself she'd done this a hundred times before. That much was true. Yet she'd never done this with Andrea. If they were to silently pursue their target, they needed complete symmetry in their movements, something that normally took months of training to acquire. Her only hope was that the level of intimacy they'd established would guide them on a different level.

"I still think we should have chosen a different spot."

"Shut up."

And there was no further conversation, just the sounds of the footsteps and the labored breathing that they could now hear. Cameron could feel how tense Andrea was as the trio approached their position. She reached out a hand, squeezing tight on Andrea's forearm.

As if sensing their presence, it was Patrick who stopped and tilted his head, listening.

"What is it?"

"Thought I heard something."

Cameron could just make them out through the trees. Patrick was in the lead with the girl between them. It appeared her hands were bound behind her back, and she was indeed gagged. The man in the back—Charles—was armed. Not that this surprised her, but it did complicate things. Patrick swept his flashlight back and forth, then continued on up the trail. Once the group was in front of them, Cameron again leaned close to Andrea.

"We follow, but not too close," she whispered in her ear.

Andrea nodded.

"The one in the back has a gun," she added.

Cameron waited until they were thirty yards or so in front of them before moving from their hiding place. She hoped the group's own footsteps would muffle the sound of hers and Andrea's. She watched them, counting the rhythm of their steps before heading out, her pace even with theirs.

The microphone was all but useless now, the sound of their steps on the rocks loud and distorting. But she kept it on. Once Patrick stopped, they had to be prepared to take action. She feared the girl would have little time.

She jumped, as did the others, as the loud, high-pitched scream of a mountain lion pierced the quiet night.

"What the hell was that?"

"Cougar, maybe."

"It sounded close. Let's get this over with."

"There's a stand of trees up ahead. It's a good spot."

"Can I do it this time?"

"No, Charles, you cannot do it. But you can play with her afterward, if you want."

Again, the gagged whimper of the girl was loud. Charles grabbed her hands from behind, jerking them up as the girl tried to get away.

"Now don't go getting all scared on us, little girl. It'll be over soon enough."

"Not too soon," Patrick added, a sickening laugh echoing across the rocks. "Come on."

Cameron knew they didn't have much time, but they had to be careful. Patrick, obviously, was the one wielding the knife. Charles, on the other hand, had a gun. Either weapon could kill the girl.

She withdrew her own weapon from the holster on her hip, silently following them off the trail. She stopped when they did, again hoping Andrea would follow her lead. They had no way to communicate, and she assumed Andrea's vision was limited.

"Now, Tiffany—that's your name right? You've been chosen to join a very long list of beautiful women," he laughed. "And a few not so beautiful men."

"Good one," Charles said with a chuckle.

Cameron saw that he held the gun loosely, his attention on Patrick and the ritual that was about to occur. She could make out the girl's eyes, wide with fear—fear Cameron could nearly smell.

"By taking your life, I'm adding to mine. I've become

invincible. I have the power," he said loudly as he raised the knife high.

"The hell you do," Cameron yelled.

Andrea stood frozen to the spot, squinting into the darkness. The flashlight that Charles held swung their way, but Cameron fired her weapon, both shots sending Charles backward onto a mesquite, where he slumped to the ground. The girl sank to her knees, her muffled screams loud in the dark night.

"Back away from her or you are a dead man," Cameron instructed as she walked closer, her gun pointed at Patrick's head. "Drop your knife."

"Agent Ross, we finally meet," he said. "I thought your little fall might have done you in. You surprise me. I was certain you'd have thought you had scared me off of this trail." He stared at her gun. "And there's no need to threaten me. I doubt you'll shoot."

Andrea fumbled with the light, finally snapping it on, the strong beam illuminating the darkness. Cameron took off her night vision goggles as Andrea shone the light at Patrick, watching as he dropped the knife on the rocks.

"You're a scrawny little shit," Cameron said. "How the hell did you get Collie?"

"Oh, yes, Agent Collie. What a pussy," he said. "I'm the brains. Charles is the muscle. He didn't stand a chance."

"*Was* the muscle," Cameron corrected. "Looks like you're running out of brothers," she said, obviously taking a guess on their relationship. By Patrick's startled look, Cameron's guess was correct.

"John was expendable, Charles was not."

"Expendable because he was slow?"

Patrick laughed. "He was a retard, yeah. But he had his skills. No, he became expendable when he developed a soft spot for that detective." He sat down nonchalantly on a rock and crossed his legs. "I should have killed her when I had the chance."

"Why Collie?"

He laughed again. "I got sick of seeing him on TV. The

arrogant fool thought he could take me down. He ended up begging for his life and crying like a baby. Big, tough FBI agent my ass. He was nothing but a pussy."

Cameron took a step closer and Andrea saw the tight grip she had on her gun. "Shut the fuck up."

"Or what? You're going to shoot me?" He smiled, showing off even, white teeth. "You have such a lovely little kitten in that rolling home of yours. I'd recommend you not leave her alone. Taking the lives of pretty, young girls is my passion. Toying with animals is my hobby."

Andrea felt the bile rise in her stomach at his words. She glanced at Cameron, hoping she wouldn't let Patrick get into her head, hoping she wouldn't allow him to make this personal. The thought that he'd been near the rig, near enough to see Lola, caused her to want to shoot him herself. But Cameron didn't fall into his trap. Instead, she smiled at him.

"You won't get the chance to *toy* with anything. You're a dead man."

"So shoot me then," he challenged.

Cameron held her gun only a foot from his head. "You think I won't?"

"You don't have the guts."

"I have so many deaths on my conscience, one more won't hurt me."

"Then do it."

Andrea saw Cameron's finger tighten on the trigger, saw her eyes narrow and she was afraid Cameron would send this miserable little man straight to hell right then and there. As she'd told Andrea, she'd done it countless times before. It was what she was trained to do. But this time, Andrea wasn't going to let her go through with it. Cameron was no longer that person, no longer a sniper for the military. No longer their assassin

"Agent Ross, stand down." Cameron didn't so much as blink. "Agent Ross," she said again.

Her stern, yet calm voice finally seemed to penetrate Cameron's senses. Cameron took a deep breath, relaxing the hold she had on her weapon, but Andrea knew the smile on her face was forced.

"No, I'm not going to shoot you," Cameron said. "That would be too easy of an end for you. Killing a federal agent got you in all kinds of trouble as it is. Of course, we can just haul you back to Texas. They'll stick that needle in your arm. Lethal injection," she said slowly as she lowered her gun. "It's a shame states have gotten away from the electric chair. Because you deserve to fry."

"I can guarantee you it won't end that way."

"No? You going to jump off the cliff again?"

"Will you follow me again?"

"Not this time. Now get up. I'm tired of talking." She glanced at Andrea. "Cuffs?"

Andrea unclipped them from her holster, tossing them to her. She kept her weapon at the ready as Cameron holstered hers.

"Stand up."

Just as Andrea was thinking it was too easy—far too easy to apprehend him—she saw the shiny blade of the knife he held. He whipped it from behind his back quickly, taking an expert stab at Cameron. Andrea dropped the flashlight as she fired her weapon three times, her training taking over as her mind tried desperately to process what was happening. As if in a vacuum, she vaguely heard Cameron's cry of pain. Her focus was totally on Patrick as he stumbled into the shadows, one hand clutching his chest, the other still holding the knife.

She walked toward him, standing just outside the halo of light. He was gasping for breath and—as if an afterthought—the bloody knife fell from his hands. Their eyes met, his filled with pain and disbelief. His mouth moved as he tried to speak but no sound came out. Then he turned, struggling to walk. She lowered her gun when she realized his intention. She wasn't going to stop him.

She let him stagger to the edge of the rocks, then his body gave way, collapsing, and he soundlessly fell from her view as he disappeared into the vast emptiness of the dark, dark canyon—three hundred feet below. Her mind's eye followed his progress, his now lifeless body floating aimlessly as it continued its journey into the canyon, waiting to be swallowed up by the darkness.

Cameron.

Jolted from her stupor, she turned and hurried over to her. Cameron, too, was clutching her chest and Andrea panicked when she saw her shirt darkened by blood.

"Oh, dear God," she whispered. "How bad?"

Cameron shook her head. "I'm fine."

"You're bleeding."

"It's my arm, that's all. It's not my first knife wound."

"Let's hope it's your last," Andrea said, now seeing that Cameron was clutching her left arm to her chest, trying to stop the bleeding. She grabbed the discarded flashlight, gasping at the amount of blood. "Christ, Cameron."

"There's a first-aid kit in my pack. Bring that to me. Then check on the girl."

"We need to stop the bleeding."

"Check on the girl," she said stubbornly.

Andrea found the pack and tossed it to Cameron. The girl was curled in the fetal position, her hands bound behind her back. A faded blue bandana was used as a gag. The girl was trembling and tried to scream when Andrea touched her shoulder.

"It's okay, Tiffany. FBI. You're going to be fine." She met the girl's frightened eyes and Andrea smiled gently. "It's okay," she said again as she loosened the bandana.

"FBI?" the girl asked weakly.

"Yes."

"Is he...is he gone?"

"Yes. They're both gone."

Andrea untied her hands, then was surprised when the girl flew into her arms, clutching her hard. Andrea held her tightly, knowing the girl needed to feel safe and secure.

"He was going to kill me," she sobbed. "He was going to kill me."

"You're safe. He can't hurt you now."

Andrea glanced behind her, seeing Cameron holding a gauze wrap with her teeth as she tried to bandage herself. She was torn between comforting the girl and doing what her heart told her to do—go to Cameron. She decided she'd do both.

She pushed the girl out of her arms, meeting her eyes. "Come with me now. Agent Ross is injured and I need to tend to her.

Can you help me?"

Andrea held her hand as they went to Cameron, keeping the light away from the body of the dead brother.

"Tiffany, this is Agent Ross," she said, positioning the girl on the rock beside Cameron. She ignored the scowl Cameron gave her as she took the gauze from her. "Be nice," she whispered.

"I was managing."

"You're so stubborn." Andrea peeled the shirt away, revealing a deep, six-inch gash across her forearm. "And you're going to need a doctor."

"I told you—"

"You need stitches," she said, no longer trying to keep her voice low. "Don't argue with me." She glanced quickly at Tiffany. "Sorry. Agent Ross is a bit cantankerous."

"What's your name?" the girl asked, her voice still shaky.

"Andrea. Andrea Sullivan," she said. "Can you hold this for me?"

Tiffany came closer, holding one end of the gauze as Andrea wrapped Cameron's arm tightly.

"Do you have tape?"

"In the pack," Cameron said. She looked at Tiffany. "Are you okay?" The girl nodded, but didn't speak.

Andrea found the tape and tore a piece off, cutting it with her teeth. Cameron flinched when Andrea pressed it against her arm. "I'm sorry," she whispered.

"We need to call the guys."

"Yes. I'm surprised they haven't radioed," Andrea said. "Surely they heard the shots."

"We told them not to call unless they had something," Cameron said. "They're following instructions."

"I'll report it," Andrea said as she stood up, taking the radio off her belt. "I'm ready to get the hell out of here."

CHAPTER THIRTY-TWO

The morning broke slowly in Coyote Canyon, the shadows clinging to the night as if not yet ready to hide and sleep for the day. Night merged with day, owls giving way to hawks, bats to songbirds. The sounds of the horses' hooves was soon relegated to the background as the sweet calls of birds, the scream of a red tailed hawk and the familiar cackling of busy ravens filled the air.

They were taking the long way into the canyon at Devil's Rock Trail, the normal route was too steep and rocky for the horses. The trail through the lower end of Sycamore Canyon would intersect with it, and they'd reach Devil's Rock from the north.

Andrea glanced at Cameron, who, after much debate and a few not-so-idle threats, had finally relented and let Andrea take her to the minor emergency facility in Sedona. The gash took twenty-three stitches to close and Cameron was still dutifully wearing the sling the doctor had provided. Her ankle was another story. X-rays showed no break or fracture, but the doctor had produced a walking boot for her to wear. This was met with a "the hell I will" followed by "just tape the goddamn thing."

"What?"

"What...what?" Andrea asked.

Cameron raised an eyebrow. "You were staring."

"I was thinking."

"What were you thinking?"

"I was thinking how stubborn you are."

"I went to the doctor, didn't I?" She pointed to her arm. "And I'm wearing this damn silly sling."

"Which tells me it really hurts or you wouldn't be wearing the damn silly thing."

Cameron smiled. "You're a little cranky this morning."

"Missing a night's sleep tends to do that."

"We've missed sleep before," Cameron said quietly, and Andrea quickly glanced behind them, hoping Randy and Joey couldn't hear their conversation.

"At least we were in the prone position."

Cameron laughed. "Yes, a far more enjoyable way to miss a night's sleep than what we just did."

"You think that girl will be okay?" Reynolds and his team had descended on Sedona and were still debriefing her when they'd set out to find Patrick's body.

"I would imagine it's going to take some time. Depends how strong she is."

"She was so close," Andrea said. "If we hadn't gone with your gut feeling and instincts on which trail to take, she would be dead."

"Yeah, she would."

They rode on in silence for a few moments then Andrea asked, "Were you really going to shoot him?"

"Yes. If you hadn't been there to stop me, yes."

"I'm sorry that I stopped you," she said. "If I hadn't, you wouldn't have a knife wound. He could have killed you just as easily."

"You did the right thing. This was no covert military

operation. I have no license to kill. Despite the monster that he was, he was entitled to a judge and jury."

"Was he?"

Cameron held her gaze. "Does it bother you that you killed him?"

"No. And *that* bothers me a little." She shook her head. "But no, his death won't be on my conscience, if that's what you mean. He was trying to kill you."

Cameron nodded. "Thanks for having my back."

"Well, that's what partners do, right?"

Cameron again cocked an eyebrow. "The last time I referred to us as partners, you got pissed off and wouldn't speak to me for the rest of the day," she reminded her.

"True." Of course, that was when she was still smothered in guilt over Erin, and long before she'd developed an affection for Cameron. "You were arrogant and conceited."

"Still am."

"Not so much."

"A bully?"

Andrea laughed out loud, no longer caring if Randy and Joey heard them. "You *try* to be. I think I can handle you."

Their eyes held for long seconds, and Andrea saw that her affection for Cameron was returned. That made her feel both happy and sad. It was nice to know someone cared for you like you cared for them. But the end of the case signaled the end of their relationship. Oh, they might keep in touch through e-mail or the occasional phone call, but the brief affair they'd enjoyed would come to a halt. And that made her feel very sad.

"Is that it?" Cameron asked, eyeing the huge slab of rock with a lone, smooth spiral rising from its base some fifty feet high.

Andrea nodded. "Devil's Rock."

Cameron checked her GPS settings again. "The trajectory from the ledge should put him here."

Andrea nudged her horse on, stopping at the five-foot-thick

rock. She used the fallen boulders as stepping stones, climbing on top of the slab. Cameron wanted to follow but didn't think her ankle could make it. She stayed in the saddle as Randy and Joey scampered after her.

The rock slab was large, but not so large that you couldn't spot a body. She again checked her calculations. She bent back, looking up the cliff wall to the ridge far above them—Tower Ridge. She'd logged the GPS coordinates before they'd left the ridge. They were in the right spot.

"Got blood," Andrea called. She, too, looked skyward. "He fell here." She smirked. "On Devil's Rock. How ironic."

"Or appropriate," Cameron said. "But where's his goddamn body?"

"Is this a blood smear?" Randy asked.

Andrea inspected where he was pointing and nodded. "Yeah. Looks like he was dragged this way," Andrea said, walking slowly toward the opposite end of the slab.

"Who the hell would have dragged him? There's nobody out here," Cameron said.

"So you think he may have gotten up and walked then?"

"I wouldn't put it past him," she said, acknowledging Andrea's sarcasm.

Andrea motioned for her to join them on the other side and Cameron kicked her horse lightly, trotting to the back side of Devil's Rock.

"And it's most likely *what* dragged him, not who," Andrea said.

"Animals?"

Andrea nodded. "They don't call this Coyote Canyon for nothing. Coyotes are scavengers. Or a mountain lion could have found him. They prefer fresh kill, not carrion."

"You're not telling me we might not find a body, are you? Because I have to have a body, Andi."

"And I think you will." She pointed into a stand of mesquites. "Ravens."

Cameron reined her horse around and rode over to the trees where a group of ravens were gathered, leaving the others still standing on Devil's Rock. What was left of Patrick Doe hardly seemed human. His ribcage was exposed, with little flesh remaining on the bones. He'd been disemboweled, his torso mostly eaten, his clothes shredded by sharp claws. His face was distorted, no doubt from the fall, but enough remained to confirm his identity. All in all, it was a fitting end to this man's life.

She turned in the saddle and waved the others over. Randy's mule would serve to haul the body out. Then Reynolds and his team would head back to Phoenix to wrap things up. And hopefully identify Patrick and Charles Doe.

She led her horse away from the body, watching Andrea as she gracefully hopped off the rock slab and climbed back on her horse. She wondered how much longer they would have together. A couple of days at most, she suspected. It was going to be hard to say goodbye to her, but that was her own damn fault. She knew better than to get so involved with her. Hell, she'd been down that road before. But it was just so easy with Andrea, so easy to be with her...so easy to fall in love with her. And so hard to leave her.

"Well?" Andrea asked as she rode up. "Anything left?"

"Not a lot."

Randy and Joey walked closer, then Joey turned away quickly, his face white as a sheet.

"Oh, my God, that's disgusting."

"Jesus," Randy murmured. "He's been eaten."

"Pretty much, yeah," Cameron agreed.

"A fate well deserved," Andrea added. Then she smiled broadly. "Okay, guys. Bag him."

Randy and Joey looked at her with wide eyes.

"Bag him?" Randy asked. "Why us?"

"Because Agent Ross is injured. And I shot him. I think you guys can participate a little, don't you?"

"Oh, man," Randy muttered as he looked again at what was left of Patrick Doe. "This part of the job sucks."

Joey followed his gaze. "I'm glad I didn't eat anything."

Andrea glanced at Cameron, smiling as their eyes met.

"Case closed, Agent Ross?"

Cameron nodded. "Case closed, Deputy Sullivan."

"Do you want to call Dallas and give them the good news, or should I?"

"You can have the honor. That Agent Hunter was a bit hard to deal with. A little on the arrogant side."

Andrea laughed. "You would know."

CHAPTER THIRTY-THREE

"Does it hurt?"

"I've had worse wounds," Cameron said.

"That's not what I asked."

Cameron smiled. "Okay, yes, it hurts like a son of a bitch," she said.

Andrea leaned closer and kissed her. "Now was that so hard?"

"Yes."

Andrea laughed quietly as she snuggled closer to Cameron, making sure not to bump her injured arm. After they'd delivered Patrick Doe to Reynolds, who was waiting for them at Cutty's funeral home, they'd gone back to the office to fill Jim in on everything. Their field notes and case report would have to wait. They were both too exhausted.

There wasn't any discussion when they'd left, as Cameron had just said, "meet you at the rig" and Andrea had. She was starving and knew Cameron must be too, so she stopped for burritos and they had a late lunch. They ate them silently as they sat on the loveseat, Lola purring continuously as she went from lap to lap. Apparently, they'd left her alone for too long and she was letting them know.

But exhaustion had set in and Cameron stood, taking Andrea's hand, limping down the short hallway to the bedroom. Andrea wanted a shower, but she was too tired. She fell in bed beside Cameron, where she now snuggled next to her sleeping form.

She closed her eyes, but sleep wouldn't come, even as tired as she was. The uncertainty of tomorrow loomed and she hated that they were potentially spending their last night together sleeping. Finally, she let Cameron's even breathing relax her, their fingers lightly entwined and eyelids heavy. She gave in to sleep.

Through the foggy haze of sleep, Cameron realized a warm, wet tongue was teasing her nipples, moving from one to the other. She moaned, feeling how aroused her body was. Even in sleep, Andrea could elicit a response from her. She opened her eyes enough to see the sun was fading from the sky then shut them again when Andrea's fingers moved lower. She spread her legs, letting Andrea have her way.

Andrea left her breast, sitting up and straddling her thigh, stroking herself against Cameron as her fingers found their target. Cameron moaned again, her hips arching higher. She reached out, cupping Andrea's hip with her right hand, moving against the smooth skin of her rounded backside. She felt Andrea's wetness against her thigh as Andrea pleasured herself, all the while her fingers moving slowly—deeply—in and out of Cameron, her thumb brushing her clit with each stroke.

The leisurely, deliberate strokes became faster with each pass, Andrea's hips keeping the pace of her fingers as she ground herself against Cameron. They were panting together, their moans intermingling. Cameron opened her eyes, meeting Andrea's, wanting to memorize them, storing away the image of hungry eyes dark with passion as they climaxed together.

Andrea collapsed on top of her and with her good arm, Cameron held her close as their breathing returned to normal. Again, they drifted off to sleep, their bodies still damp with perspiration and desire.

CHAPTER THIRTY-FOUR

Cameron walked through the quiet motor home, her ankle feeling surprisingly better after nearly eighteen hours in bed. Those hours in bed, however, did little to douse her exhaustion, and the morning shower hadn't helped much either. She yawned widely as she poured water over ice then smiled as she felt Lola rub against her leg.

"You hungry?" she asked, bending down to pick her up. She kissed her little face, loving the constant purring that always emanated from Lola. She sat her back down, then noticed the nearly full food bowl. "I see your other mommy has already fed you."

She paused as those words sunk in. No, there was no other mommy. There was just her. Andrea was only a temporary fixture in their lives. One that, she feared, was coming to an end. Murdock had e-mailed. He wanted a video conference. That meant he had an assignment for her.

They'd had a brief conversation that morning with Reynolds which ended with her promising to complete her field report and submit it to him within forty-eight hours. So a video conference meant he was sending her on another case. It was something she'd not mentioned to Andrea.

Andrea had left at daybreak with a promise to meet up later in the day. She had her own reports to do. They hadn't talked about Cameron's impending departure, but it was on Andrea's mind as well. She could tell that by the way Andrea had kissed her goodbye. Hell, she could tell that by the way Andrea had made love to her. She wondered if Andrea sensed Cameron's reluctance to leave by the way she'd clung to Andrea at the door.

They had nearly slept through the afternoon and night, getting up only to shower and order their usual pizza before falling back into bed at midnight. But their passion overrode their exhaustion and they reveled in each other's lovemaking, hands and mouths pleasuring each other until sleep claimed them again. Cameron woke to Andrea's warm body snuggled tightly against her, arms still entwined. The sense of contentment, of sheer delight at having Andrea at her side was overwhelming, overpowering. Because that meant she'd lost control.

She knew better, of course. She knew better than to get so involved, she knew better than to fall in love with her. But fall she did. It was out of her control. It always had been with Andrea. And it was going to break her heart to leave this town. She wondered if her leaving would break two hearts.

A soft beeping on her laptop told her Murdock had signed in to their session. She sat down in her recliner and brought the laptop to life, quickly typing in her password for the video link. Murdock greeted her with a broad smile.

"Agent Ross, I trust you got some sleep," he said.

"Eighteen hours, yes."

"Good. And your arm?"

"It's fine," she said. It was a bitch taking a shower, but there wasn't really much pain. Much less than her ankle.

"Great. Then I hope you're ready to head out. I've got an assignment."

She nodded. "Sure," she said as Lola did a graceful leap from the floor to the arm of her chair. She tried to move her out of camera range but failed.

"What the hell is that?" he asked. "A cat?"

"Yes."

"You? You have a cat? What the hell's wrong with you?"

"And why can't I have a cat?"

"No offense, Cameron, but you don't seem like a pet person. Okay, maybe a Rottweiler or Doberman, but definitely not a cat."

Cameron scowled. "There's nothing wrong with having a cat. Besides, I didn't exactly go out and intentionally get her. I found her at a stop in Utah. Starving little kitten. So I took her with me."

"Wow. So you do have a soft side. Amazing."

Cameron ignored his comment. "What about this assignment? You don't have anyone else to take it? I could use a couple of days," she said, hoping to delay her departure.

"It's up in Utah, actually. Canyonlands National Park. They found a decomposed body. Sent to Salt Lake City for autopsy and ID."

"And? Foul play?"

"Either that or suicide. There was no pack, no personal belongings found on the body. He was found out in the backcountry that requires a permit to hike and camp. He had none."

"And you want me to go?"

"Well, I'd thought of flying out someone from Denver, but you know, with budgets cuts and all, you're the closest."

"Reynolds has a whole goddamn team to choose from," she said.

"True. But Reynolds was the senior agent after Collie. I wouldn't trust any of the others to do a solo. That's your gig," he said. "Besides, I figured you'd be ready to hit the road. You've been stuck there almost a month."

She kept her expression even as she nodded. "Okay. Send me the details."

"I've got the file ready to go. You need to head out as soon as possible. I've included a name of a forensic specialist from

230

Salt Lake. He's expecting your call. He's agreed to meet you out there to go over the scene."

"How long has the body been there?"

"No way to be sure yet. The ranger guessed two to three weeks."

She sighed. "Okay. I'll get the rig ready to run. It'll take me the morning."

"Contact Mark Canton when you get there. He's got a spot for you to park her."

"I'll be in touch."

"Safe travel," he said as the screen went dark.

She stared at it for several seconds, her fingers running silently across Lola's fur. Now what? She'd been given the expected assignment. By all accounts, Murdock expected her to depart today. Which was feasible. It would only take an hour or so to get the rig ready to travel. Then stop to dump the tanks and refill with fresh water. Stop for diesel fuel. Stop to replenish supplies, which, truth be told, were sorely lacking to begin with. She should be able to be on the road by noon.

"Noon, Lola," she whispered. She brought the kitten up to her face and kissed her. "Telling Andrea is not something I'm looking forward to."

But tell her she must. So she spent the next hour securing the inside of the rig, putting things in their traveling place and locking down the computers in her office. She piled dirty clothes in the small washer and set it to run, hoping she didn't run out of water before all the chores were done.

Finally, she could put it off no longer. She grabbed her keys and left, making the short drive into town using the now familiar Red Rock Loop Road. She took in her last sights of the beautiful country surrounding Sedona, trying to memorize the colors, the smells. Knowing she would pull those memories out often and examine them, she wanted to tuck them away safely. But how she was going to say goodbye to Andrea, she had no idea.

Andrea was just reading through her report when Randy tossed a wadded up piece of paper at her.

"Looks like you have a visitor, Andi."

She glanced up, seeing Cameron's familiar truck pulling to a stop in front beside her old Jeep. She couldn't help the smile that shot to her face, and she didn't try to hide it. But as soon as Cameron opened the door, as soon as their eyes met, her smile faded. Cameron was leaving.

"Hey," she said. "I didn't expect you so early."

"Yeah. I know." She motioned outside. "Can we talk?"

"Sure."

Andrea's feet felt like lead as she walked around her desk and out into the open entryway. She glanced back at Randy, finding him watching them with interest. She followed Cameron outside and stood still as Cameron leaned against her truck with a heavy sigh. Andrea studied her, seeing a myriad of emotions cross her eyes. Even though they both knew it would come, it seemed it was as hard for Cameron to say goodbye as it was going to be for Andrea.

"When?" Andrea finally asked.

"Now. The rig's all packed."

Andrea nodded and tried to force a smile to her face. "Well, I guess you're ready to hit the road anyway. You're not used to being stuck in one place so long."

"No, Andi, I'm not ready." Cameron shoved off the truck and ran a nervous hand through her hair. "I was hoping we'd have more time." She took Andrea's hand and squeezed it. "Murdock called this morning. I've got to head up to Utah—Canyonlands."

"I see."

"Maybe...well, maybe if it's a quick trip, maybe I could come back here," Cameron said.

For a moment, Andrea's blue mood faded, a part of her hoping that maybe they would see each other again. But reality set in. Any time they spent together would always be temporary.

"Or maybe that assignment will end, and you'll have another

one even farther away," she said. "Let's don't try to pretend we'll be able to see each other, Cameron."

"I'm not ready to say goodbye."

"Neither am I. But, the reality is, we have to." She cleared her throat. "I have a lot to thank you for," she said, holding up her hand when Cameron would have protested. "You brought me out of my funk. You made me feel alive again. I won't ever forget you."

Cameron bit her lip and looked away, and Andrea was surprised to see that Cameron was fighting to control her emotions.

"I didn't think it would be this hard," Cameron said.

Andrea slipped into her arms, wrapping her own around Cameron's strong shoulders, holding her tightly.

"Oh, Cameron, me either," she whispered. "I'm going to miss you."

They pulled apart, their mouths only breaths away from each other. Cameron hesitated as she must have known that Randy and the others were watching. Andrea didn't care. She leaned closer, her lips finding Cameron's with ease, memorizing their taste, their softness, her mouth saying its own goodbye.

She felt tears dampen her eyes when she stepped away. She blinked several times. "You know, you could send me the occasional picture of Lola," she said, the mention of the kitten's name bringing a whole new set of emotions to the surface. "Let me know how she's growing and all."

Cameron nodded. "You know I hate that name, right?"

Andrea smiled. "No, you love it."

Their eyes held for a long moment then Cameron smiled too. "Yes, I love it." She squeezed Andrea's hand again, then let go completely. "I should get going."

"Yes. Please...please be careful," she said. "I won't be there to watch your back."

"And I'll miss that." She paused at the door to her truck. "Take care of yourself, Andi."

"I will."

Cameron backed away without another word and Andrea stood there, watching her drive out of her life as quickly as she'd come into it. She crossed her arms and leaned against her Jeep, staring up at Thunder Mountain, seeing...not the red rocks, but images of Cameron as she filtered in and out of Andrea's life so easily, it was almost as if she'd always been there, leaving Andrea to wonder how she could possibly exist without her now.

How long she stood there, she didn't know. Long enough for Randy to come out and check on her.

"Andi? You okay?"

She rolled her head to the side, trying to smile and failing. "Yeah, I'll be okay."

"Is she gone?"

She met his eyes, noting the concern there. "Yes. She's leaving."

He nodded. "That's why you look sad again."

"Again?"

"When you first got here, your eyes...you always looked so sad. Since Cameron's been around, well, you were happy. There wasn't any sadness there."

She just stared at him, saying nothing.

"But it's back," he said quietly.

She looked away, back to Thunder Mountain. "For a completely different reason though."

He leaned against the Jeep beside her, saying nothing for the longest. Finally, he bumped her shoulder lightly. "So, did you fall in love with her or what?"

She gave him a half-smile. "What makes you think we can start discussing my personal life now?"

He shrugged. "I thought you might need someone to talk to. You know, girl talk."

She smiled again, then linked her arm with his, resting her head on his shoulder.

"I think maybe I did fall in love with her."

She felt him nod. "It shows," he said. Then he paused, as if considering his next words carefully. "I think maybe you weren't the only one."

Andrea closed her eyes. No, probably not. And she could tell herself that Cameron probably did this at every stop she made, but Andrea didn't believe that. She could see it in Cameron's eyes when they made love. She could see it each time Cameron looked at her. And she knew it the other night when Cameron chased her down in bare feet, not wanting her to leave. She knew it then. But none of that mattered.

Cameron was leaving her.

CHAPTER THIRTY-FIVE

Cameron sat at the steering wheel, staring out into the desert. The four slides were pulled in, the leveling jacks were up, the diesel engine was idling, yet there she sat, her hands gripping the wheel tightly.

"Stupid, stupid, stupid," she whispered. She took a deep breath. "Stupid." She glanced over at Lola who sat importantly in the passenger's seat, staring at her. "I don't want to leave her."

She leaned back in the seat, taking her hands off the wheel. "Rules, Lola. There are rules. Never, ever fall in love with them. Rule number one. It's there for a reason." She raised her hands. "*This* reason. Because I can't leave."

She stood up, pacing in the small confines of the motor home, made much smaller with the slides closed up. "What am I going to do? Just what the *hell* am I going to do?" She stared at Lola who was watching her every move.

She ran her hands through her hair, trying to decide. Of

course, she and Andrea hadn't talked about anything. Their affair had blossomed so quickly, the attraction so strong, there wasn't really any chance to back away from it. It had taken its natural course. And now she was just supposed to pack up and leave and pretend it had meant nothing to her.

Well, she couldn't do it. She'd had plenty of affairs in her day, some short and some lasting months. But she'd always been able to leave. In fact, she had a hard time recalling names and faces of the women who passed through her life.

Not this time. She couldn't do it.

She quickly grabbed her headset from the console and called Murdock. She walked back and forth, impatiently waiting for him to pick up.

"Murdock."

"It's me."

"Are you on the road already?"

"No. I need to talk to you about something."

"Okay. What's up?"

"Well, I've been thinking," she said.

"Oh, great," he said dryly. "That's never a good sign."

"Very funny, Murdock. I sometimes forget you have a sense of humor."

"Well, I try."

"Yeah." She paused, then, "I need a partner."

"You? You hate partners."

"I know. But since this case, I realized I work better with a partner. You know, someone to bounce ideas off of," she said, again pacing as there was a lengthy silence.

"Okay," he said slowly, drawing the word out. "So who do you have in mind?"

Again she hesitated. "Andrea Sullivan."

"Oh, Cameron, please say you didn't get involved with her."

She smiled. "No, of course not. What do you think I am? Stupid?"

"Well..."

"No, Murdock. It's just...we worked well together. She's the best partner I've ever had. I think we would make a good team."

"And she would travel in the rig with you?"

"It's big enough for two people. And the loveseat folds out into a bed," she added, hoping to appease him. "Of course, I haven't asked her yet. She may say no."

"And this is strictly professional?"

"Of course. Absolutely," she lied, knowing he would kill her if—when—he found out.

He laughed. "Do you seriously think I believe you, Cameron?"

"You know me, Murdock, there's never anything personal."

He sighed. "I don't suppose you want to give me time to think about this?"

"No. I'd like her to go with me now."

"Okay, let me get this straight, you've not even talked about this with her? What makes you think she'll agree?"

"Because she's a good cop with elite training from LA. Her skills are wasted here." That much was true, at least.

"Okay, Cameron. Trial run. Entry level."

"Entry level? Come on, Murdock, she's got more than ten years experience."

"Not FBI. She hasn't been through our training."

"Neither have I."

"Cameron, don't try to compare your military training with that of LAPD. And she gets temporary credentials."

"Jesus, Murdock, is this like super secret probation or something?"

"I can only pull so many strings."

"You always tell me you can pull whatever strings you need. Give her mid-level, not entry. She'll fit in perfectly with your teams, Murdock. She's as dysfunctional as the rest of us. Hell, she pulled her weapon on her captain," she reminded him.

"Yes, and let's hope you don't piss her off to the point where she pulls it on you."

She smiled. "Thanks, Murdock. You'll e-mail me with her account information and access credentials?"

"I'll see what kind of clearance I can give her. When you get settled in Utah, I want a video conference with her. I want to know who the hell I've just hired."

"You'll love her. We'll call."

She disconnected, knowing she had a damn silly grin on her face but was unable to stop it. She got back in the driver's seat, this time her grip on the steering wheel was light and effortless as she was no longer dreading driving away.

"Now let's go see if Andrea wants to go with us," she said, pausing to scratch Lola behind the ear. She was still smiling as she pulled the big rig onto the service road and headed out of Red Rocks Park.

CHAPTER THIRTY-SIX

Andrea splashed water on her face, trying to wash away the evidence of her tears. Yes, she knew it would be hard when Cameron left. She just didn't realize it would be this hard. She met her eyes in the mirror, acknowledging the sadness in them. It never occurred to her that Cameron would take her heart along with her when she left. And now Andrea was left to wonder what could have been. Was Cameron the one? Andrea had dated enough to know that she was still left searching for that one person to fill her soul completely. Erin wasn't that person, and Andrea hadn't been content enough to pretend she was, even though after her death Andrea tried to hold on to some belief that they'd had a loving, lasting relationship.

Could Cameron be that person? Was Andrea just letting her walk away without telling her how much she'd come to mean to her? Did Cameron have any idea how deeply Andrea's feelings went? Yes, she supposed she did. But what could Cameron do?

She had a job. She had an assignment. At least she'd offered to come back. Maybe she should have taken Cameron up on that. She could come back after her assignment and they could see where they were. Of course, she would just leave again, and they'd have to say their goodbyes all over again.

"Andi?"

She turned and stared at the closed door, her eyebrows drawn. Then she moved, jerking it open quickly.

"What are you doing here? I thought you'd be on the other side of Flagstaff by now."

Cameron studied her face, and Andrea cursed her earlier tears. She turned her head away, but Cameron touched her face, forcing her to look at her.

"You've been crying," she stated unnecessarily.

Andrea shrugged. What could she say to that?

Cameron moved into the bathroom and closed the door, giving them privacy. She leaned back against it, watching her. Andrea's mind was buzzing as she tried to read the look in Cameron's eyes.

"Why are you still here?" she finally asked.

"Why were you crying?"

Andrea tapped her chest. "I get the first question."

Cameron nodded. "Fair enough. I got a call from Murdock," she said. "I tried to talk him out of it, but he's forcing me to get a partner."

Andrea's heart fluttered to life as her eyes locked with Cameron's.

"Come with me," Cameron said quietly. "Be my partner."

Andrea felt tightness in her chest and she leaned back against the sink. "Just like that?"

"Do you want to?"

"Just pack up and leave? Right now?"

"Right now."

Dear God, was Cameron really asking her to go with her? Could she just walk away from her life here on a moment's notice? Her head was spinning as Cameron looked at her expectantly. Apparently, Cameron took her silence to be indecision, not shock.

"Just for a trial run," Cameron said quickly. "If you don't like it, you can come back. I'd imagine Jim would hold your position for you."

Andrea met Cameron's gaze head on, letting everything sink in—Cameron's words, the look in her eyes, the offer she'd extended. Cameron wanted her in her life. She wanted her to go with her.

"And we'd live—," Andrea said, clearing her throat. "We'd live in the motor home together?"

Cameron nodded. "I know it's small, but, well, the loveseat makes into a bed. I don't want to assume that our relationship would—"

"The loveseat?" she asked, interrupting her. "You want me to sleep on the sofa?"

Cameron stepped away from the door. "No. I want you in my bed. Our bed. But it occurred to me how this must sound to you, as if I want you along for sexual favors. That's not it. We made a good team, good partners. We can keep this strictly business between us, if that's what you want." Cameron took her hand, squeezing gently. "But honestly, I don't want to leave without you."

Andrea released her hand and moved away, wanting to talk, wanting to make sure they were both on the same page. Sexual favors or not, she wanted to make sure Cameron knew how emotionally invested she was already.

"I was crying because you were walking out of my life," she said, answering Cameron's earlier question. "I didn't want you to leave, but of course I knew you had to. And I felt so empty." She took a deep breath. "When Erin died, I at least had my guilt to fill me. As you know, it did more than fill me. It consumed me," she admitted. "You allowed me to let go of my guilt in my own time. You made me see how it truly felt to care about someone. Yet, you were leaving me, and I felt my heart breaking."

"I don't want to break your heart, Andi. I want to heal your heart. For the first time in so very long, I know what love feels like. I want—need—you in my life."

Andrea's breath caught. *Oh, God, she mentioned the L word.* Dare she believe Cameron's words? She met Cameron's eyes, searching for the truth.

"Love?" she whispered.

Cameron held her gaze. "I'm sorry. Was it too soon to mention that?"

Andrea laughed nervously, her head spinning. "No. Why do you think my heart was breaking?"

Cameron smiled too, reaching for her and tugging her closer. "So? Will you come with me?"

"As long as you don't make me sleep on the loveseat...yes," she said, giving in to her desire to kiss Cameron, their mouths meeting.

Their kiss was one of joy, love, contentment. No longer the last kiss of goodbye, rather the first in what Andrea hoped was a long and adventurous life together.

A life on the road. With a cat. She smiled against Cameron's lips, pulling away finally.

"So? What's this assignment we have?"

Cameron took her hand and led her out of the bathroom. "Three-week-old body found in a canyon at the bottom of a cliff," she said.

"Cliffs again? You don't do so well with cliffs, Cameron."

"I fall off of one, and now I have a problem?"

"Fall? Sweetheart, if only you had fallen. Then I wouldn't have to question your sanity."

Cameron stopped up short, her eyes on fire.

"What?"

"You called me sweetheart," she whispered. "I think I like it when you do that. It makes me feel—"

"Loved?"

Cameron nodded. "Yeah. Loved."

"Good." Andrea ignored the curious glances of Randy and Jim as she squeezed Cameron's hand. "Because you are. And I do."

Cameron grinned. "I do too."

Andrea laughed. "I'm glad we got that out of the way." She let her fingers slip away from Cameron's hand. "Let me tell them what's going on."

Andrea watched her walk away in that familiar, confident stride of hers, albeit with a slight limp from her gimpy ankle.

Cameron paused to speak briefly with both Randy and Jim before leaving. They then turned expectant looks her way.

She went closer, unable to wipe the smile from her face. "She kinda offered me a job," she said.

Jim nodded. "You're leaving then?"

She grasped his big, calloused hand, holding it tightly. "As much as I love it here, I can't *not* go with her. She's become...well ...she's very important to me." She met his eyes. "I let her inside my heart," she whispered. She glanced quickly at Randy, then back to Jim. "I didn't think I'd ever find this."

He nodded again. "I only want what's best for you, Andi. I always said your talents were wasted here anyway."

"You gave me a chance, Jim. Everything I have now, it's because of you."

"No, I just—"

"You took me in when no one else would. I'll never forget that. I'll never forget *you*." She hugged him, squeezing tight before placing a quick kiss on his cheek. "Thank you."

She turned to Randy, playfully punching his arm. "And you," she said with a smile. "Thanks for being my friend. I know it was hard. Especially at first."

"Hell, yeah. I was scared of you," he said with a laugh. He then reached for her, surprising her by pulling her close into a hug. "I'll miss you."

She squeezed him back. "I'll miss you too."

They parted, both slightly embarrassed by their display of affection.

"If you could keep an eye on my house," she said. "I'll have to see about getting my stuff later."

"No problem. I'll take care of it."

She stepped back, knowing Cameron was waiting for her. "I should get going. I'll be in touch," she said. She gave Jim's hand one last squeeze, then headed out into the sunshine.

Cameron was leaning against the rig, watching her. Andrea paused, letting her gaze travel over her, stopping when their eyes met. What she saw there caused her heart to tighten, her breath to catch. How did she ever think she could let this woman walk out of her life?

"All set?"

Andrea nodded, climbing the three steps into the rig. Once Cameron shut the door, Andrea moved into her arms.

"I'm so in love with you," she murmured against her lips.

Cameron released her, her fingers softly brushing the hair away from Andrea's face. "And I'm in love with you," Cameron whispered. "I couldn't leave without you."

Andrea's eyes slipped closed, loving the gentle pressure of Cameron's touch. As she'd told Jim, she never thought she would find this. She took a deep breath, finally moving away from Cameron's touch. They had some cliffs to get to.

Andrea smiled, allowing herself one more quick kiss.

"Okay then. Let's get this show on the road."

Publications from
Bella Books, Inc.
Women. Books. Even Better Together.

P.O. Box 10543
Tallahassee, FL 32302
Phone: 800-729-4992
www.bellabooks.com

THE GRASS WIDOW by Nanci Little. Aidan Blackstone is nineteen, unmarried and pregnant, and has no reason to think that the year 1876 won't be her last. Joss Bodett has lost her family but desperately clings to their land. A richly told story of frontier survival that picks up with the generation of women where Patience and Sarah left off.
978-1-59493-189-5 $12.95

SMOKEY O by Celia Cohen. Insult "Mac" MacDonnell and insult the entire Delaware Blue Diamond team. Smokey O'Neill has just insulted Mac, and then finds she's been traded to Delaware. The games are not limited to the baseball field!
978-1-59493-198-7 $12.95

WICKED GAMES by Ellen Hart. Never have mysteries and secrets been closer to home in this eighth installment of this award-winning lesbian mystery series. Jane Lawless's neighbors bring puzzles and peril—and that's just the beginning.
978-1-59493-185-7 $14.95

NOT EVERY RIVER by Robbi McCoy. It's the hottest city in the U.S., and it's not just the weather that's heating up. For Kim and Randi are forced to question everything they thought they knew about themselves before they can risk their fiery hearts on the biggest gamble of all.
978-1-59493-182-6 $14.95

HOUSE OF CARDS by Nat Burns. Cards are played, but the game is gossip. Kaylen Strauder has never wanted it to be about her. But the time is fast-approaching when she must decide which she needs more: her community or Eda Byrne.
978-1-59493-203-8 $14.95

RETURN TO ISIS by Jean Stewart. The award-winning Isis sci-fi series features Jean Stewart's vision of a committed colony of women dedicated to preserving their way of life, even after the apocalypse. Mysteries have been forgotten, but survival depends on remembering. Book one in series.
978-1-59493-193-2 $12.95

1ST IMPRESSIONS by Kate Calloway. Rookie PI Cassidy James has her first case. Her investigation into the murder of Erica Trinidad's uncle isn't welcomed by the local sheriff, especially since the delicious, seductive Erica is their prime suspect. 1st in series. Author's augmented and expanded edition.
978-1-59493-192-5 $12.95

BEACON OF LOVE by Ann Roberts. Twenty-five years after their families put an end to a relationship that hadn't even begun, Stephanie returns to Oregon to find many things have changed...except her feelings for Paula.
978-1-59493-180-2 $14.95

ABOVE TEMPTATION by Karin Kallmaker. It's supposed to be like any other case, except this time they're chasing one of their own. As fraud investigators Tamara Sterling and Kip Barrett try to catch a thief, they realize they can have anything they want—except each other.
978-1-59493-179-6 $14.95

AN EMERGENCE OF GREEN by Katherine V. Forrest. Carolyn had no idea her new neighbor jumped the fence to enjoy her swimming pool. The discovery leads to choices she never anticipated in an intense, sensual story of discovery and risk, consequences and triumph. Originally released in 1986.
978-1-59493-217-5 $14.95

CRAZY FOR LOVING by Jaye Maiman. Officially hanging out her shingle as a private investigator, Robin Miller is getting her life on track. Just as Robin discovers it's hard to follow a dead man, she walks in. KT Bellflower, sultry and devastating...Lammy winner and second in series.
978-1-59493-195-6 $14.95

LOVE WAITS by Gerri Hill. The All-American girl and the love she left behind—it's been twenty years since Ashleigh and Gina parted, and now they're back to the place where nothing was simple and love didn't wait.
978-1-59493-186-4 $14.95

HANNAH FREE: THE BOOK by Claudia Allen. Based on the film festival hit movie starring Sharon Gless. Hannah's story is funny, scathing and witty as she navigates life with aplomb—but always comes home to Rachel. 32 pages of color photographs plus bonus behind-the-scenes movie information.
978-1-59493-172-7 $19.95

END OF THE ROPE by Jackie Calhoun. Meg Klein has two enduring loves—horses and Nicky Hennessey. Nicky is there for her when she most needs help, but then an attractive vet throws Meg's carefully balanced world out of kilter.
978-1-59493-176-5 $14.95

THE LONG TRAIL by Penny Hayes. When schoolteacher Blanche Bartholomew and dance hall girl Teresa Stark meet their feelings are powerful—and completely forbidden—in Starcross Texas. In search of a safe future, they flee, daring to take a covered wagon across the forbidding prairie.
978-1-59493-196-3 $12.95

UP UP AND AWAY by Catherine Ennis. Sarah and Margaret have a video. The mob wants it. Flying for their lives, two women discover more than secrets.
978-1-59493-215-1 $12.95

CITY OF STRANGERS by Diana Rivers. A captive in a gilded cage, young Solene plots her escape, but the rulers of Hernorium have other plans for Solene—and her people. Breathless lesbian fantasy story also perfect for teen readers.
978-1-59493-183-3 $14.95

ROBBER'S WINE by Ellen Hart. Belle Dumont is the first dead of summer. Jane Lawless, Belle's old friend, suspects coldhearted murder. Lammy-winning seventh novel in critically acclaimed mystery series.
978-1-59493-184-0 $14.95

APPARITION ALLEY by Katherine V. Forrest. Kate Delafield has solved hundreds of cases, but the one that baffles her most is her own shooting. Book six in series.
978-1-883523-65-7 $14.95

STERLING ROAD BLUES by Ruth Perkinson. It was a simple declaration of love. But the entire state of Virginia wants to weigh in, leaving teachers Carrie Tomlinson and Audra Malone caught in the crossfire—and with love troubles of their own.
978-1-59493-187-1 $14.95

LILY OF THE TOWER by Elizabeth Hart. Agnes Headey, taking refuge from a storm at the Netherfield estate, stumbles into dark family secrets and something more... Meticulously researched historical romance.
978-1-59493-177-2 $14.95

LETTING GO by Ann O'Leary. Kelly has decided that luscious, successful Laura should be hers. For now. Laura might even be agreeable. But where does that leave Kate?
978-1-59493-194-9 $12.95

MURDER TAKES TO THE HILLS by Jessica Thomas. Renovations, shady business deals, a stalker—and it's not even tourist season yet for PI Alex Peres and her best four-legged pal Fargo. Sixth in this Provincetown-based series.
978-1-59493-178-9 $14.95

SOLSTICE by Kate Christie. It's Emily Mackenzie's last college summer and meeting her soccer idol Sam Delaney seems like a dream come true. But Sam's passion seems reserved for the field of play...
978-1-59493-175-8 $14.95

FORTY LOVE by Diana Simmonds. Lush, romantic story of love and tennis with two women playing to win the ultimate prize. Revised and updated author's edition.
978-1-59493-190-1 $14.95

I LEFT MY HEART by Jaye Maiman. The only women she ever loved is dead, and sleuth Robin Miller goes looking for answers. First book in Lammy-winning series.
978-1-59493-188-8 $14.95

TWO WEEKS IN AUGUST by Nat Burns. Her return to Chincoteague Island is a delight to Nina Christie until she gets her dose of Hazy Duncan's renown ill-humor. She's not going to let it bother her, though...
978-1-59493-173-4 $14.95